RISE
AND
SHINE

STEVE KIRBY

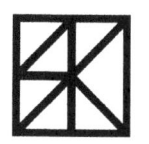

RISE
AND
SHINE

Text Copyright © 2024 Steve Kirby

The right of Steve Kirby to be identified as the author of this work has been asserted by him in accordance with the Copyright, Designs and Patents Act 1988.

All rights reserved. No part of this publication may be reproduced or transmitted in any form or by any means, electronic or mechanical, including photocopy, recording, or any information storage and retrieval system, without permission in writing from the author.

First published by Steve Kirby 2025

Contact; **steve_kirby_rise_and_shine@btinternet.com**

ISBN 9781068470202

Also available as an eBook

e-ISBN 9781068470219

Cover design by Steve Kirby

Dedicated to

Harry James Bruschan Kirby

I hope you have a life full of happy adventures

Background

This project began in April 2009 after a chance conversation with a neighbour. It led me to research the family history of an elderly spinster known simply as 'Miss Cox' who had lived nearby.

I soon realised that there was a story to be told about the fascinating life of the Cox family. Originally it was going to be a biography, but I then I thought, that with a bit of creative licence, I could create a work of fiction based on the real-life characters I had discovered. I laid out my plan and wrote the first paragraph. There it sat, on my computer's hard-drive untouched for the next 14-years - life just got in the way.

In 2023, due to the Writer's Guild of America strike, my son found himself out of work and in need of a project to keep himself busy. He asked if he could have a look at the research I had done, with a view to writing a book or screenplay of his own. Spurred on by his interest and the discovery of fresh information that was previously unavailable, we spent most of that year digging into the extraordinary lives of Harry and Cecily Cox.

Now retired, I decided it was time to write the book, so on the 1st January 2024 my new year's resolution was to write one page a day. By the end of April, I had fulfilled my task.

The vast majority of the characters in this book were real people and many of the events actually happened, but not all.

Chapters

1 - Training Ship 'Wellesley'	1
2 - Harry's Future	10
3 - Success at the Shipyard	16
4 - Harry's First Day at Work	26
5 - Making His Way	33
6 - A Death in the Family	38
7 - A Bright Future	43
8 - Apprenticeship Comes to an End	49
9 - Harry Goes to College	53
10 - New Opportunities	56
11 - Eshott Hall	59
12 - Royal Corps of Naval Constructors	81
13 - A Weekend in London	86
14 - Holmwood	98
15 - To Greenwich	102
16 - Home for Christmas	114
17 - A Visit to London	132
18 - Wedding Plans	135
19 - The Admiralty	139
20 - An Unexpected Visitor	143

Chapters

21 - Unexpected News	149
22 - Arrangements Made	154
23 - Mr. & Mrs. Cox	159
24 - Life in Perivale	166
25 - Lloyd's Register of Shipping	168
26 - New Job and the New Arrival	172
27 - Cecily	178
28 - Early Casualties	180
29 - Atlantic Crossing	184
30 - A Close Call	198
31 - Reunited	204
32 - All Together	208
33 - New Horizons	216
34 - New Beginnings	226
35 - Old Friend	231
36 - Love at First Sight	235
37 - A Visit to England	239
38 - Life in Japan	247
39 - That's What Friends Are For	261
40 - Storm Clouds Gathering	275

Chapters

41 - It's War	283
42 - The Summons	288
43 - Home in Sight	301
44 - To Canada	309
45 - Cecily Signs Up for Adventure	317
46 - Peter's War	323
47 - A Trip to Bakers Street	325
48 - Peter Saves the Day	330
49 - Cecily Starts Basic Training	332
50 - Fortress Singapore	334
51 - Cecily Moves On	335
52 - Peter Gets a Promotion	337
53 - Cecily Gets the News	339
54 - Peter's Escape	341
55 - Cecily's First Mission	353
56 - Andaman Islands	364
57 - In the Bag	368
58 - The Interrogation Officer	376
59 - What Next?	386
60 – Epilogue	396

1 - Training Ship 'Wellesley' – Newcastle upon Tyne – 1894

Like so often when it's very hot, a sort of calm descends. The calm and almost silence of very hot people going about their business trying to conserve energy and stay cool. The brightness and heat of the sun made everything seem to shimmer and glow like liquid gold, not a colour normally associated with the Tyne.

On the Wellesley, it was that time in the afternoon when the day watch did their utmost to look busy under the constant scrutinising gaze of the junior officers. Today however, it was even too hot for them to bark orders at the boys. Instead, they casually walked around the poop deck concentrating their efforts in the shadier areas of the ship. Only a few hours to go before the night watch reported for duty, then it was a quick swim in the river to cool off, supper and bed.

A sound pierced the near silence. Those working near the bow of the ship, would have been forgiven for thinking it was just the high-pitched squawk of a passing gull. Seaman Pringle on the other hand thought differently. Having grown up with five younger siblings, he knew the shriek of a young child when he heard it. From that moment on, everything seemed to be in slow-motion. All he could feel and hear was the sound of his own pulse throbbing inside his head. He ran to the starboard side of the ship and looked over the rail. Slowly drifting away on the afternoon tide, he could see what looked like a white blouse floating along. He looked around, no one else was there. Am I the only person who heard it? he thought to himself. As he processed that thought, he climbed over the rail, and shouted at the top of his voice, "Man overboard", and jumped.

Despite the sweltering heat of the midday sun, the water was cold, very cold. His body went into spasm as he hit the water. He had always thought he was a good swimmer, but now, just bobbing to the surface, it became a struggle and treading water was nigh on impossible. His legs felt heavy. If only he had had time to take his boots off. The baggy bell-bottomed trousers and middy were now saturated and clung to him, restricting movement. He shivered violently as he tried to fill his lungs with the warm air. Lifting his head up long enough to see in what direction he needed to swim, he saw a flash of white material in the water about fifty-yards away. This time an arm waved frantically from it.

Fortunately, he was going with the tide. Using every ounce of strength in his body, he managed to kick his arms and legs and fight the clawing water trying to drag him down. Once he was horizontal, his powerful front crawl, with arms and legs going like steam pistons, he was able to close the distance between himself and the person in trouble.

The muscles in his shoulders and thighs were burning. He could still see the waving hand. He was nearly upon it when it slowly sank beneath the water and out of sight. The white cotton material was still visible on the surface. He grabbed a handful of it and pulled. He could hardly keep himself afloat let alone someone else. Somehow, he found an inner reserve and pulled again. A head appeared. It came up quick and nearly headbutted him in the face. Both of them were now coughing and spluttering and trying to get their lungs full of air. Despite the flailing limbs, he managed to get his left arm around the persons head and under the chin.

The tide was taking them closer to the river's edge where a number of coal barges were moored. He managed to grab hold of one of the mooring ropes with his free right hand. The person he was holding onto couldn't see anything. Their hair was plastered down over their face, but sensed the taught rope and took hold of it with both hands. After a few moments the feeling of panic subsided and his stinging muscles started to ease. His heart, that felt as if would burst through his chest, now just pounded in his ears. He said "Are you all right?" The person that was clinging to him and the rope wiped the hair out of their face and gasped; "Yes, I think so".

Pringle's eyes widened in disbelief. His heart started beating fast again and he felt his cheeks flush with embarrassment. It was Captain Baynham's twelve-year old daughter May Helena.

The following morning, Pringle stood in the corridor outside the captain's office. Dressed in his number-one uniform, every inch of it pressed and starched, and his boots, now dry from the soaking they'd got yesterday, polished to a mirror like finish.

He'd never been summoned to any of the officers before. He'd always kept his nose clean and out of trouble. A different story when he lived in London and worked at the Covent Garden fruit and veg market.

He was easily led astray by the older boys, whose acceptance he always sought. They, on the other hand, showed no loyalty whenever the rozzers were about feeling collars. Since his father had walked out, he was the main bread winner in the family. His mother took in laundry but it didn't pay very much. Then she met her new fella. He was nice enough, a clerk at an insurance company in the city. The trouble was, he didn't want young Pringle around, especially if he was going to get into trouble with the police every five-minutes. The last brush with the law he had was a serious one. He'd got caught with a barrow full of King Edwards, hawking them around the posh hotels in the west End. It was made clear to him in no uncertain terms that it would be time in prison for him. His mother would kill him when she found out.

Fortunately for him, there was one of those Christian types at the police station that afternoon. One of those do-gooders, who like to offer boys like him a chance to repent and offer them an alternative way of life. Much to his surprise, he was offered a place on a naval training ship. He didn't have to think about it for very long. Free board and lodging, a chance to get out of London and away from all the trouble he was getting into, and a chance to learn a trade and travel to far off places he'd never even dreamt about.

He was given bail and a third-class train ticket to Newcastle-upon-Tyne. If he didn't report to the training ship 'Wellesley', he'd be hauled in front of a magistrate and sent to prison.

He went home later that afternoon and told his mother. After a bit of shouting and a lot of crying, he left home with his worldly goods in a sack over his shoulder and walked to King's Cross station.

Now he was standing in the corridor outside the captain's office. He had a knot in his stomach. Captain Baynham, the ships superintendent, was a ferocious looking man. His dark, almost black beard made him look like a bear. He'd spent a lifetime in the navy but due to ill health, this was a semi-retirement job for services rendered. His family lived on board the ship with him but they were hardly ever seen. He was a stickler for the rules and 'Discipline, Discipline, Discipline', was his mantra. It was drilled into the junior ratings every day. I hope I haven't mucked things up, he said silently to himself. Dereliction of duty, jumping over board without tying a line around himself, putting himself and the captain's daughter in harms' way, bringing the navy into disrepute, were all the scenarios whirling around in his head. He didn't know what to expect. I didn't even know it was his daughter; he tried to reason with himself. How could I have known, I didn't see her face until we were holding onto the rope, together. Oh Christ, I'm going to be for the high jump, he muttered under his breath.

The suddenness of the captain's door opening made him jump and he stood bolt upright to attention. Lieutenant Stocker, the Captain's adjutant, stepped into the corridor and with his usual stern face, looked Pringle up and down. "In", he said nodding towards the opened door.

The office was dark and gloomy on account of the ceiling height being quite low. He could see the silhouette of the captain against the large window sitting at his desk. As he approached, his eyes became accustomed to the light and he could see that the captain was looking down at a report on his desk. Pringle stopped and saluted about a yard from the desk. He then stood to attention and looked straight ahead, his eyes taking in the view outside of the early morning fog coming up the Tyne from the sea.

The captain put the lid on his fountain pen, blotted the signature he had just signed with it and rose to his feet. The room got noticeably darker as his large frame blocked the light from the window. He walked around the desk and stood immediately in front of Pringle, towering over him. The captain's eyes seem to burn straight through him and out the other side. Pringle swallowed, his mouth was so dry he thought his tongue would stick to the roof of his mouth and choke him.

Captain Baynham held out his right hand. Not at all sure what would happen next, Pringle held out his and the two shook hands. Pringle thought that his arm would be pulled from its socket, such was the captain's enthusiasm.

Henry Baynham's features softened. He said, "My dear boy, I owe you a debt of gratitude I fear I will never be able to repay". Pringle was stunned; he stood there with his mouth wide-open. The captain continued; "Your quick thinking and presence of mind, let alone your physical prowess, saved the life of my daughter, May Helena. It was a truly heroic effort, and my wife and I thank you from the bottom of our hearts".

Pringle wanted to cry, not because of the touching words from the captain, but of the sheer relief that he wasn't going to be in any trouble. Always being good at thinking on his feet, he replied to the captain; "Thank you sir, I've been trained by the best and I have you to thank for that sir".

The captain roared with laughter; he knew a crawler when he met one. "Well said young man, well said". With a hand on his shoulder, he turned Pringle around to face the way he had come in. "There's someone here who would also like to thank you".

Presumably, she had been sitting there all the time, May Helena was sitting on a stool in the corner of the room. She stood as her father and Pringle approached. In a soft and almost inaudible voice she said, looking at her shoes, "Thank you Mr. Pringle. Thank you for saving me. I was a very silly girl and I promise not to cause a nuisance ever again".

"That's alright Miss, no harm done", replied Pringle. "How did you come to fall overboard Miss?"

"I was playing with a kite, and the string got caught in the ship's rigging. So, I climbed up on the handrail to untie it and slipped", she said sheepishly.

"It was a miracle you didn't dash your brains out", interjected her father, which made her go very red and look at her shoes even harder.

After saluting the Captain, Pringle stepped back out into the corridor. He was just about to close the door, when the captain called out to him, "Oh, Pringle, next time you jump overboard to save someone, tie a line around your waist, there's a good chap".

2 - Harry's Future

"Well, I don't know where he gets it from", said Charlie Cox. "Nobody on my side of the family spent a moment longer in school than they needed to, let alone be any good at it. All our father ever wanted for us, was to get out a earn a wage".

Mrs. Cox sat at the dining room table looking down at the letter young Harry had brought home from school that afternoon with a perturbed look on her face.

Charlie was sitting at the end of the table, collar and cuffs removed from his shirt. He stubbed out his cigarette and took the last draught of beer from the bottle. "Give us another look at it", he said, and held out his hand. "I always imagined he'd leave school and go and join his brothers at the shipyard. It says here, he's academically gifted and has a natural talent when it comes drawing and sketching. The last thing we want is an artist in the house. We can't afford any of this *la-di-dah* nonsense".

"Oh Charlie, can't you find him something? He won't last five minutes at the yard. He's half the size of his brothers. Even some of the younger lads at school push him around. Can't he work with you?"

"Don't be daft woman, I'm a travelling salesman, he'll be of no use to me. I'll tell you what, I'll go down to the school and have a chat with this Miss Thirkettle, and ask her if she has any suggestions. She shouldn't be putting ideas into the heads of these youngsters".

A few days later, Charlie Cox got off the train at Newcastle upon Tyne station. Suited and booted in his best apparel, he had a smile of satisfaction on his face having had a successful morning in Middlesborough. There was a boom in the shipbuilding industry, north and south of the border, and that translated into more thirsty men in need of a good pint, and he sold the best. New pubs and alehouses were springing up all around the shipyard area and some of the posher areas too.

His walk home took him past Harry's school. All the children would have left by now, but the teachers might still be there. He walked through the playground towards the imposing looking building. He'd never liked school. So long as you can read, write and count, he couldn't see the point of the rest of it. If a man can get a decent job with fair pay, that's it, he's cracked it. Charlie had left school at the age of ten and had gone off to work with his father, a shipwright at the Southampton docks. He hadn't enjoyed the work, much to the annoyance of his father. When the opportunity came along, after a chance meeting in a local alehouse with Mr. Crowley, he grabbed it with both hands. Less hours, more money and all the beer he could drink, within reason, what young man wouldn't take it? He'd felt guilty about breaking with tradition, but now that his own sons were working at Swan Hunter on the Tyne, his conscience was clear. It had certainly pleased his father.

As he got to the door, two lads came running out and nearly collided with him.

"Sorry mister", one said. "Careful you boys" replied Charlie. "Is Miss Thirkettle still here?"

"She's in the hall" said the other lad and both quickly disappeared.

Charlie walked along the main corridor, his nose filling with the scent of a freshly disinfected tiled floor. He could hear the cleaner moving desks and chairs around in a nearby classroom.

He knew exactly where the hall was. He'd been there many times over the years, usually at Christmas for the nativity. Two years ago, his third oldest lad had played Joseph, much to the delight of his mother. Christmas was always a busy time for a brewer's agent, but he knew these little trips to the school meant a lot to his wife and the children and he always made the effort to be there.

Miss Thirkettle was two-rungs up a short stepladder, hanging a picture on the wall. It was obviously done by one of the pupils, a rather naïve landscape with the shipyards in the distance, but the perspective was very good. That's why it was being

hung in the main hall, for all the children to see and aspire to.
Charlie kept quiet until she got down from the steps. He didn't want to startle her in case she fell. When she'd got down, he gave a little cough and said "Miss Thirkettle?"

Miss Thirkettle was about thirty-years old and the picture of respectability. She wore a long-sleeved white blouse, a long navy skirt that came down to black ankle-length boots. Her hair was a mousey brown and tied back in a simple pony-tail, that crowned a pale face with high cheek bones which gave the impression she had a permanent smile. Despite her diminutive size and slight build, she had presence, and Charles got that feeling in the pit of his stomach like he was back at school again himself and had done something wrong for which he was about to be punished.

"Yes, how can I help you?"

"I'm Mr. Cox, Harry's father" he stammered.

"Ah, very nice to meet you Mr. Cox. Harry is one of my best pupils, you must be very proud of him". It wasn't really a question but a statement of fact.
"Yes, yes, he's a good lad, doesn't give us any bother, well, not until now that is".
Miss Thirkettle looked at him quizzically with a raised eyebrow. Her look said; tell me more.

"It's like this Miss; we're a hard-working family like most folks in these parts. We have a lot of children to cloth and feed. His brothers are earning a wage at the shipyard and we need him to do the same. We can't afford to keep him at school any longer than need be. And if you don't mind me saying Miss, putting fanciful ideas into his head, will only lead to disappointment on his part".

"Mr. Cox, I have not, nor would, put ideas into the heads of any of the pupils here without consulting their parents first. I fully understand your concerns. My letter to you was to merely say that Harry has shown potential and that work as a manual labourer ought not to be his, or your, first choice for him. He can earn just as good money working in an office as he can down a pit or at the shipyards. That is all I was trying to say".

Charlie, now disarmed and feeling a bit guilty for having got the wrong end of the stick, said "Oh, well, er, we thought you were saying he should be an artist or a writer or some such".

"Goodness gracious me" she laughed, "I can see why you were concerned. Well, I hope I've put your mind at rest?"

"Yes, you have. I'm sorry if I came across a bit rude just then. It wasn't my meaning".

"That's quite alright Mr. Cox. Now would be a good time to start asking around. I feel certain that an office job with a reputable company would help him to achieve his potential".

"Right, you are miss" said Charlie with a bit more enthusiasm in his voice. "Er, the only trouble is, I don't actually know anyone who works in an office. Except for my gaffer that is, and I know he don't want anyone".

Miss Thirkettle looked past Harry into the distance as if looking for the answer to the problem. After a few seconds, she looked Charlie in the eye and said "You've got lads working at Swan Hunter, haven't you?".

"Yes" he replied, "But I thought you said he weren't cut out for a manual job?".

"My father was an acquaintance of Mr. Swan prior to his passing. Mr. Swan that is, not my father" she smiled. "The business is going from strength to strength and I know for a fact they employ many young men in their offices. And train them too, why in a few years, he could be taken on as a draftsman. Building ships isn't all about welding and riveting you know".

She stood there looking at him with an air of satisfaction and her chin held high. He returned the gaze with a new feeling of respect for the lady. He thought; Blimey, she makes it sound so easy. Perhaps it is. He said, "That's a grand idea miss, I'll certainly give it a go. I won't take any more of your time. It's much appreciated. Well, goodbye".

"Goodbye Mr. Cox".

3 - Success at the Shipyard

A few weeks later, Charlie returned home from work and found the house in its usual teatime disarray. Mrs. Cox, or Laura as she was known to friends and family, or Lols, the name that only Charlie called her, was shouting at the younger children to stop making a racket in the back yard. She gave instructions to the older girls on how to prepare the evening meal whilst the older working boys just loafed about getting in everyone's way making the tablecloth grubby with their filthy hands. "I don't know why I bother with a cloth on this table" she said. Why can't you leave all that grime at the shipyard?"

"It's ground in mum, you can't just get it off with a bit of soap and water" said Charles, the eldest. "We wash before we come home, you should see what it's like beforehand".

"I shudder to think", she replied crossly.

Charlie knew that the best thing to do was keep out the way. After shouting out a "Hello, I'm home", which everyone ignored, he climbed the stairs and sat on the bed and removed his tie, collar, cuffs and boots. He leant back against the headboard, lit a cigarette and started to read the evening paper. "Trouble in South Africa, trouble in China, the world is falling apart", he said to himself.

Half an hour later there was a yell up the stairs, "Dinners ready dad". He put his slippers on and went down to a scene of quiet domestic bliss. Everyone was tucking into beef stew and dumplings. He sat down at one end of the large pine table opposite Lols. I don't know how she does it, he thought.

Cecil broke the silence. He put his hand in his shirt pocket and pulled out a piece of paper. He tossed towards his father and said, "This is for you pa".
Charlie looked down at it suspiciously. "What is it?" he said.
"A note" replied Cecil.
"Who from?" said Charlie
"The gaffer at work asked me to give it to you".
"What for?"
Lols banged her tea cup down on the table, "For heaven's sake Charles, open it. It might be important".
"Alright, alright, give me a chance". Charlie gingerly picked up the note as if it might explode and carefully unfolded it. His lips moved and his head went from side to side as he read it. When he'd finished it, he folded it back up and put it down on the table. He looked at Cecil and said "Who's Mr. Peskett?"
I don't know" he replied.
Charles piped up and said, "I think he works in one of the offices, I think he's management".
"That would make sense" Charlie replied.
"For the love of God, what is it all about" Lols cried in exasperation, "What's happened?"

"This Mr. Peskett has asked if I can go in and see him tomorrow about a job in the drawing office".

Everyone around the table stared at him, some with their mouths open, Cecil said "You're applying for a job at the yard?"

"No, not me you clot, Harry".

Everyone one around the table gave a sigh of comprehension and continued to eat.

"That'll be good won't it Harry?", said Lols, "Drawing boats and things".

"Yes mum" replied Harry.

The Cox household consisted of Charlie and Lols and ten children. Lucy was the eldest at twenty-four-years of age, and Phyllis, the youngest, was five.

Charlie's job took him all over the country, including a spell in Scotland where the last five of the children had been born at a town called Bothwell, south-east of Glasgow. He had worked hard all his life and put a roof over their heads and there had always been enough food on the table. Now that he was knocking on the door of being fifty, he was looking forward to the day, in about 10-years' time, when he could take it easy and enjoy his retirement with Lols. By then, all the children would be out at work, those who hadn't gone off and got married at least, and will all be bringing money in.

Life was looking alright for the Cox family. There may be troubles in the world but he had a good job,

people will always need beer and his boys were working at the
shipyard. People would always need ships, especially if there's trouble in the world.

Like Charlie, Lols had been born and raised in Southampton. The only child of local watchmaker, she had received a modest inheritance when both her parents had died four years ago. It allowed them to buy a bigger house in Victoria Square near Newcastle city centre. An imposing 4-story terraced house with steps and iron railings up to the front door. It took a bit of the day-to-day financial pressure off but their feet were firmly on the ground. They'd worked hard all their lives; nothing was going to change that.

"There's nothing wrong with being working class", Charlie would often say when the conversation turned to politics and the social reforms forever being debated in the national press. "Nor, is ambition or the desire to improve one's position. What the upper classes have got to realise is, that without the working classes, they'd have nothing. So, it's no use them looking down their noses. We've got to live together and get on". It was usually at this point, if he was in the pub, that someone would shout; "Thank you for the lecture Mr. Campbell-Bannerman, would you please put a sock in it, it's your round".

The following morning Charlie got up early and walked the mile or so to the shipyard with his two sons,

Charles and Cecil. Charles had been there for over ten years and Cecil coming up for five. Both were welders. Cecil had another couple of years to go on his apprenticeship and then he would start to earn good money with the opportunity of plenty of overtime. Charlie's father had been a shipwright at the other end of the country in Southampton. The only difference was, the ships he worked on were the old ones made of wood and a lot smaller.

He felt proud of his two lads as he walked through the gates. The place was enormous and a hive of activity. Already the air was filled with the sounds and smell of heavy industry. Some parts of the yard looked like a scene from Dante's Inferno. Masked men walking through showers of sparks, some carrying red hot slabs of iron with tongs. Smoke and steam hovered in the still morning air and the cacophony of hammers, drills and pneumatic riveters would continue for the rest of the shift.

Charles and Cecil clocked in and walked off to their respective building berths while Charlie followed a group of men towards the main offices set further back from the water's edge.

Showing the note that he had received the previous night to a man sitting at the desk in the entrance hall, he was given directions to the office of Mr. Peskett.

He walked down a very long corridor with a highly polished floor. On the right-hand side there were endless doors, presumably offices. On the left, a procession of glass partitioned offices with large tables in the middle stacked with plans and technical drawings. Dotted down the far wall of the offices, under large angled windows, stood an army of men, young and old in their shirtsleeves, standing at drawing boards. There must have been dozens and dozens of them. My God, Charlie thought to himself, Our Harry would be in his element.

At the end of the corridor Charlie found what he was looking for. A polished oak door with 'Leonard Peskett – Senior Architect' written in gold leaf paint upon it. It instantly conveyed the message; I'm important, I'm probably very busy, so please don't waste my time. Charlie had knocked on many doors in his capacity as a brewery agent. He had a genial manner about him and getting new business came easy to him. Anyway, he thought, He invited me. He took off his hat, straightened his tie, took a deep breath, pulled his shoulders back and rapped on the door with three satisfying knocks.

Almost immediately, a man's voice called out. "Come".
Charlie turned the highly polished brass knob on the door, and entered.

The office was flooded with light from a huge window. The view from it looked across the shipyard, the Tyne and over towards Jarrow. Wooden bookcases and shelves lined one wall. An oak desk sat by the wall at the opposite end to the window. A large bench occupied the middle of the room and was covered in architect's drawings, and by the window stood two draughtsman's boards. Behind one of these stood a man. Charlie could only see his legs. He said "Er, Mr. Peskett?".

A head appeared from around the side of the drawing board, "Yes, how can I help you?"

Leonard Peskett was a man of about forty-years. A fair, boyish complexion with a round face and receding hairline. The bushy moustache suited him and gave him an air of authority. He wore shirt sleeves with armbands and a waistcoat with pocket watch and chain. He had a pencil behind his right ear and was holding a set of dividers. He couldn't have looked more like an architect if he'd tried.

Hello Sir, my name is Charlie Cox and I'm …"
"Ah, Mr. Cox", he interrupted, "Thank you for coming in. Now I understand your son wishes to join us in the drawing office?".
"Yes, that's right sir. You see, his teacher thinks it would be a good place for him to learn a trade. You see sir, what with him not being, well, you know, let's just

say he was the runt of the litter. Prefers, reading, writing and drawing".

"Sounds like the kind of lad we're always looking for. She must be well connected this teacher. I got the message about your lad from Mrs. Swan".

"Blimey" replied Charlie.

Whilst Charlie stood there dumfounded with his mouth open, scratching the back of his head, Mr Peskett walked over to the desk and scribbled on a piece of note paper.

"Here" he said. Take this note to Mr. Henshaw, you'll find him in the drawing office across the corridor and he'll discuss the terms of employment with you".

"Well Sir, I don't know what to say, thank you" Charlie stammered.

"Nice to have met you. You must excuse me; I need to press on".

Charlie said his goodbyes and closed the office door behind him. He stood there for a few moments and thought to himself, as easy as that. He then went to find Mr. Henshaw.

Charlie got home from work later that afternoon and was greeted by the domestic mayhem he was accustomed to. He did his usual routine of going upstairs and waiting until he was called down to dinner. He considered that his presence was unnecessary and that he'd only be in the way.

Lols looked a bit red in the face as she served up dollops of mashed potato on to everyone's plate. She kept looking at Charlie as if waiting for him to say something profound. He thought he'd done something wrong and she was about to blow her top at him when she said "Well?"

"Well, what?" he replied.

"Well how did you get on at the yard this morning, what happened?".

Trying to make himself sound nonchalant, as if it were a regular occurrence, he said "Well, I went and had a nice chat with the senior architect, what's his name, oh yes, Mr. Peskett, and I told him our Harry would like a job in the office, drawing boats". He looked around the table where a sea of faces stared at him. "Of course, he was only too happy to oblige".

He turned to Harry and said "You can start on your birthday and you'll be getting five-shillings a week to start off on. If you stick at it and do well, you'll be earning as much as me in ten-years' time".

"Oh Harry, that is good news isn't it" said his mother with a voice full of pride and relief in equal measure. "What do you say to your father?".

"Thanks dad. Does that mean I won't have to do welding or stuff like that?"

"And what's wrong with welding?" chimed his elder brothers Charles and Cecil together.

"Nothing, I just don't think I can do it. I'm not as tough as you two".

Don't you worry son, the heaviest thing you are going to have to lift is a roll of paper and a box of pencils", said his father in a jovial way that garnered a ripple of laughter around the dinner table. Harry looked around the table sheepishly. He didn't like being the centre of attention, even at home. School was ten-times worse. When Mrs. Thirkettle made him stand up in class and read aloud from a book, or was made to show one of his drawings, he just wanted the ground to open up and swallow him. The general hub-bub around the table returned and Harry took a bite of his minced beef and onion pie.

4 - Harry's First Day at Work

Harry's birthday fell on the day after Easter Monday. The newspapers were full of the ongoing war in South Africa against the Boers'. In Newcastle, Harry Cox was pulling on his socks and preparing for his first day at work. Naturally, he was very nervous but at the same time, curious. It would have felt a lot worse if he'd had to go there on his own, but at least he could walk with Charles and Cecil. They would show him which gate to go through and point him in the direction of the drawing office.

As the three boys were about to leave, Mrs. Cox came out from the kitchen. She put her arms around Harry and kissed him on the cheek. "Have you got your sandwiches?".

"Yes Mum. Don't worry, I'll be alright".

This brought a tear to her eye. "Look at you, so grown up. Go on, off you go, you'll be late".

Charlie came out of the kitchen just as he was about to go down the steps to the pavement. He held out his hand and shook Harry's. "Make us proud son. Do what your told and do it the best you can. That's all anyone can ask of you. See you tonight and you can tell us all about it".

"Will do, dad".

Harry was met in the reception area by one of the first-year apprentices and shown to the office of Mr. Henshaw. The office was more like a partitioned off area within the main drawing office. One side of it was glass, the rest of oak panelling covered with shelves containing large books, ledgers and a vast array of rolled up charts and drawings.

Mr. Henshaw seemed an amiable sort of man. He explained what they did in the drawing office, the things that Harry would learn there, what was expected of him and his long-term prospects if he successfully completed his apprenticeship. Harry sat there in silence for most of it. Some of what was said he didn't understand and went in one ear and out the other. One thing that he did remember was that he would get a pay rise on his birthday every year. That'll please his parents he thought, especially his dad.

Sitting there in that office, he realised that he was no longer a child. Doing and saying childish things would no longer be tolerated. At least not here. For the first time in his short life, someone was talking to him as an adult. If he was going to get anywhere in life, today was the day that journey began. He'd been given a chance and he was going to do all he possibly could to make a success of it.

Mr. Henshaw got up and stepped over to the door. He opened it and said "Come with me and I'll introduce you to the senior apprentice, who will show you the ropes".

Harry walked behind Mr Henshaw as they made their way to the far end of the drawing office. He must have counted at least forty large drawing boards. Each one occupied by a man so totally engrossed in what he was doing, they didn't even look up as he passed. They reached the far corner of the office. Some of the tables here had two or three young men sitting around them in silence, concentrating on the task in hand. Standing with his back to them, a young man was at a table with two younger lads either side of him obviously receiving some instruction.

Mr. Henshaw walked up behind him and put his hand on the shoulder of the eldest one and said something to him. There was an exchange of words and Mr. Henshaw returned to Harry. "If you'd like to sit here for a minute", indicating a vacant table and chair, "Joe will be with you in a minute. Do everything he tells you, and you won't go wrong".

"Thank you, sir,", replied Harry. Mr. Henshaw walked off back to his office.

Harry sat there and looked around. He felt like a very small fish in a very big ocean.

The table at which he sat was bare save for a piece of notepaper and a few blunt pencils. As was his want, He picked up the sharpest looking of the pencils and began to doodle. After a minute of two, he turned the paper over and started to sketch the view before him. The rows of desks, bookcases, windows, and the people working at them. This was his new world, and so far, he liked it.

Suddenly, he was clapped on the back, making him jump. "Harry Cox, I presume?", said the young man. "Er, yes, yes Sir, I am" replied Harry looking slightly dazed.

"Nice to meet you. My name is Joseph Mulcare, but you can call me Joe. No need to call me 'sir', I'm an apprentice, just like you". As he said this, he leant over Harry's shoulder and picked up the paper he'd been drawing on. "I'm impressed", he said, "The perspective is spot on, there's detail, the scale is right and you did all this in a couple of minutes. I'm very impressed". He put the paper back down on the desk and said "Right, come with me and we'll go for a walk round the yard. It's a big place, but don't worry, we'll be back in time for lunch".

The ship yard was enormous. It was the size of a small town. Somehow, being on the inside made it seem bigger. He'd walked past it plenty of times. He had occasionally sat on the other side of the river and viewed it from there.

"Does your father work here?" asked Joe.
"No, my two older brothers do though".
"What department are they in?"
"Welding and riveting".

"Oh, right. We won't go over there; it can be a bit dangerous. We'll get shouted at if we're in the wrong place. People can get killed if they're standing in the wrong place. I heard that someone got his head knocked off once".

Harry turned slightly green, but it didn't put him off his lunch.

As Harry walked home later that day, his head was buzzing with all the information that had been given to him. Joe seemed to know everything about the place. Six years hard graft, and he was now looking after all the apprentices and was tipped to be a supervisor in a couple more years. If Harry could emulate what Joe had done, he would be very happy with himself.

He decided that he was going to like it in the drawing office. The work was going to start off a bit boring, but he half expected that. Filling ink wells, sharpening pencils, cutting paper, burning rubbish, running errands, putting away equipment, generally keeping the place tidy. And then slowly, he would be taught how to read drawings and plans, setting out boards and doing calculations. He wouldn't mind any of it. Harry had a logical and well-ordered mind. He always liked things to be in the right place, and here everything had to be in the right place and done at the right time or it just wouldn't work. Yes, he was going to like it here.

Day by day, week by week, month by month, Harry's confidence grew. He had only been the general dog's body in the office for three-months before another young lad had joined and relieved him of those thankless tasks. Now, he had a year under his belt and things were beginning to get really interesting. On top of that, he would be getting a pay rise. He gave a third of his pay to his mother, and the rest of it, he kept in a tin under his bed. He hardly ever went out, preferring to stay at home and read or sketch.

Later in the day, he was given a copy of his first report. It was written by Joe and signed off by Mr. Henshaw. He knew what it was going to say, as Joe had discussed it with him beforehand. It said he was punctual, conscientious and hard-working, and displayed a natural ability for the job. He would go far.

The coming year would see him doing more of the same; copying and duplicating plans. Some of the older lads found it boring, but he was happy to do it. He was fascinated by the way the different classes of ship were designed and constructed and how different they could look when complete. Every day he was learning, and the more he learnt, the more he wanted to know. This was going to be his future, and the future looked bright.

The following twelve-months saw Harry grow in confidence. He was no longer the new boy, or even a first-year apprentice. The older draughtsmen in the office liked him. He was always looking over their shoulders and asking sensible and pertinent questions and generally showing an interest in whatever it was they were working on. He had an insatiable thirst for knowledge. He was like a sponge, he absorbed everything that was said to him and most importantly of all, he remembered it.

Joe Mulcare had finished his apprenticeship and was now a proper member of the staff. He was working on the team drawing up the 'Carpathia'. Something that he hoped he would be able to do himself one day.

The apprentice boys, were now looked after by the new senior, Thomas Bainbridge. He was nice enough, but didn't have the charm or personality as Joe, but he was a good draughtsman. He would often try and join Joe at lunchtime and they would eat their sandwiches together. Usually in the canteen, but if it was warm outside, they would go and sit on a jetty by the water's edge and talk about ship design. Joe was his mentor, a bit like a brother. Although his real brothers worked at the yard, they never talked about their work at home. As they got older, all they seemed interested in was supping beer with their mates and going to a dance in the hope that they might meet a girl.

Harry thought he would have time for all that later. What was more important now was, learning his trade, honing his craft. Girls would have to wait, at least until he'd finished his apprenticeship. Nothing was going to stand in his way.

5 - Making His Way

In the summer, he'd gone down to the yard where the rubbish was being burned and saw one of the maintenance men taking an axe to a couple of old desks. "What are you smashing those up for?" he asked the man.

"Firewood", he replied.

Harry frowned, and said "But why, what's wrong with them?"

The maintenance man rested his axe on the top of the one desk that was still intact. Pushed his flat cap back, took a long drag of the cigarette sticking out of the corner of his mouth and said, "They're old, a bit knackered, not worth mending and they've been replaced with new ones. I've been told to get shot of them". "Now young man" he continued, "If there are no more questions, I'd like to get on. "I'll be late for my lunch".

"Can I have the top of one?" said Harry, hopefully.

The man thought about it for a moment and said, "I suppose. What do you want it for?"

"I'd like to take it home and use it as a drawing board. I work in the drawing office, and I could use it to practice on".

The man mulled it over. "Alright", he said. "I'll leave it by the gatehouse. You can collect it from there on your way out tonight. If anyone says anything, just say Arthur let you have it".

"Thanks Arthur". Harry turned and went back to work.
"What on earth have you got there Harry?" Said his mum as he started to climb the stairs when he got home.
"It's the top of an old desk. I'm going to use it as a drawing board".
"And where's it going to live?"
"Under my bed, mum, it won't get in anyone's way, I promise"
As Harry looked down at his mother, he noticed that she looked very pale. He gave her a quizzical look and said, "Are you all right mum?".
"Yes" she snapped back, "I've just got a bit of a cold, that's all". She scuttled back into the kitchen and started to cough. A loud, rasping, chesty cough, that sounded horrible.
"She's going to cough her guts up, one day", said one of his elder brothers a couple of nights before. Many people living in the city had a bit of a cough, but hers was definitely getting worse. If it was a cold, it was one of those lingering ones.

Harry shared a room with his three younger brothers; Geoffrey, Reginald and Ian. They wouldn't mind. They were always out, in all weather, kicking a ball about. Football mad they were. Harry's bed was by the window. He could put it on top of the bed when he wanted to use it, and slide it back under in the evening.

Just before his seventeenth birthday Harry came home from work. The house was unusually quiet. He went into the kitchen and was met by the sombre looking faces of his father, two elder brothers and his elder sister. There was one noticeable absence.
"Where's mum?" he said. There was a moments silence, and his father said,
"There's nothing to worry about Harry, your mother has gone to hospital. It's that cough of hers. The doctors want to keep an eye on it. She'll be out before you know it".
"Can we go and see her?" Harry said quietly.
"Not just yet", replied his father, "She needs to have a bit of rest. Perhaps next week".

Dinner was a quiet affair that night. Lucy cooked the dinner with help from Laura. The seriousness of their mother's illness was kept from the younger children. Everyone went to bed early that night.

Harry's seventeenth birthday fell on a Friday. He'd been looking forward to it all week. The pay rise would be nice, but more importantly, it would be another year crossed off his apprenticeship.
In the afternoon, Tom Bainbridge came to the drawing board he was working at. Harry looked expectantly at him, thinking he was going to get his end

of year report. Tom said, "Mr. Henshaw has your report and he would like to see you".

"What, now?" replied Harry a little surprised.

"Yes, now. Go on, don't keep him waiting".

"Come in Harry, take a seat". Mr. Henshaw was standing at his desk. He rolled up a blueprint, put a rubber band around it, and put it on the shelf where many others lay.

Harry sat there smiling and wide-eyed, wondering why he was there.

"Firstly, happy birthday. Seventeen years old, eh? A lot has changed in the world since I was seventeen, I can tell you. When I began my apprenticeship, steel hulls were a rarity, now they're commonplace. Everything is getting bigger and faster. The lord only knows where it will end. Anyway, I digress". He sat down in his chair and continued. "Congratulations on your latest end of year report. Everybody in the office, not just Joe and Tom, think you're a good lad. I've seen how hard you work for myself. Don't think things like that go un-noticed". Harry's smile got a bit wider and he could start to feel himself blush. "Thank you, sir," he said in his usual calm, soft tone.

"Now, what I want to tell you is, and this doesn't go beyond these four walls", he looked around conspiratorially as he said it and lowered his voice, "The company is in negotiations with its biggest customer and the government, and is hoping to bid on two new ships that will be the biggest and best we have ever built". Harry's eyes widened and he swallowed hard in amazement.

Mr. Henshaw continued, "If we get the contract, there will be some significant changes around here. I have no doubt that you will be head apprentice when your time comes, and I'm sure there will be a place for you on one of the teams working on the new projects".

Harry could have burst into tears with elation. This is exactly what he wanted. All his hard work and commitment had led to this point. I better not get ahead of myself, he thought. It might not happen. But what an opportunity. "When might this happen, sir?

"Soon, hopefully sometime in the next six-months".

6 - A Death in the Family

In early June, Harry was working at his drawing board in the office. There was still no official word on what was going on with the company and its potential new contracts, but it did seem more people knew about the rumours and that they were being openly discussed in the office. There was a tap on his shoulder. It was Tom. Harry looked up and saw that Tom was looking at the office door with a concerned look on his face. Harry followed his gaze and saw his brother Charles standing in the doorway. He was very grubby. He had his flat cap rolled up in his hand and his bag over his shoulder. The look on his face said that all was not well.

Harry walked across the office towards him. In the three-years he had worked there, he had never seen one of the welders in the drawing office. Others in the office turned to look.

"What are you doing here?" Harry whispered sharply at his brother; aware he had an audience.

"It's mum", he replied in a low voice. "Dad sent a message; he wants us to come home now".

Harry felt a knot in his stomach and the sound of his heartbeat ring in his ears. For a moment he thought his legs were going to give way under him.

Tom appeared at his side. "Is anything the matter Harry?"

"It's our mum" he said shakily. "She's been in hospital for ages, our dad wants us to go home".

"Well go, you must. I'll tell Mr. Henshaw, I'm sure he won't mind. Leave it to me, and go".

Harry and Charles left the building. Cecil was waiting outside for them. After punching their timecards by the main gate, they ran all the way home. In normal circumstances, Harry would have been lagging behind his stronger and more athletic brothers, but on this occasion, probably fuelled with adrenaline, he kept pace with them.

When they arrived home, they found their father in the kitchen with Lucy, Laura and Geoffrey. All were sat around the table, in tears. Before Charles, Cecil or Harry could say anything, their father stood up and in an emotionally strained voice said, "I'm not long back from the hospital. They sent a messenger to me at work saying I ought to get round there as your mum had had a turn for the worse". More tears welled up in his eyes and started to run down his cheeks. "By the time I got there, she was gone". He wiped the tears away with his handkerchief. "They said it would have been a blessed relief. She's at peace now, no more pain and suffering".

Everyone sat at the table in silence except for a few gentle sobs and sniffing. Charlie sat there with his head in his hands. "We're going to have to be strong, he said defiantly. "The four youngsters will be home from school soon. They probably won't know understand what any of it means".

Life in the Cox household had changed forever. The feeling of joy and happiness had gone. and had been replaced with melancholy. It certainly felt that life would never be the same again. Their mother had been the lynchpin holding everything together. The two eldest girls had taken over the responsibility of running the household. Cooking, cleaning, laundry, shopping, making and repairing clothes. They had enough money for the day-to-day things, but they weren't wealthy by any stretch of the imagination. Charles' employer had given him a permanent office job, so he wouldn't need to spend days away from home.

Only the youngest children carried on with anything resembling normality. They seemed to relish their new found freedom. Lucy and Laura were far less strict with them than their mother ever had been. Perhaps it would hit them later. Grief affects different people in different ways, even the young.

The funeral had been a quiet family affair. Lols had been an only child, and both her parents had died some years ago. She only had distant relatives on her side, most of whom lived on the south coast. They were never going to traverse the full length of the country for a thirty-minute service. Charlie's younger brother, also called Harry, made the effort. They hadn't seen each other for a number of years, so it turned out to be quite a tearful reunion. Young Harry enjoyed talking to his uncle. He was aa urban architect in Southampton, so there was a lot of common ground between them. He'd tried to talk about ship design and engineering with his father, but he didn't have the basic knowledge to have a worthwhile conversation about it. Even his elder brothers who worked on the ships displayed little interest. He'd felt a bit isolated. His uncle knew the right questions to ask, and they talked long into the night.

Life went on at the shipyard. The three brothers seemed a little closer. The constant joking and ribbing one another had stopped and they chatted to and from work more like adults than teenagers. Everyone had seemed to suddenly grow-up. It all happened very quickly.

Everyone in the office had been very kind to Harry. He even received a note from Mr. Peskett, offering his condolences to Harry and the family. The whole shipyard felt like one big happy family. Each department looking after its own, working and co-operating with the others, all for the benefit of the customer. Business was booming, and it was about to enter its golden period.

Harry no longer saw very much of his first mentor, Joe Mulcare. He was in demand and always kept busy.

Harry was becoming good friends with Tom. He had taken good care of Him when his mother had died, sorting out his time off work and easing him back in when he returned.

Tom came from a well-to-do family up in the north of the county. The family seat was Eshott Hall, but they also had a more modest residence in Clayton Road, about half a mile from where Harry lived, up the Jesmond Road. His father insisted that he make his own way in the world. A family friend got him into Swan Hunter, as he expressed an interest in becoming an electro-mechanical engineer.

None of this was apparent to the casual observer. He was just, good old reliable Tom. One of the drawing office lads who was surely earmarked for greater things. Nothing was too much trouble, nothing fazed him. A born leader of men, or at least, soon would be.

At the weekend, he was the archetypal socialite. Attending dinners with other members of his family at all the fashionable houses in the north-east. Very well connected indeed. He had invited Harry along to some of the more local functions in the city, but he had politely refused, saying he was needed at home those particular weekends. Harry was confident at work in familiar surroundings, but still a bit socially awkward. He only had one good suit, and that was last worn to his mother's funeral. He knew nothing about the latest fashions but felt others did and they would look down on him in social gatherings that were far above his station.

7 - A Bright Future

It was the end of June, and Harry was at his drawing board with the midday sun flooding into the office. He became aware of murmurings at the far end of the office. The murmurings got louder. Everyone in the office all seemed to be talking at once. What on earth? he muttered to himself. All the senior men were now starting to crowd around the main door to the office. Harry craned his neck to see what all the fuss was about.

The door opened, and there was an almighty cheer from the assembled crowd. The 'Governor' walked in. None other than George Burton Hunter himself. Closely followed by Mr. Peskett and Mr. Henshaw. The three men were positively beaming from ear to ear and basking in the hurrahs directed at them.

Mr. Hunter was wearing his trade mark yachting cap and blue suit. He was a large, tall man with a thick grey beard. He looked more like a sea Captain than any Harry had ever seen. He'd never been this close to him before and the great man's presence in the room was palpable.

Mr. Hunter raised his arms and motioned with his hands for the cheering and applause to stop. As it did so, Harry and the other apprentices took Tom's lead, and slowly edged forward.

"Gentleman, gentleman", said Mr. Hunter in a deep loud voice that entirely suited his persona. "Thank you, thank you, I am very much obliged". He looked around at the assembly, still smiling. "Today will go down in this company's history as a day to remember. I am pleased to announce that this morning, we have gone into partnership with our neighbours, Wigham Richardson". There was a round of applause. As it went quiet again, Mr. Hunter continued; "Now gentlemen, that is not all. For some time, we have been in discussions with His majesty's Government and our biggest customer, the British Cunard Line, and have just secured a contract for a new cruise liner, which will be the biggest and fastest the world has ever seen". Everybody in the room cheered and clapped, including all the apprentices who were now all standing on tiptoe, trying to see over the throng of people surrounding Mr. Hunter.

Amidst the euphoria in the office, Mr. Hunter went round and shook the hand of everyone in the office. When he got to where Tom Bainbridge and the apprentices were standing, Mr Hunter gathered them round into a huddle and said, "Now then, you young gentlemen, I want you to do everything Tom here asks of you. I know his father, and he's a good man".

Harry and the others were impressed. They all turned to Tom, who looked embarrassed. "There is going to be a lot of hard work coming up and I know you will all rise to the challenge. Will you give me your best?"

"Yes sir". Echoed around the room.

Within days, work had begun in the yard to build an enormous scaffold, with a roof over one of the dry docks, in order that the new ship could be built undercover, away from the elements. Soon, it was the size of three football pitches laid end-to-end. It was colossal.

By the end of the year, another neighbouring business had been bought up by the company, which meant they now had an uninterrupted river frontage of three-quarters of a mile. The place had doubled in size since he started with the company a little over three-years ago. Mr. Henshaw's forecast of the company's future had proved wholly accurate and so had the role he expected Harry to play.

The best of the apprentices, of which Harry was one, were to act as assistants to the senior draughtsmen. This meant that everything they did, would be a direct contribution to the construction of the vessel. If the rumours were true, it really was going to the biggest and fastest in the world and not just the exaggerations of Mr. Hunter. It was going to be something to be really proud of.

Harry became the assistant of James Bell. He'd been with the company for over twenty-years, and was the best man in the business for the keel and cradle calculations. He spent a lot of time in Mr. Peskett's office, who was the designer of the new ship, thus leaving Harry to get on and draw from the notes he'd leave him. His friend Tom had got his wish and was assisting the electrical engineering team.

Everybody worked hard. From the draughtsmen to the welders to the canteen staff. There was a real sense of community at the yard. A real sense that everyone was pulling together for a common purpose. There was plenty of overtime on offer, which Harry would have done without the extra payment if he'd had to, such was the pleasure he was getting from it all. Often, the three brothers would get home late after extra hours at work, eat their supper and go straight to bed, they were so tired. Their father, Charlie didn't mind. He was proud that his three eldest sons were at the shipyard working on the new contact. The whole city was talking about it. He told them that they could keep all the extra money they earned for themselves. This went down very well. Harry decided he would soon need to get a bigger tin in which to save his money.

In April 1904, Harry celebrated his twentieth birthday. At work, Mr. Bell gave him his end of year report which, as always, was exemplary. A pay rise and another year knocked off his apprenticeship was all the encouragement he needed. Only two more years to go.

That lunchtime, Tom came and joined him, sitting on one of the jetties near the river's edge. "Happy birthday old chap" he said in his relaxed, jovial manner. He dropped a small package into Harry's lap.

"What's this?" said Harry putting down his cheese sandwich to examine it more closely.

"It's your birthday today, isn't it?"

"Yes".

"Well, what do people get on their birthdays?" replied Tom with a note of sarcasm in his voice.

"Er, presents?", replied Harry feeling a bit embarrassed.

"Got it in one. Go to the top of the class. Yes, it's a present you clot"

Harry had never received a present from a friend before. Only from his mother and father. Now that his mother was gone, he doubted if he would ever get another one again. Buying presents wasn't really something his father would ever think about.

The package was tied up in blue paper and string. It was a bit smaller in size than a packet of cigarettes. He untied the string and removed the paper. Inside was a cardboard box, bearing the name 'Davidson's Jewellers'. Harry looked at Tom wide eyed and back at the box. As he opened it, a glint of silver shone in his eyes. I was a little case. Engine turned and engraved on the front were his initials; 'HJC' – Harry Jasper Cox.

"Wow" said Harry, "It's beautiful".

"I'm glad you like it. It's a card case. When you start going to important meetings, people will be impressed when you take that out of your pocket and hand them one. And you will be important one day Harry, of that, I am sure".

When Harry got home that evening, His sister Lucy had made a cake for him. They all waited until after dinner, and had a slice with a cup of tea. As expected, he didn't receive any presents.

8 - Apprenticeship Comes to an End

The following two-years went by very quickly. Harry was already working with the minimal of supervision. The various teams he worked with were more than happy with his contribution and were no longer treating him as a young apprentice, but more as an equal. A few times during the build, Mr. Peskett dramatically changed the design, often with short notice, but they all rallied round and came up with the solutions and the plans. The customer had changed the specification for the power plant and an extra funnel had to be added to accommodate it. Not something that can happen overnight. It had been a long six-years, but Harry had enjoyed every moment of it. His aptitude, dedication and constantly expanding knowledge did not go un-noticed.

On the final day of his apprenticeship, Harry received a message from Mr. Henshaw to meet him in Mr. Peskett's office. No longer a shy, first-year apprentice he was back then, he confidently strode off to the office, rolling down his shirtsleeves and straightening his tie on the way.

He knocked and entered. Both men were standing at the drawing board. Mr. Peskett did the talking; "Ah, Harry my boy, come in, come in". As Harry approached, Mr. Peskett held out his hand and shook Harry's warmly. "Congratulations. It's a very special day in one's career to successfully complete your apprenticeship".

"Thank you very much sir" replied Harry, then turning to Mr. Henshaw to shake his hand, "And to you too sir".

"Well done, Harry" he replied.

"Come and sit down" said Mr. Peskett, walking towards his desk. Harry followed.

"First of all, here is your certificate confirming you have successfully completed your apprenticeship. Secondly, here is your final report, Thirdly, here is a letter confirming your position in the company, which includes your new pay scale. Finally, and this is not something we do for everybody, only the particularly good ones; here is confirmation from Newcastle College that you are enrolled on their next course in 'Naval Architecture', which starts in September".

Harry looked shocked and bewildered in equal measure. Before he had a chance to speak, Mr. Peskett went on, "It's a full-time course for one-year. All your expenses will be paid by the company and of course, you will still be drawing your salary. All I ask is, you come back to see us once in a while and tell us how you are getting on and what you have learnt. It's a marvellous opportunity, and you greatly deserve it".

Harry looked from one man to the other. Tears of joy welled up in his eyes. He thought he was going to explode. "I don't know what to say sir, I'm completely overwhelmed", he stammered, his voice slightly breaking with emotion. "I've always s tried to do my best sir, and I will continue to do so, you have my word".

"We should be launching the new ship later in the year, you must come back for that", said Mr. Henshaw.

"Of course, sir, I wouldn't miss it for the world".

Harry walked back to the main office in a state of shock. "I can't believe this is happening" he muttered under his breath. Tom Bainbridge came bounding over.

"Happy birthday old chap and congratulations on finishing the apprenticeship. I say, are you alright, you look like you've seen a ghost".

"They've just given me a year's scholarship to the college, studying Naval Architecture".

"You're kidding? that's incredible Harry. You must be over the moon? Those scholarships only go to the best of the best. Just think what this will do for your career".

"I know" said Harry, now sporting an enormous grin. "It feels like I'm in a dream".

Harry didn't get much work done for the rest of the day. There was a seemingly endless procession of people coming up to him and offering their congratulations. In a quiet moment, he thought about his mother and how excited she would have been and all the fuss she would have made.

When he got home later that day, he was the last to arrive. As he walked into the dining room, everyone started singing 'For He's a Jolly Good Fellow'. When the singing had finished, his father stood up and handed him a glass of beer and said, "Congratulations son and well done, I'm very proud of you, oh, and happy birthday as well".

"Thanks, dad. I got a good pay rise today, and I've got some news to tell you".

Harry told them about his meeting with Mr. Peskett. His elder brothers ribbed him a bit and said "Harry's going back to school", which got a snigger around the table. But Harry had the last laugh when he told them what his new salary would be.

"Forty bob a week" snorted Charles and Cecil in unison. "For sitting in a classroom, flaming 'eck" continued Cecil. "That's more than what Charles gets, and he's been there twice as long as you have. I think we're in the wrong job".

9 - Harry Goes to College

In early September, Harry started his course in Naval Architecture at the Rutherford Memorial College in Newcastle. It was much closer to his house than the shipyard, which meant he could have a bit of a lie-in each morning.

On the 20th September, he left college at lunchtime and walked to the shipyard. Today, the biggest ship in the world, would be launched, and he had worked on it. The streets around the shipyard were very crowded, with all the people making their way down to the river, in order to get a view of the spectacle. On both sides of the Tyne, huge crowds had gathered. Harry fought his way to the shipyard and walked along the waterfront until he caught sight of Tom Bainbridge, standing with others from the drawing office. He went and joined them.

It was the most impressive thing Harry had ever seen. It was colossal. "Just imagine how big it will look once the four funnels are fitted", he said to Tom, both craning their necks.

"They are saying that it's the biggest ship ever built, and at twenty-thousand tons, I should think so too" He replied.

After a bit of pageantry, the guest of honour made her way to a specially erected platform from which to carry out the naming ceremony. After a few speeches from Mr. Hunter and other members of the board of directors, the champagne bottle was handed to the Duchess of Roxburghe. "Who is she exactly?" whispered Harry.

"My dear fellow, don't you know anything? She's a politician, the sister of the old Chancellor of the Exchequer – Randolph Churchill. You're going to have to do better than that if you want to get on in polite society" Tom said mockingly. Harry looked at him blankly. "You remember that chap who escaped from the Boers in South Africa a few years ago? Came home to a hero's welcome? Winston Churchill?"

"Oh yes, I remember him".

"Well, she's his aunt".

The bottle was attached to a length of chain. Somewhere on the bow of the ship. In a loud, clear voice she said "I name this ship the Mauretania. God bless her and all who sail in her". She let the bottle go and it smashed against the ship, champagne spraying everyone standing nearby, and a tremendous roar went up from the many onlookers. There were a few creaks and groans, and then it felt like the earth was moving. As if sliding on rails, the massive structure started to inch its way backwards towards the river. It picked up speed and with an almighty whoosh, the stern hit the water, sending a huge wave across the

Tyne to the south side. Cheering could be heard all around, on both sides of the river. People were waving flags and nearby ships sounded their claxons. A truly momentous day for the people on Tyneside.

10 - New Opportunities

Harry worked hard at college. Absorbing and retaining everything. He seemed to have a photographic memory, always remembering, never forgetting. Invariably top of his class, other students would seek him out to explain complex technical issues that their instructors sometimes failed to do. As a result, he made a lot of new friends. There were people from all over the country studying there, London, Portsmouth, Liverpool, Glasgow, all the great port cities. A number of his fellow students were hoping to join the Royal Navy once they had received their qualification. Harry had grown up surrounded by commercial shipping and had never really given much thought to the Royal Navy. Now he came to think of it, a merchant ship was built the same way as a military one. Britain at the time, had the biggest military navy in the world with the Japanese second and America third. The more he looked at the opportunities in the Royal Navy, the more he became interested. He had no plans to leave Swan Hunter & Wigham Richardson, but going forward, he would certainly keep his options open.

With extra money in his pocket, he decided to invest in some smart clothes. He was always being ribbed by his good friend Tom Bainbridge about his appearance. Of course, Tom could afford the latest fashions, he had a clothes allowance from his father that kept him impeccably dressed. Harry always had an old-fashioned, slightly stiff look about him, always practical but never stylish.

From time to time, he would meet up with people he knew from the shipyard and they would go for an early evening drink, usually on a Friday. Tom would usually be there, before going off to see his family in the North of the county. One evening as he was about to leave, he said to Harry, half in jest, but actually meant it, "Now that you've finally taken my advice and smartened yourself up a bit, I might invite you up to Eshott one weekend and teach you how to shoot".

"That would be nice" replied Harry in a deliberately non-enthusiastic way. "I'll try not to shoot the gamekeeper, or you". The both laughed and Tom went on his way.

Harry's twenty-first birthday fell on a Monday. He was back at college after the Easter break and didn't really want to go out and celebrate until the Friday. As he walked out of the college main gate, a familiar voice called out behind him. "Happy Birthday old chap".

It was Tom, who had diverted there on his way home from work.

Harry stood and smiled as Tom strolled up to him, then shook his hand. "Thank you, kind sir".

"Fancy a swift half before you go home, celebrate reaching manhood unscathed and all that".

"Not tonight thank you Tom, my sisters are putting on a special dinner for me tonight. I'll be alright for our usual Friday night soiree".

"Ah, I was going to talk to you about that. I can't make this Friday, but I was wondering if you'd like to come up to Eshott for the weekend?

Harry was slightly taken aback. Tom had threatened to invite him for some time, but he never thought it would actually happen.

"Oh, er, well, er" Harry stammered.

"I'm not taking no for an answer" said Tom forcefully. "It's your birthday, we will eat, drink and be merry. With any luck my sister will have a few friends to stay, so we won't have to dance together". They both chuckled like schoolboys.

Suddenly looking a bit serious, Harry said "Will I have to shoot anything?"

Tom laughed even louder, "Not unless you want to eat a Roe Deer for your supper. The season doesn't start until December. I thought you were educated".

"I shall look forward to it, thank you very much. Oh, just one thing, I don't have a dinner jacket" Harry said looking mildly embarrassed.

"Don't worry, just bring the best gear you have, and I'm sure we can sort out what you need when we get there".

They agreed to meet at Newcastle station at six o'clock Friday evening.

11 - Eshott Hall

The two friends met at the allotted time and boarded the northbound train. Tom had bought the tickets and much to Harry's surprise, they were first class. He couldn't really see the point of paying the extra for a journey that was only going to take about an hour, but he supposed that Tom went everywhere first class. Harry hadn't travelled very much at all really. From his birthplace in Stockton, the family had travelled to Scotland when his father had got a job there. They lived for a few years in a small-town south-east of Glasgow and then to Newcastle. He often thought that he'd like to travel but as yet, had never had the opportunity to do so. Perhaps one day, he would get to go on one of the ships he built and go somewhere interesting and exotic. It would be later in the year that the Mauretania would go on its maiden voyage to America.

The train stopped at Chevington Station. Harry and Tom were the only passengers to get off. They were met by the station master, who greeted Tom by name, "Good evening, Master Tom. Ambrose is waiting for you". He took their bags and led the way around the station house to the road. A horse and carriage sat there, with a very old looking man sat at the front, holding the reins. He looked every inch a farmer. All he needed was a piece of straw in his mouth and the picture would have been complete.

"Good evening, Ambrose" called out Tom in a voice louder than his usual.

"Evening Master Tom" the old man replied, doffing his cap.

Tom turned to Harry, "Ambrose has lived on our land and taken care of the farm since my grandfather's day. He's a bit deaf now, poor old chap. I don't know what we'd do without him". He repeated the last bit again in a loud voice for Ambroses' benefit, "I don't know what we'd do without you".

"You'll manage alright" he replied.

With the luggage loaded and the two passengers sitting either side of the carriage, Ambrose gave a flick of the reins and click of his tongue and they were on their way. The sun was getting low, but it wouldn't be dark for at least another hour.

"How long will it take to get to the house?" enquired Harry.

"About fifteen-minutes" replied Tom. "I'll show you around the grounds tomorrow, it'll be too dark tonight". Harry nodded in appreciation.

The carriage turned left off the main track and made its way down the private drive of Eshott Hall. Tree-lined and beautifully manicured, nobody could fail to be impressed. At the end of the drive stood the most beautiful and elegantly proportioned Georgian house.

"Good grief" Harry blurted out, "I had no idea, it's enormous. How many bedrooms does it have".

"Er, twenty-six, I think" replied Tom, "Do you know, I don't think I've ever actually counted them".

They stopped outside the front entrance. The door was open, and standing just outside on the gravel drive, stood what Harry presumed to be a butler and a groom. He wasn't entirely sure, as he had never actually been anywhere before that had one.

Harry and Tom got down from the carriage. The groom went to get the luggage while the butler approached Tom. "Good evening, sir, I trust you had a pleasant journey?".

"Yes, thank you Bradders". He turned to Harry, "This is Bradshaw, better known as 'Bradders'. If you want anything, he's your man. The best batman in the business".

"Thank you, sir, you are too kind. Your father is in the drawing room, sir".

"Right Harry, let's go and see the old man".

They walked across the entrance hall that had a highly polished stone floor. Tom opened the door to the left of the staircase and entered the room, with Harry three-steps behind.

As expected, the drawing room was large. Rectangular in shape, a marble fireplace graced one wall with three large sash windows on the opposite. There was a liberal scattering of sofas, armchairs, and occasional tables, all in the modern style. At least twenty guests could sit comfortably in here Harry thought to himself. Despite the failing light outside, the room had a bright and airy feel to it. Fresh, colourful paintings adorned the walls with the occasional portrait of a family member. His first impressions were good ones. This was a home, not just a large old country house to rattle around in. It would appear, the Bainbridges' were men of taste and embraced modernity. All this went through Harry's mind as he walked to the centre of the room and looked around in awe.

"Good evening father," said Tom. His father was sitting in a comfortable looking leather armchair near the bookcase at the far end of the room. He put down the book he was reading, removed his pince-nez, and stood up. "Thomas, my boy, how the devil are you? Working hard I hope?"

"Of course, I am my father's son", he replied rather flippantly.

"Good, good, good. Now then, who do we have here?" the old man enquired, walking past his son and towards Harry.

"Father, allow me to introduce, my good friend, the second-best employee of Swan Hunter and Wigham Richardson, Mr. Harry Jasper Cox esquire", Tom said rather theatrically.

Harry smiled broadly as he shook the hand of Mr Bainbridge senior. "A pleasure to meet you sir" Harry said, trying to sound as confident and relaxed as Tom. "Thank you for inviting me into your beautiful home".

"It's a pleasure my boy, Thomas has told me all about you. He tells me your one of the best. He's always been a shrewd judge of character". Mr. Bainbridge put his arm around Harry's shoulder and steered him towards a nearby sofa. "Come, sit down and have a drink. You can tell me all about yourself. What line of work is your father in?".

They sat and talked. Tom pulled the bell-pull next to the fire place and was quickly attended to by Bradders. who left and returned post-haste with a decanter of whisky, a soda syphon and three glasses.

After Harry had recounted his humble life story to Mr. Bainbridge, the three men got up and went to prepare for dinner. "It's just us tonight" said Mr. Bainbridge, "Your mother and sister will be arriving tomorrow afternoon. They've been in London for a couple of days. Alice is bringing an old school friend with her".

Tom showed Harry to his room. His bag had been unpacked and everything neatly folded and put away in the chest of drawers and wardrobe. Laid out on the bed was a dinner jacket. "Excellent" said Tom, "Looks like Bradders has come up trumps again". He picked up the jacket and held it open for Harry to try on".

"Where did he get it from?" asked Harry inquisitively.

"I expect it belonged to one of my brothers. It may not be the latest fashion, but it is perfectly serviceable and will be good enough for the next couple of nights".

Harry stood in front of the long mirror, "It's a perfect fit", he smiled. I'll try not to spill gravy all down it" he said in jest.

"We'll make a gentleman of you yet". Retorted Tom. "Right, see you downstairs in half an hour".

Tom left, and Harry sat on the end of the bed looking around at yet another large, stylish room. "How the other half live", he said quietly to himself. He'd never considered his life-style before. He had lived with his mother and father, brothers and sisters in various houses over the years. He knew they weren't poor but neither did they have money to spend frivolously. Not that he was implying the Bainbridges' were frivolous, far from it. They had worked hard, and created a very profitable business empire that included farming, coal mining and had the largest drapers store in the north-east. They also had something that no amount of money could buy; taste, charm and charisma. Harry was pleased that a man like Tom was his friend. That in itself was quite a compliment. Tom didn't suffer fools gladly, and the fact that he had brought him here to stay, did nothing but boost his confidence. He felt that if Tom believed in him, he could believe in himself.

Dinner that evening was a quiet affair, with a main course of pork chops courtesy of Ambrose from the home farm. The three men sat at one end of the large dining table. A modest amount of claret and, port was consumed with the meal as they conversed about business, politics and world affairs. Just before they were about to retire to the drawing room, Tom had got up and proposed a toast to his good friend Harry and wished him a belated happy twenty-first birthday. This prompted Mr. Bainbridge to open a box of his favourite cigars and pass them round. Sitting back on one of the sofas, puffing on an enormous cigar and sipping his brandy, Harry thought to himself, this is the best birthday I've ever had.

The following morning, after a hearty breakfast, Tom took Harry for a walk around the estate. Most of the gently rolling landscape was given over to arable interspersed with cattle and sheep, not forgetting the pig-pens, that had graced the dinner table the previous evening. It was a warm sunny day with a moderately cool breeze coming from the east, off the North Sea. Walking was easy over the dry ground, and by lunchtime, their circuitous route had led them to the village of Felton. which sat on the river Coquet. They decided to stop for lunch at the Northumberland Arms, an old coaching inn on the south side of the river. Judging by the reception he got, Harry formed the opinion that Tom was a regular. A ploughman's lunch was served to them, along with two foaming pints of ale, which they consumed sitting on the wall outside the pub.

The route back, took them past one of the family's coal mines. A small affair, but nonetheless profitable. They finally got back to Eshott at about three o'clock. As they walked down the drive, in the shade of the trees, they heard the sound of a carriage behind them. They stepped to one side to allow it to pass. Once again, it was being driven by Ambrose. There were three passengers; a well-dressed woman of about sixty years of age, which Harry took to be Tom's mother and three much younger, fashionable ladies of similar ages to himself, which he took to be Tom's sister and entourage. Which one was which, he had no idea.

As the carriage went past everyone waved to one another Tom shouted out. "Hello mother". To which he received a "Hello darling".

Tom and Harry caught up the now stationary carriage outside the front of the house. Bradders was assisting the passengers to alight, and the footman was removing the luggage. Harry couldn't help but think that there seemed to be an enormous amount of it for only three passengers.

Tom's mother walked to wards them and she embraced Tom affectionately, kissing him on the cheek. "My darling boy", she said warmly to him, "I am sure you get taller and taller every time I see you".

Mrs. Bainbridge was a very elegant, petit woman, impeccably dressed in the latest fashions. Harry could see now where Tom got that sparkle in his eye from.

"How was your trip to the metropolis?", enquired Tom.

"The travelling to and fro is exceedingly tedious but once there, we had a lovely time, thank you darling".

Tom turned to face Harry. "Mother, allow me to introduce Mr. Harry Cox, a first-class draughtsman and an all-round, thoroughly good egg".

Harry, feeling a little embarrassed, didn't know whether to bow or hold out his hand. He did the latter. "Ah, Harry, so lovely to meet you. I have heard so much about you from Thomas". Harry found this hard to believe. Whether it was true or not, Harry was charmed.

"A pleasure to meet you Mrs. Bainbridge", said Harry shyly as he gently shook her delicate hand, "Thank you for allowing me to stay in your beautiful home".

"You are most welcome, but please, do call me Kate, I insist".

She took Harry's arm and wheeled him around to where the two young ladies were standing. "This is my daughter, Alice". She indicated a tall slender woman, not much older than Harry. He could see the family resemblance. Alice and Tom both had their mother's facial features. "Alice, this is Harry".

The two shook hands, and Harry said, "Very nice to meet you miss".

"This, continued Mrs. Bainbridge, is May".

"An old school friend of mine", interjected Alice.

"Delighted to make your acquaintance miss", said Harry.

May was of similar age to Harry, perhaps a year or two older. She was slim and attractive and had a healthy complexion Her chestnut brown hair was pulled up under a wide-brimmed straw hat, decorated with dried flowers, held in place by a pale blue silk ribbon.

All three women were dressed to a high standard and would not have looked out of place on the cover of 'La Mode Illustrée'. "Harry suddenly remembered that the family owned 'Bainbridge's' in Eldon Square in Newcastle, a fancy draper where such fashion could be obtained. His sisters would often go there to get ideas about the latest fashions to incorporate into their own dressmaking.

Introductions over, the ladies went straight to their rooms to change out of their travelling outfits while Tom and Harry went and sat in the ornamental garden at the rear of the house. It was that awkward time of the day. It was too early for a gin and tonic, and too late for a cup of tea. They just sat there and chatted for a while, and after about half an hour, they were joined by Alice and May. An impromptu game of croquet was organised and as it was still quite warm in the afternoon sun, a jug of refreshing lemonade ordered from the kitchen.

Tom's partner was May and Harry joined forces with Alice. The game was light-hearted, but Harry could sense an element of competition between Tom and his sister. Much to his surprise, as he had only ever played once or twice before, he and Alice won the game.

As they left the field of play, they were joined by Mr. and Mrs. Bainbridge. The ever-resourceful Bradders followed behind, pushing a trolly loaded with gin and tonics, which sparkled in the late afternoon sun.

Harry sat back in his chair and watched the interaction between the others. It doesn't get much better than this, he thought to himself. If he was at home, he'd probably be sitting in his room working, whilst the younger children would be running around the garden squabbling with one another and his two eldest sisters would be banging around in the kitchen preparing dinner. His father would be snoring away in his armchair and the older boys would probably be at St. James' watching the football. But this, this was paradise.

"A penny for them". Harry was brought back to reality from his little daydream by a nearby, soft feminine voice directed at him.
He sat upright in his chair, and glanced around, feeling a little embarrassed.
"Er, I'm sorry?" he stammered.
"A penny for your thoughts", replied May, sitting in the chair next to him.

Harry replied quietly so as not to interrupt the conversation that was going on between the Bainbridge family, "I'm terribly sorry, I was miles away then, it must be the gin. I was just thinking what a wonderful place this is and what a glorious day it has been".

"Yes, it is, you're absolutely right. Is this your first time?"

Yes, what about you?

"I've been here quite a few times over the years. Alice was my best friend at school. I love it here. Mr. and Mrs. Bainbridge really are quite wonderful people".

"Yes, I can see that", agreed Harry

Before either of them could say another word, Tom had got to his feet and announced that there would be time for another game of croquet before dinner and a chance for him to regain his honour. "Same sides as before", Mother, you can join Alice and Harry, father, you're on my side. We'll show them".

Harry joined Alice, May and Tom in the drawing room at the appointed time of a quarter to eight. Whist Bradders served the sherry, Tom gave a blow-by-blow account of his team's victory on the croquet lawn. Mr. and Mrs. Bainbridge joined the assembly and at eight o'clock, Bradders appeared and announced that dinner was served.

The three ladies were dressed in yet another elegant outfit. No wonder they travelled with so much luggage, Harry mused to himself. He'd only been in their company for about five hours, and they were in their third outfit. Wives and daughters must be very expensive to keep, he concluded.

There was plenty of room around the large oval dining table. Harry sat between Mrs. Bainbridge and May. As the soup arrived, Mr. Bainbridge asked after May's father, "How's that old sea dog of a father of yours, Miss Baynham?".

"He's very well, thank you sir. He is still the Superintendent of the Wellesley, but plans to retire in a few years".

"Good show, the man has served his country well, he deserves a rest. Please give him my regards".

"Thank you, sir, I will".

Harry's ears had pricked up when he heard the word 'Wellesley'. He turned to May, who was sitting on his right-hand side, "Would that be the naval training ship, formally HMS Boscawen, moored over in North Shields?", he enquired.

"Yes, it is", May replied, looking at Harry questioningly.

"I used to go up that way when I was a young lad, to draw all the different types of ships". explained Harry.

"There's nothing Harry doesn't know about ships", piped in Tom, I expect he could tell you how many rivets hold the thing together", he added jokingly.

"I've spent more than half of my life living on that ship", said May.

"Fascinating", said Harry. Do you ever get seasick?", No sooner had the words left his mouth, he realised that was probably not the question to ask a young lady at the dinner table. He looked around the table apologetically, and said, "I'm sorry, where are my manners?".

"No offence taken, I'm sure Harry", said Mrs. Bainbridge in a cheery voice, in an attempt to put Harry at ease.

"Why, I'd wager that May here, has the best sea legs of all of us", chortled Mr. Bainbridge.

"It wasn't always the case, was it?" Said Alice in a slightly mocking way, designed to embarrass her friend. "Tell Harry about the time you went overboard".

"Darling, I think you are being cruel, it's not becoming of a young woman in your position", said Mrs. Bainbridge, who looked wide-eyed at her daughter as if looking at a troublesome child.

"It's quite alright", said May unperturbed. She turned to Harry, "As a child, I was playing with a kite on our private deck at the stern of the ship. The string got caught on some rigging. So, I climbed up to free it, slipped, and ended up in the water. One of the ratings had to jump in and rescue me".

"You must have been Terrified", Harry replied, with concern.

"I was more terrified about what my father would do when he found out", she said light-heartedly.

"And what did he do?" asked Mr. Bainbridge.

"Nothing really, I just had to apologise to all concerned. I think my father was more embarrassed about the incident than I".

"And did it make you afraid of water?", asked Harry.

"Not at all, you cannot afford to be afraid of water, if you live on it", she said rather matter-of-factly. A ripple of laughter went around the table.

The following morning, Harry went down to breakfast, the least formal meal of the day. Tom and his father were already sitting at the table. Both were reading newspapers and didn't notice Harry until he sat down next to Tom with a plate of scrambled eggs and bacon.

Pleasantries exchanged; Harry tucked into his meal.

The three ladies arrived and were all dressed for riding. "Outfit number four", Harry said to himself and smiled.

"What are you boys doing today?", enquired Mrs. Bainbridge.

Tom lowered his newspaper, "I'm going to teach Harry how to shoot. You never know, it may come in handy one day especially if this 'Triple Entente' that Campbell-Bannerman has got us into doesn't stack up".

"Keep your friends close and your enemies closer still", came from behind the newspaper of Mr. Bainbridge. "Not sure if the man is a genius or a complete fool".

"I have absolutely no idea what any of you are talking about", exclaimed Alice in a disinterested way.

"Politics, my dear sweet, uninformed sister. Don't let it worry your pretty little, empty head".

"There's no need to be sarcastic Thomas", she retorted.

"Children, please, we have guests, they haven't come here to listen to your squabbling", intervened Mrs. Bainbridge.

"I expect your father keeps a close eye on world affairs", said Mr. Bainbridge, addressing May.

"Yes, Sir, he does. It seems that whenever there is trouble in the world, the Royal Navy are always the first to go", she said in a well-rehearsed manner. "He last saw active service during the Nile Campaign", she added proudly.

Harry sat there and observed the interaction between Tom and Alice. It was just like being at home. He was one of life's listeners. He preferred it much more than talking. Being lost in the crowd of a big family, he was happy not being the centre of attention. He could talk quite freely about subjects that interested him, but as for general chit-chat, he usually found it a bit of a bore. Not that he found his present company boring in the slightest, far from it. It was that he felt, just a little bit, of an outsider. He never went to a public school or had a private education. His parents were not wealthy or held positions of authority. They were just, ordinary. He was ordinary, but the people around him seemed to have something special about them. What, he could not yet fathom, but he knew he wanted to be one of them.

After breakfast, the ladies went out on their horses, Mr. Bainbridge went to his study and Tom took Harry out to the fields of Home Farm where they found Ambrose waiting for them with a couple of shotguns.

Tom proceeded to give Harry a crash-course on gun safety. "Basically", he said, "Don't point this end at anyone, unless you want to kill them".

A few minutes were spent on grip and pulling the weapon into your shoulder. Stance, aiming and tracking was next and, as with anything technical, Harry fully grasped what was being said to him.

Tom picked up the other Armstrong 12-bore and loaded it. Making sure Harry was standing well behind, he shouted "Pull".

There was a metallic clang and a twang. Then, from nowhere, a small black disc flew across the horizon. Tom raised the weapon, followed its trajectory and pulled the front trigger. The disc disintegrated in a cloud of black dust. No sooner had it vanished when another one followed in its path. A loud crack from the gun and the second disc splintered into many pieces. Tom broke the breach and two smoking cartridge cases flew out and over his shoulder. Harry managed to catch one but dropped it very quickly. On account of it being hot.

Tom turned around and looked at Harry, "There, it's as easy as that. Right, let's get you loaded up".

Harry got into position with Tom standing directly behind him, so that he could see exactly where the gun was being aimed. "Don't forget", he said, "Squeeze the trigger, don't yank it".

Once again, Tom shouted "Pull".

A disc scudded across the sky, Harry had it in his sights, tracking, tracking, boom. The gun sounded like it had exploded. It kicked back into Harry's right shoulder so hard, it felt like he had been kicked by a horse. He fell backwards. He thought he was going to go flat on his back but was held up by Tom. There was a loud ringing in both his ears and for a few seconds he was completely disorientated.

Tom took the gun from him and opened the breach.

"What happened?" gasped Harry, still reeling from his ordeal and clutching his painful shoulder, "Did it misfire?"

"Not, it," laughed Tom, "You. You pulled both triggers at the same time and gave it both barrels".

Harry would have laughed as well if his shoulder wasn't in quite so much pain. "The question is, did I hit the target?".

"Yes, you buffoon, you could hardly miss it with shooting like that. I think you'd be better off with a blunderbuss in future".

Harry persevered with the shooting despite the pain in his shoulder and Tom displayed the patience of a saint and his ability to instruct. By the end of the session, both were pleased with what they had achieved. They walked back to the house for lunch, Harry with his right arm hanging lifelessly beside him.

Harry had time to have a soak in a hot bath with Epsom salts. The colour of the bruise on his shoulder was now a deep plum. He gingerly rubbed in the liniment left by Bradders, got dressed, and went down to the dining room. Lunch was to be roast beef and Yorkshire pudding in honour of Tom and Harry, who would be returning to Newcastle on the late afternoon train.

"I hear you had a bit of a mishap this morning, young Harry", announced Mr. Bainbridge as everyone sat down to eat.

"Oh dear, what happened, are you alright?", added Mrs. Bainbridge.

"A schoolboy error, I'm afraid Sir. I let off both barrels at the same time. It nearly knocked me off my feet".

"And nearly broke your shoulder into the bargain", laughed Tom.

"Often happens with a novice", said Mr. Bainbridge in a conciliatory manner. "Well, I'm sure you learnt from it eh?".

"Most definitely, sir".

"How is your shoulder now?", asked May Baynham, sitting to Harry's left.

"Fine thank you, just bruised".

After lunch, they all retired to the large conservatory. Mr. Bainbridge nodded off and was gently snoring within minutes of sitting down. Tom read a newspaper, Alice and her mother did needlepoint, while Harry and May went for a stroll around the ornamental garden.

As they walked across the neatly manicured lawn, Harry asked May if she had any brothers and sisters. "Four brothers and two sisters", she answered. "I'm the eldest. What about you?".

"I'm one of ten", Harry replied. "I have two older brothers and two older sisters. Have you always lived in the north-east?

"Not really. I was actually born just south of London. We lived in Kent for a while, then we went to Birkenhead, just outside Liverpool, and then Newcastle. It was wherever my father was stationed".

"Similar story with my lot, only my father works for a brewery, not the Royal Navy", smiled Harry. "I hope to travel myself one day. There are plenty of opportunities out there for qualified naval architects. What about you? do you have any hopes or aspirations for the future?"

May thought for a moment, "I suppose I will marry a naval officer one day; they're the only types I seem to meet socially, and go wherever he goes", giving Harry the impression that that was not her ambition whatsoever.

For a moment, Harry looked at May and felt sorry for her. It was almost as if she was resigned to her fate. Her future was preordained, and she had no control over it or any say in the matter.

They finished their circuit of the garden and returned to the conservatory, just as Bradders was pouring the tea. A pleasant afternoon was had by all. The ladies read magazines and commented on the latest styles of haute couture, while the men worked their way through the voluminous selection of newspapers. It was very relaxing. Harry couldn't remember the last time he hadn't spent a weekend with his head in a text book reading about naval architecture.

At the appropriate time, Bradders entered the room and informed Tom that Ambrose was out front with the carriage.

"Good lord", exclaimed Tom, rising to his feet. "Is it that time already? Get your skates on Harry, it's time to go".

"I haven't packed my bag yet" he replied, jumping up from his seat.

"Don't worry, Bradders will have done all that".

Farewells were said, and the offer to come anytime was extended by Mr. and Mrs. Bainbridge. Harry shook hands with Alice and was about to do the same with May, when she leant forward and kissed him on the cheek and said, "It was lovely to meet you, I wish you well in your studies".

"Thank you, Miss Baynham", he replied, a little taken aback and colour rising in his cheeks.

The two men climbed aboard the carriage, and with a flick Ambrose's wrist on the reins, they were off with plenty of shouted farewells and waving as they proceeded down the driveway and off to the station.

The train arrived on time and in just less than an hour, they were back in Newcastle city centre. Harry, who had a considerably smaller case than Tom, decided to walk home, whilst his travelling companion, hailed a hansom cab.

Harry laid on his back in bed that night with a grin on his face like a Cheshire cat. What a wonderful weekend he'd had. He really ought to do it more often. He turned onto his right side. Wincing in pain, he rolled over onto his left side, and went to sleep.

12 - Royal Corps of Naval Constructors

The next few weeks saw Harry preparing for his end of course exam. It was not only important for him to pass, but to pass with flying colours. He was at the top of his class and there was already talk among the teaching faculty, that he was a potential candidate for the Royal Corps of Naval Constructors. Entry was competitive, and was open to civilians.

The more he thought about it, the more it made sense. Joining the Royal Navy would give him the opportunity to work with the largest navy in the world, that operated in every corner of the globe.

On his last day at the college, he was called to the principal's office to receive his results. Doctor Radnor, the principle, was positively beaming as harry entered the room. Short and plump, with a round balding head and spectacles, he was the image of 'Mr. Pickwick' the Dickens character. He had a soft, educated voice that immediately put one at ease. He had been a ship's doctor in Her Majesties Navy but had decided to re-train as an engineer. He hadn't lost his bedside manner.

"Come in my dear fellow, sit down", he said, rising to his feet and indicating a chair.

"Thank you, sir,". Harry was understandably nervous. The result of this exam could decide where his future lay.

"Well, young Harry, I'm pleased to tell you that you have passed, with distinction, and that you are the top student of the year. Congratulations".

Harry took a deep breath, and let it out slowly. The knot in his stomach relaxed and the weight on his shoulders lifted. He suddenly felt six-inches taller. "That is wonderful news sir", he replied, his voice slightly choked with emotion.

"I've heard nothing but good reports about you. The teaching faculty and the students, all hold you in high regard. Well done". Doctor Radnor handed Harry a certificate as he spoke.

Harry tried to read it, but was unable to on account of the tears in his eyes. He just said "Thank you".

The doctor put his elbows on the desk and steeled his hands. Looking over the top of his spectacles, he said, in a now more serious tone, "Well, how would you like to take this to the next level?".

Harry looked at him questioningly, "Sir?"

"You've no doubt heard of the 'Royal Corps of Naval Constructors'?"

"Yes, I have, sir".

"Well, I have no doubt whatsoever, that you would do very well in the entrance examination. I could arrange for you to sit it this year. As you will probably know, it is a very competitive exam. Only the best of the best will go through. I think you are eminently capable, but it would require a great effort and total commitment on your part. It would mean studying and doing your job at Swan Hunter at the same time. Would you be prepared to take on such a challenge?".

"Oh, yes sir. I would".

"The Royal Navy is a fine institution. The training and experience you'll receive there will be second to none. Is it what you really want?"

"Yes sir. I have thought about this for some time now, and it is where I see my future. I will not let you down sir, I promise".

"I was hoping that that would be your answer. A wise decision. I have in fact already enrolled you, your exam will be in June".

Harry returned to Swan Hunter the following Monday. He relished the idea of getting back to work and putting to practical use, the knowledge he had attained over the previous year.

Out of courtesy, he sought an interview with Mr. Peskett, the senior architect.

"I hear congratulations are in order". He held out his hand and shook Harry's vigorously.

"Thank you, sir. Thank you for putting your faith in me. I hope I have done the company proud".

"You most certainly have". Mr. Peskett walked round his desk and sat in the chair. "Now, you've asked to see me, may I hazard a guess at what it is you want to talk about?".

Harry's eyebrows raised and he nodded slowly. "Yes" he said tentatively.

"You've come to tell me that you are going to take the 'Naval Constructors' exam, and if you pass, you will be leaving to join the Royal Navy. Am I close?"

"Very", replied an astonished Harry.

"You feel that by leaving us, you'll be letting the side down. Well don't. The company will take great pride in the fact that one of its own went on to do great things. Reflected glory they call it. I'm sure everyone here will give all the support you need. And if you don't pass this year, there's always next year. But remember, there will always be a role for you here if you want it".

"How did you know?" asked Harry, still a little perplexed.

"Oh, that was easy, Doctor Radnor is an old family friend. He's been keeping me informed of your progress all year".

Harry sought out Tom during his lunch break. It was a hot afternoon, and the pair sat by the water's edge in their shirtsleeves to consume their lunch.

Harry told Tom about his plans for the Royal Navy and the exam he would have to pass in order for it to happen. "So, it won't be Friday afternoons in the pub or weekends in the country for me for a while". Harry finished.

Tom was very happy for his friend. "I promise not to lead you off the straight and narrow, or have any corrupting influence on you whatsoever", he said jokingly. "In fact,", he said, suddenly remembering, "I have a nice little house in west London, you could stay there if you're going to be in London".

"Thanks for the offer, but it's a long way off yet. If I don't pass the exam this year, it will be another year before I can retake it".

Tom looked Harry in the eye and said, "When have you ever failed an exam?"

Harry worked like a Trojan for the next six-weeks. Unable to study at home because of all the distractions, he was given special permission by Doctor Radnor to use the college library. Using it every evening after work to study, he would spend the weekends there as well, taking a packed lunch with him. He was in good hands. His former masters would occasionally join him and pose him questions and problems to solve. One evening, he was joined by Doctor Radnor himself, who gave him a very useful lesson on naval ranks and insignia, and even how to salute. "Even though you are a civilian in their eyes, you will be expected to know these things. You don't want to blot your copybook by failing to salute an Admiral, do you?".

The exam was to be taken on a Saturday morning, to allow the non-serving members to attend Greenwich Naval College without having to take a day off work.

Harry had never been to London before, so Tom thought it would be a good idea if he went with him and showed him around. After the exam, he would treat harry to a slap-up meal at one of the finest restaurants by way of celebration. They would go on Friday and return Sunday.

13 - A Weekend in London

The two met at Newcastle station at the appointed hour, and boarded the train to London's King's Cross station. They travelled first class and had their dinner on the train. By the time they arrived in London, it was getting on for midnight. Tom hailed a cab which took them west, to Perivale Gardens. As Tom had described, the house was small and idea for occasional use. It had belonged to one of Tom's maiden aunts, who had bequeathed it to him in her will a few years earlier. Situated next to Pitshanger Park, it felt quite rural but with easy access to town on the District Railway line from nearby Ealing Broadway. The house itself was very modest compared to the other places Tom and his family resided in. The aunt had never actually lived in it. Purchased on the suggestion of her financial adviser as a property speculation in an ever-growing suburb of capital, it would prove a shrewd investment. The area was later to be referred to as 'Metroland' by the rail company who were busily buying up estates in the hinterlands of the city.

The property was in the style of a late Victorian villa, with two-reception rooms and three-bedrooms and the usual offices. It was cosy and elegant and Harry liked it. He could see himself as quite the man about town living in a Batchelor pad like this.

Both men were so tired when they arrived, that they didn't have the energy nor the inclination to make up their beds. Harry fell asleep on a bare mattress in one of the upstairs bedrooms, still in his travelling clothes, while Tom did the same, laid out on the sofa in the lounge.

Harry woke the following morning suitably refreshed. He found Tom in the bedroom next door to his, shaving. "Morning old chap, there's a jug of hot water for you in the scullery. What time is it that you have to be at Greenwich?"

"The exam starts at one-o'clock and lasts four-hours".

"Alright then", said Tom, thinking on his feet, "There's nothing to eat of drink in the house. Get yourself ready, and we'll go for a late breakfast, or early lunch, whichever you prefer, and make our way to Greenwich. Does that plan meet with your approval".

"I'm not sure I feel all that hungry at the moment. It must the nerves", said Harry suddenly feeling butterflies in his stomach.

"Nonsense", rebutted Tom, "You can't go all day without anything to eat, you'll faint".

"Alright bossy-boots", replied Harry, unconvinced.

An hour later, the two men walked to Ealing Broadway. Harry was carrying his brown leather briefcase which contained his draughtsman set and a box of fiercely sharp pencils. They found a pleasant hotel just along from the station and ordered breakfast. By now, Harry was more excited than nervous, and, after the brisk walk, his appetite had returned.

After generous portions of egg, bacon, sausages, tea and toast were consumed, they left replete.

The train took them to Victoria, where they got off and walked to the nearby tram terminus. As the tram approached, Tom said, "Well, good luck my boy", in a paternalistic fashion. "I'll meet you back here at six-o'clock tonight, and we'll go for a nice supper. Have you got some change for your fare?".

"Yes father", replied Harry sarcastically. "Thank you", he continued on a more serious note as he boarded the tram. With a wave to his friend, he climbed the stairs to the upper deck. It was a delightfully warm day, and he wanted to see more of the place that he hoped one day to call home.

A return fare to Greenwich cost him one-shilling, which the conductor duly collected. The sights, sounds and smells of the capital filled his senses. Apart from being much bigger, it didn't seem that dissimilar to Newcastle. As he went over Vauxhall Bridge, he thought it looked like the Tyne, but without the heavy industry and ship building. He sat back in his seat with a smile on his face and enjoyed the journey.

About an hour later, he was sitting on a bench inside the main reception area of the naval college. There were three young naval officers in uniform and two others like Harry, in civilian attire. Nobody spoke. They just gave each other furtive glances out the corner of their eyes. It was a competitive exam. There would be winners and losers. All were aiming to do their best, to do better than the man next to him. Harry had never been in such a cut-throat situation before. At school, at work and more recently at college in Newcastle, everyone had worked together to achieve the best result. Now he was on his own. No-one to turn to for help. If he wanted this job, he would have to fight for it. He wanted it so much he could taste it.

As the clock struck one, the click-click sound of quarter-tipped heels on a polished stone floor, could be heard coming towards them from what seemed a very long corridor. A young officer in the smartest uniform Harry had ever seen appeared. A glance around the reception with a slight nod of the head as he counted each candidate, he simply said, in a clear, loud voice, "Follow me please gentleman". He turned and walked back from whence he came. The three naval candidates quickly fell in-line behind him, sounding as one. Harry and the two others just shuffled along behind making no attempt to keep pace with the others ahead of them. Doctor Radnor didn't tell me anything about having to march, thought Harry.

The room was about thirty-feet square. Light poured in through the windows that made up almost one whole side. The opposite wall was lined with mahogany bookshelves with every volume on them, numbered and in perfect alignment. A far cry from the jumble that sat on the office shelves where he currently worked. A desk was positioned at each end of the room, overlooked by portraits of Admirals and Captains from a bygone era. The history of the place was tangible, not just here in this room, but throughout the impressive estate.

An officer sat at each desk. Both had a blank expression on their face, looking like pressed men rather than volunteers.

There were six drawing boards evenly spaced out in the room with a small desk and chair next to each. On each desk lay a sheath of paper and a bottle of ink. Along with a name badge.

"Please sit at the table that has your name on it" said the officer that had led them there.

Harry removed his jacket and hung it on the back of the chair. He opened his briefcase and removed its contents and put them on the desk. Finally, he rolled up his shirtsleeves.

"The examination with last precisely four-hours. There will be no talking among you. If you require anything, you will raise your hand, and one of the invigilators will come to you. If you need to go to the lavatory, you will be escorted by an invigilator. Your results will be posted to you in approximately one-week from today. Those of you who are not already in the service of his majesty's Navy, will also be sent a contract of employment and the start date of your service, which will be in September. Rest assured, there will be no favouritism. Civilian candidates will receive the same fair treatment as the uniformed ones. We are looking for the best of the best. Are there any questions?".

There was silence

"Good. It is now a quarter past one, and you have four-hours. Good luck to you all, you may now turn over the question paper and begin.

Harry sat there in the warmth of the late afternoon sun, reading through his answer paper and checking his drawings. He was happy with what he had done. Every question answered to the best of his knowledge and ability. Content that he could do no more, he took out his pocket watch for the first time that afternoon. Less than ten-minutes to go. He looked around the room. Two of the uniformed candidates were standing at their drawing boards, the rest were seated. The invigilators at each end of the room were reading what looked like an instruction manual and making notes. Harry surmised that they were students here at the college and had drawn the short straw.

Harry looked at his pocket watch again. At precisely a quarter past five, the door opened and in walked the officer from earlier. In a loud, clear voice he said, "Thank you gentlemen. The invigilators will now collect your papers. Any questions?". As none were forthcoming, he went on. "Please remember to take your personal belongings with you. I will now escort you back to the reception area". He turned and went and stood by the door. Shirtsleeves rolled back down, jackets on and briefcase packed, they went on their way.

Harry met Tom back in Victoria. "How did you get on, old sport?"

"Very well", said Harry modestly. "What have you been doing all day?"

"I have had an afternoon of culture, my dear fellow. A stroll through St. James' Park, a walk around the National Gallery and then a jaunt along the Thames. And now I'm a hungry boy who wants his dinner".

"Yes, I'd go along with that, I'm starving, I could eat a horse".

"Well, I don't think they eat horse in London, you may have to go to Paris for that. I don't think we'll get in anywhere too fancy dressed like this, especially you. You look like you've just come home from the office".

"Thanks", retorted Harry despondently.

"I'll tell you what, let's slum it. We'll find a nice little pub that that can offer us good fayre and a skin full of their finest ale. What say you?".

"Yes, why not", said Harry, grinning like a schoolboy.

"There's just one problem with this place of yours, Thomas", slurred Harry as they arrived back at the house in Perivale Gardens.

"What's that, old bean?", Tom slurred back.

"It's so bloody far from Greenwich. Excuse my French".

"Don't worry about it, old boy. You'll just have to rent something closer. You can use this at the weekend".

"Thanks awfully old chap".

Back in Newcastle, Harry kept himself busy at work, trying not to think about the results he was waiting so eagerly for. While at college earlier on in the year, he had been selected as the chairman of the graduate section of the North-East Coast Institution of Engineers and Shipbuilders. He had promised to stay on until at least the end of the year, or at least until he had to move away from the area. It was this work that kept his mind occupied in the evenings and at the weekend.

No post on Saturday meant that he would now have to wait until Monday for the next delivery. "Don't fret so, son", his father said to him at the dinner table that Saturday evening. "There'll be a lot of red-tape involved I expect. You'll know sooner or later, one way or the other. Whatever they say, we're all very proud of you, aren't we?" he looked around the table. There was unanimous agreement, with nods of the head and a general hub-bub, which put a smile on Harry's face.

Thanks Dad, thanks everyone" he said. "I'm sorry I've been a bit of a grump lately, but this is really important".

"If you go to London", piped up Russell, the youngest of the boys, "Can I have your bed?".

This got a ripple of laughter around the table.

"Of course, you can, you cheeky blighter, I won't be carrying that with me on the train".

Harry walked home from work on Monday, certain he would find a letter waiting for him on the table in the hall, by the front door. There was nothing there. He asked his elder sisters, but was told that there was no post at all. He climbed the stairs with his head down and sat in his bedroom feeling miserable.

The following day, Harry met Tom at their usual lunchtime spot, down by the water's edge.

"Any news?", enquired Tom

"No. I should have heard by now, it's not looking good, is it?"

"I wouldn't be so hard on yourself. There could be a dozen reasons why there's a delay".

"Really, such as?".

"Well,", Tom looked around for inspiration, "I expect that, because you did so well, they want the king to sign your letter himself. And what with his majesty having had a busy weekend, it's got delayed".

"Nice try", said Harry, now with a smile on his face.

After lunch, Harry returned to the office. A message was pinned to his drawing board asking him to see Mr. Henshaw.

"This came for you Harry", said Mr. Henshaw, holding up a large brown envelope. Harry looked at it questioningly. "It was dropped off at the main gate by your father". As he handed it to Harry, he added; "The postmark is Greenwich". He gave Harry a knowing smile as he handed the envelope over. "Open it here in private. I'll be back in ten-minutes. I hope it's good news, I really do".

Harry was left in the office alone. His throat went dry, as he slit the envelope open. It wasn't just a letter, there was a sheaf of paperwork inside. As he slid the contents out, he noticed on the covering letter the words; We are pleased to inform …',

In the time before Mr. Henshaw returned, Harry had discovered that he had scored one-hundred percent and had impressed everyone on the examination board. He was formally offered the post as 'Probationary Assistant Constructor (2nd Class), there was a contract for him to sign and return forthwith and his joining instructions.

Mr. Henshaw was absolutely delighted for him. With his hand on his shoulder, he walked Harry round to Mr. Peskett's office and informed him of the news.

"You are a credit to this company, and to yourself. Please remember us, wherever you go in the world and whatever you do, you will always have friends here. Congratulations".

Harry was given the rest of the afternoon off. He was far too excited to concentrate on his work. His first port of call was to find Tom in the electro-mechanical engineering department. Tom was overjoyed at the news and promised they would go out and celebrate sometime over the weekend.

Harry was going to try and find his brothers but thought better of it. Too much noise, too much grime and far too many sparks flying about. They could wait until they got home to hear the news.

Instead of going straight home, Harry stopped off at his father's office to give him the news. "I thought as much" his father said, "They wouldn't have used such a big envelope just to say 'No thanks'".

Dinner that evening was a boisterous affair, with Harry fielding questions from all and sundry. "So how much are you going to get paid", asked Charles, straight to the point as ever.

"They're starting me off on two-pounds, ten-shillings a week".

"When do you go", asked Russell, with designs on Harry's bed.

"I start the first Monday in September, so I'll go down on the Friday or Saturday beforehand".

"Where will you live?"

"Well, I've been offered a place by my friend Tom, but it's too far to travel each day. The Navy have given me a list of recommended boarding houses in the area around the college, so I'll probably use one of those".

"Don't forget to write", said his father. "I want to hear all about it".

The subsequent weeks went by quickly. Harry had written to a couple of the boarding houses on the list furnished by the navy. He had settled on one in Lewisham, a comfortable thirty-minutes' walk from the college, and at a modest five-shillings a week full-board, it seemed like a good deal. Tom had given him a key for the house in west London, to use whenever he needed a change of scenery. It would be an ideal place for them to meet whenever Tom came to London.

14 - Holmwood

On the Friday prior to his departure, Tom had invited him to his family's town residence for dinner. "Nothing fancy", he'd said, "No need for your best bib and tucker. It will only be you, me, my sister Alice and her friend, May".

"May Baynham?", enquired Harry.

"Yes, oh of course, you've already met, haven't you. I'll ask her to bring her father along, you can talk about all thing's navy with him", Tom said jokingly.

The house in Clayton Road was only twenty-minutes' walk away from Harry's house. It was on a different scale and in a completely different league. It was the first time he had actually been invited. They normally met in town on a Friday night and went for a drink with friends from work.

Holmwood was an elegant, detached Georgian house, with a sweeping gravel drive, set back about fifty-yards from the road. Harry walked up the stone steps to the door and pulled the bell-pull. The door was opened by a young man in livery. He took Harry's hat and coat and ushered him into the drawing room.

The internal décor of the house was similar in style to what he had seen earlier at Eshott Hall, albeit on a much smaller scale.

"Here he is", announced Tom as he got up from his chair and walked over to welcome his friend. "It's just the four of us tonight. Mater and pater are on a buying trip to Paris, ordering up stock for the shop. Come through to the veranda, the girls have just opened a bottle of champagne".

They walked through the dining room and a small conservatory onto the ornate veranda. "Ladies I give you our guest of honour, Mr. Harry Cox RN". Pleasantries were exchanged and Harry was handed a glass of champagne. Tom raised his glass and proposed a toast; "My dear old friend Harry, here's to you and the next step of what I'm sure will be, an illustrious career in his majesty's Navy. And God help the noble people of Kent, as they have no idea what they have let themselves in for". There was laughter all round.

"I was born in Kent", offered May Baynham.

"That's interesting", said Harry, sitting down on a chair opposite the two women.

"My father was at Greenwich for a while before being sent to Sheerness".

"Do you know the area well?" he asked.

"I'm afraid not, we moved to Cheshire when I was four, I've been in the north ever since".

Harry found it easy to talk to May. He sat next to her at dinner and she talked about her father's long career and her two brothers that were also serving. He told her of his hopes and dreams for the future.

He hadn't noticed it the first time they met. Perhaps it was the formal setting and his shyness, but there was a definite glint in her eye. There was no doubt that she was a young attractive woman, only a fool would fail to notice that. What awful timing, he thought, it's the first time I've met someone like this, and tomorrow morning I am travelling three-hundred miles to start a new life at the opposite end of the country.

He asked her; "Would you father approve of me, now that I am in the Royal Navy?".

She looked him in the eye and held his gaze. She smiled and gently touched is hand, and said, "Yes, I believe he would".

Emboldened, Harry said in a low voice, "Would you allow me to write to you?".

"Yes, I would like that very much".

"Hey, you two", said Tom in a loud, slightly slurred voice, "It's a poor show whispering like a couple of conspirators. You'd better watch yourself Harry, her father will eat you alive".

Harry blushed. May said, "He isn't as bad as that, is he Alice?"

"Certainly not", she replied, "He may look like a grizzly bear, but he's as soft as a kitten".

Harry was glad to hear it.

Conscious of the late hour and the long journey that lay ahead of him in the morning, Harry said his farewells. Tom gave him a hearty handshake. "So long old friend, keep in touch, won't you? Try not to frighten the natives. I'll come and pay you a visit once you're settled in".

"Yes, we all will", said Alice purposefully, giving a sideway glance at May as she said it. She gave Harry a kiss on both cheeks and then led her brother away. "Come big brother, let these good people say their goodbyes".

Ah, yes, right you are little sister. Good lord, I didn't see that coming". They disappeared into the drawing room and shut the door.

Left alone in the hall, Harry said, "It would be wonderful to see you in London sometime".

"I go fairly regularly with Alice and her mother. They go to look at the latest fashions and get ideas for their shop".

"Splendid", said Harry, his heart beating a little faster.

As if prompted by some inner signal, they both leant forward and kissed each other on the lips.

Harry walked home that evening almost skipping with delight. In his pocket was May's address, it simply read; HMS Wellesley, North Shields Harbour, Tynemouth. Not something he was ever likely to forget.

15 - To Greenwich

The following morning, primed by their father, everyone in the household was on hand to see off Harry. After a hearty breakfast of sausages, eggs and bacon, he went around and hugged all those assembled. There were lots of tears from the girls and plenty of bravado from the boys. Charlie Cox was the last to put his arms around his son. Holding him at arm's length, and with tears welling up in his eyes, he said, "Make us proud son, your mother and I knew you had it in you. I wish she was here for you now".

Harry was choked with emotion. He just smiled and nodded while wiping his tears away with a handkerchief.

He stood on the pavement and looked up at the crowd standing on the steps. His worldly goods packed into two brown leather suitcases. He wondered when he was going to see them all again. It was unlikely they would ever want to go to London. Perhaps if he had time off at Christmas, he could come home for a couple of days. If he did that, he could possibly see May as well.

After a final wave, he picked up the cases and started to walk to the station. A chorus of "Bye Harry", from his younger brothers and sisters followed him down the road until he was out of sight.

Harry travelled second class to London. His compartment was empty for most of the journey and uneventful. Arriving at King's Cross, he took a City & South Line train to Oval station, where he picked up the tram that had taken him to Greenwich for the examination.

He got off at Deptford and went the short distance to Lewisham by cab, arriving at the boarding house at five o'clock in the evening.

The house was in the High Street and was of a solid looking, double fronted, red-brick construction. Many of the houses had been converted into shops and other places of commerce, but this stretch of the road was still residential. Harry paid the cab-driver, and used the highly polished brass door knocker to signal his arrival. The door was opened by the proprietor, Mrs. Dickenson. She was a small plump woman of about fifty years, with a ruddy complexion and friendly disposition. She welcomed Harry into the house and offered him a cup of tea. "My oh my", she chirped, "You have had a long journey today, haven't you? You must be worn out. You sit down there, and I'll bring you a nice cup of tea and a slice of cake". Harry sat down in the offered chair and said thank you.

The room was a well-kept lounge, with old but good quality furniture. There was the scent of beeswax polish in the air along with the perfume of the freshly cut flowers in a large glass vase on a side table. His first impressions were good. They got better when Mrs.

Dickenson returned with a cup of tea and a large slice of Dundee cake.

In the half hour they sat together talking, Harry learnt all about Mrs. Dickenson. Her husband, now departed, had been in railway construction. Having seen at close quarters, the positive impact the burgeoning network was having, and the lucrative returns on investment, he shrewdly invested his own money. Mrs. Dickenson ran the boarding house mainly for the company, but to also supplement her annuities from her late husband's railway stock. She had had no children, but now looked upon her gentlemen guests as 'her boys'.

After a second cup of tea, Harry was given a guided tour of the house. The room next door was the dining room. The centre piece was a heavy looking mahogany table that was set for four people. Breakfast was served at seven o'clock in the morning, and dinner would be at seven o'clock in the evening. Off the dining room was a veranda that opened out onto the garden. Smoking was permitted out here but not in the house. On the other side of the hall was a private sitting room and the kitchen.

The tour continued upstairs. The first floor consisted of three large bedrooms and a modern bathroom with separate water closet. "I've given you the room at the back", said Mrs. Dickenson. "It has a pleasant view of the garden, and is quieter. You said in your letter that you would be studying; this room has my husband's old desk in it, which you are very welcome to use".

"This is absolutely charming Mrs. Dickenson", said Harry as he looked around the room and out of the window. "It's a home from home. I know that I am going to be very happy here".

"The two rooms at the front are occupied by Doctor Campbell and Mr. Spence, both professional gentlemen. You'll meet them at dinner time. They are both out at the moment. Doctor Campbell sometimes has to work weekends". Mrs. Dickenson fumbled around in the pocket of the apron she was wearing. "Here is your key to the front door".

"Thank you", said Harry, pulling a white envelope from his inside jacket pocket. "Hear is your first weeks rent money as discussed. Will it be alright to pay you every Saturday? I'm not sure what day of the week I will be getting paid by the navy yet".

"Of course, my dear. Now, I'll leave you to get your things unpacked. There are plenty of hangers in the wardrobe. If you want to reposition any of the furniture, I'm sure the other gentlemen will help you. Don't forget, dinner is at seven".

Harry sat on the bed and looked around. This was probably going to be home for the next year while studying at Greenwich. After that, he could end up anywhere. He would be at their disposal.

After unpacking his things, he sat at the desk and read through some of the documentation that was sent to him by the navy after receiving his acceptance letter and signed contract.

One of the documents was a job description of his new role. Issued by the Admiralty in 1883, it was titled 'Instructions for the Royal Corps of Naval Constructors - Duties';

'Assistant Constructors of the Second Class will be employed in the office of the Controller of the Navy to assist in the preparation of drawings and specifications; as Overseers or Assistant Overseers of works in progress at contractors' premises; as professional secretaries to the Chief Constructors at the Home Dockyards; in the supervision of the record of weights of materials worked into ships in process of construction; in the preparation of returns of weights carried, and other estimates of the draught and trim of ships; and in giving such assistance to the superior officers of the Corps as may be directed by the Controller of the Navy, or by the Superintendents of the Dockyards to which they may be attached'.

Very grand, thought Harry, but I can't regurgitate that every time someone asks me what I do for a living. 'Naval architect', would probably best describe it.

Harry went downstairs at a quarter to seven. He could hear the sound of men's voices coming from the lounge. He opened the door and entered. "Good evening gentlemen, my name is Harry Cox, I'm the new boy".

Rising to their feet, the two occupants, held out their hand and introduced themselves. "Nice to meet you, I'm Alastair Campbell. I'm a doctor at Lewisham Hospital.

"Glad to make your acquaintance", said the other. My name is Albert Spence. I am a land surveyor with the Ordnance Survey".

As the three men sat down, Alaistair said, "You're the navy chap, aren't you? Mrs. D told us you were coming to stay".

"I will be, as of Monday" replied Harry.

"I deduce from your accent, that you are from the north-east?" enquired Albert.

"That's right, said Harry, "Born in County Durham and lived in Northumberland, with a few years in Scotland in-between".

"Ah, whereabouts in Scotland?" asked Alaistair, in his broad Scots accent.

A place called Bothwell, near Glasgow".

"I know of it", replied the doctor, "I did my training at the Glasgow Royal Infirmary. I'm originally from Striling".

The three men conversed happily together. Their friendly conversations continued in the dining room, where they were joined by their host who had prepared a meal of pork chops, potatoes, peas and gravy. Standing at the head of the table and serving the food, Harry thought how much she reminded him of his mother and of home.

After dinner, Alaistair rose to his feet and said, "I have a fine single malt upstairs, can I interest anyone in a wee dram? for medicinal purposes, of course". Harry and Albert nodded with approval. "What about you, Mrs. D? something to keep the cold out?

"No thank you dear, I will have a cup of tea".

Alaistair went to his room to get the whisky while Harry and Albert helped carry the dishes into the scullery. Mrs. D put three whisky glasses on a tray with a small jug of water and placed it on a side table in the lounge.

Alaistair poured out three good measures of the whisky, adding a splash of water to each. He then raised his glass and said, "Here's to new friends", and turning to Harry he added, "Here's to the Royal Navy and your new job".

The following morning, after breakfast, Albert Spence offered to go with Harry on a walk to Greenwich. He had wanted to get the lie of the land and work out the best possible route. Who better to go with he thought, than somebody who draws maps for a living. He had already established that. In the event of inclement weather, he could get a tram all the way to the college from the high street. It was a pleasant late summer morning, so armed with an up-to-date map, they set off.

They walked at a leisurely pace. Albert was excellent company and a walking encyclopaedia. He knew everything about the landscape, where the buses, trams and trains went, the places to go to and the places to avoid. A man in his mid-thirties, he was originally from Exeter in Devon. His work took him all over the south of England. The landscape was changing fast, especially around London. Places that were once villages and hamlets fifty-years ago, were growing into towns. The ever-expanding railway network, meant that more and more people were on the move, and all this meant work for the cartographers, to keep track of it all.

Albert was keen to show Harry Greenwich Park. On this clear sunny day, from the elevated position, there was an excellent view of the east end of the city across the Thames. After looking at the Royal Observatory, they meandered down to Blackheath, where they stopped at a cosy little pub to quench their thirst with a pint of beer each and a pickled egg.

They got back to the boarding house mid-afternoon to find the doctor sitting on the veranda smoking a pipe and reading the Sunday paper. At three o'clock, Mrs. Dickenson appeared with a large pot of tea and another sizeable slice of the Dundee cake.

Before going down to dinner that night, Harry wrote a quick letter to his father, just to let him know that he had arrived safely and was in the good care of Mrs. Dickenson.

For much of his first day at the naval college, Harry spent a good deal of time with a chief petty officer, who gave him a tour of the college. Before lunch, he was measured for, and issued his uniform. Although technically a civilian, he would have the equivalent rank of lieutenant. Once he had passed the course, it would be up to his commanding officer, wherever he was posted, to decide if he stayed in uniform or could wear 'civvies'. The only difference between his uniform and that of a regular officer, was the silver/grey band between the two gold braid strips on the badge of rank.

A lot of kit was issued to him. Cap, tie, socks, shoes, PE kit, overalls and wet weather gear. Fortunately, he was given a locker in which to keep everything. The only downside to wearing a uniform, he would have to learn to march and salute. It was going to be a lot more regimented than working at Swan Hunter or going to Newcastle College, but it was going to be a small price to pay for being in the greatest training establishment in the world.

He got home after his first day with his head buzzing with all the information that had been given him that day. His homework that night; to read various publications on naval traditions, identification of ranks, etiquette and customs.

Over the next couple of weeks, once all the induction activities had been done, Harry settled back into academia. It was made clear to him that once he had completed this course, he would be set up for life. There would be no examination at the end, he just had to do well all year long in order to get his constructor's certificate.

Having heard that Albert Spence had a camera, he asked if he would take a photograph of him in his uniform, in order to send to his family back up north. Albert was pleased to oblige, so one Saturday morning, he set up a makeshift studio in his room and took the portrait. Once developed and a few copies printed, Harry wrote again to his father telling him the latest news with the photograph enclosed. He also wrote to Tom Bainbridge and May Baynham, again with photograph enclosed. He wasn't quite sure how he should pitch the letter to May. In the end, he decided to be friendly but not too familiar.

A week after he sent the letter to May, he received her reply. She was so happy to hear from him and to hear his news. She thought he looked wonderful in his uniform. So much so, she showed the photograph to her parents. Both agreed he looked a handsome young man. The letter filled his heart with joy. It was affectionate without being gushing and it gave him all the encouragement he needed to write back in slightly more familiar terms.

Harry found the work fascinating. The basic structure of navy vessels was no different to any other ship. The challenge was, ships for military use carried heavy guns, armour plating, uprated engines, ammunition magazines, and all that had to be factored into the design and construction of them. Only the year before, HMS Dreadnought had been launched, Bigger and better than anything that went before it, it was now the blueprint for all future projects. Harry had good experience on big ships. The RMS Mauretania that he had worked on was soon to go on its maiden voyage to America. It was the biggest ship on the ocean and heralded the beginning of the golden era of British shipbuilding. Regular trips were made by train to the Royal Navy Dockyard at nearby Chatham for hands-on experience in building, maintenance and repair of all types of vessels in service. The importance of the place was not lost on Harry in terms of its history. For three-hundred and fifty years it had built and maintained the fleet, it was now just as important as ever.

Most weekends were spent reading, but whenever possible, Harry, along with one or both of his house mates, would go for a ride into London to see the sites and occasionally the theatre. He was learning his way around the city and was becoming quite adept at traversing the endlessly growing network of trains, trams and buses. London seemed to have so much more to offer than Newcastle. He had no idea how long he was going to be in the south east for, but he was certainly going to make good use of it while he was.

On Friday 6th December 1907, all the national newspapers carried the story that, on the previous evening, the RMS Mauretania had won the eastbound Blue Riband and set a new record for the Atlantic crossing. The previous record was held by its sister ship, the Lusitania. Everyone at the college knew that Harry had worked as a draughtsman of the project, and congratulated him. That evening, he wrote to his father, Tom and May. Apart from the news that all of Tyneside was talking about, he told them that he would be home for Christmas.

16 - Home for Christmas

Harry arrived back in Newcastle late afternoon on the Saturday before Christmas. Everybody was pleased to see him. During dinner, he told them all about his trips into London and all the things he saw; Buckingham Palace, Trafalgar Square, Westminster Abbey, The Houses of Parliament, Marble Arch and many other places in-between. They were all captivated, especially the younger members of the family, who vowed to go and visit him sometime.

Later in the evening, when just the elder brothers and sisters were sitting in the parlour in front of the fire, Cecil asked, "What are the girls like down there, have you met any yet?".

Before Harry had a chance to answer, his father started chuckling, "I can assure you son, the women down south are no different to the women up north. Your mother was a southern lass, remember?".

"I haven't socialised with any yet, but I am writing to a fine young lady that I have feelings for. Her name is May".

Everybody's ears pricked up; Harry had never spoken about a girl before. "So, who's the lucky girl?" asked his eldest brother Charles.

"Her name is May Baynham and she is the daughter of a Captain in the Royal Navy".

"Blimey", said Cecil, "She sounds a bit posh. Does she live in Greenwich?".

"No", replied Harry, "Here in Newcastle".

Everyone looked around in amazement. "Well, you kept that quiet". Said Charles.

"I didn't really know anything about it myself until I got to London".

Harry's sisters wanted to know all about the girl, and whether it was love at first sight.

"Not at first sight, I was too shy and nervous the first time I met her. It was the second time I saw her that I thought she was a handsome woman".

"Handsome?", questioned Laura, "Men are supposed to be handsome; don't you mean beautiful?".

"Yes, of course I do".

Harry spent Monday morning calling on friends from his old workplace. Everyone would be at home as the shipyard would be closed for the Christmas shutdown. Whilst out, he did a bit of shopping, and walked up to Tom Bainbridge's house, only to find that he and the rest of the family had already gone to Eshott Hall for the Christmas holiday. On his arrival back at his father's house, he found a letter addressed to him on the hall table. It was in the now familiar handwriting of May. In it, she welcomed him back to Tyneside and invited him to afternoon tea on board HMS Wellesley on Boxing Day. Uniform would be optional, but she would like to see him in it, and it would certainly be looked upon favourably by her father. Fortunately, he had it with him. Harry couldn't miss this opportunity to impress her father.

Christmas Day in the Cox household was subdued. It had been that way since their mother had died. She has always been the life and soul of the house, especially at Christmas. Charlie did his best, but it was just as hard on him as it was everyone else. The decorations about the house didn't look the same. The goose and apple stuffing didn't taste the same as their mother made it, despite the girls using the same recipe. It wasn't an unhappy occasion; it just wasn't as jolly. Harry went to bed that night with a feeling of melancholy and excitement in equal measure. Sad that his mother had left such a big hole in everyone's life, but happy that he would see May tomorrow afternoon.

In his uniform, Harry cut a dashing figure. He'd put it on after lunch in preparation for his visit to North Shields. Everyone wanted to try is hat on and be taught the correct way to salute and march. He left the house at two-o'clock and made his way to the tram terminus. There were plenty of people about, walking off the previous days' excesses. Harry felt a bit self-conscious walking along in his spotless uniform and highly polished shoes. It wasn't an unusual sight-seeing a man in a naval uniform, but it was Harry's first time here in his home town. He didn't think twice about it when in London.

He got the tram to the Fish Quay in North Shields, and then a short walk to where the Wellesley was moored. Two young sentries were posted on the shore-side of the aft gangplank, in unison they stood to attention and saluted him. That was something else that made him feel slightly uncomfortable.

He returned the salute and said, "I'm here to visit Miss, er, I mean, Captain Baynham. I'm Lieutenant Cox".

With a slight smirk, the taller of the two said, "Yes sir, you are expected sir, please follow me sir". Harry followed the lad along the gangplank, saluting the ensign as he stepped aboard. Harry was asked to wait on the poop-deck while the sentry went to the captain's quarters. Moments later, he returned, saluted Harry and said, "The Captain will be with you shortly, sir", and marched off.

Harry was nervous. He'd heard stories about Captain Baynham. He was a big bear of a man, a stickler for the rules, a disciplinarian, but above all, had had a well-earned reputation as a good sailor. Harry was convinced that the captain would keep him waiting out in the cold for a considerable time. No sooner had he thought it, the captain came out of his office and onto the deck.

Harry stood to attention and executed the best salute he could muster. Captain Baynham returned his salute and then held out his right hand. He took Harry's out-stretched hand and shook it vigorously and said, "Lieutenant Cox, I am very pleased to meet you. I have heard nothing but good reports about you from my daughter, May. Welcome to the Wellesley".

"Thank you very such sir, it's an honour to meet you, and thank you for inviting me to tea", Harry blurted out with relief.

"Well, that was more of my daughters' doing", replied the captain replied with a wry smile. "Let's go down below, I know my wife is looking forward to meeting you, and you can tell me all about Greenwich. I haven't been there for years".

The captain's private quarters were modest in size but comfortable. Alterations had obviously been made to the interior of the ship in order to accommodate Captain and Mrs. Baynham and there eight children, six of which still lived with them. Mrs. Baynham rose from her chair as Harry walked into the room. The captain introduced his wife, who said, "My dear young man, welcome to our humble home, you are so very welcome". Holding the fingers of her out-stretched hand, Harry gave her a little bow. Mrs. Baynham turned and introduced the assembled members of the family. "William, Lucy, Arthur, Pauline, Annie, and of course, you have already met May. The room was warm, but it alone, did not account for the perspiration that now showed on his brow, nor the redness of his cheeks. He smiled at May, bowed his head and said, "It's lovely to see you again".

He could feel his heart beating inside his chest. May looked positively radiant. She began to blush herself, which didn't go un-noticed by her mother and father. He hadn't seen her for four-months. She was every bit as beautiful as he remembered. He wanted to throw his arms around her and kiss her and profess his undying love for her. All this went through his mind in an instant, but decorum dictated that that wasn't going to happen here, not now. His mission today, was a charm offensive, to win over May's parents. If he could do that successfully, and get them on his side, they hopefully wouldn't have any objections to her seeing him again.

"Right then", said the captain in a loud voice, that brought Harry out of his momentary day-dream, "Let's have that tea. Will you pour mother?".

Tea and Christmas cake was served. Harry sat perched on the edge of a sofa, fielding questions, mostly from the Captain and Mrs. Baynham, some from May and her siblings. It was, Harry thought, the toughest examination, of his life.

After tea, Harry was invited by the captain for a tour of the ship. Mrs. Baynham and May also went along.

Although Harry was trained on the new method of construction with regards to naval architecture, he was also knowledgeable about the construction of wooden hulled ships such as the Wellesley. As they got back to the captain's private quarters, May said, "This is where I had my little accident".

May's father looked at his daughter aghast. "You haven't told him that story, have you?".

May shook her head defiantly, "Actually, it was Alice Bainbridge, but I don't see why I should hide it from anyone".

Captain Baynham turned to Harry, "I have never been so embarrassed in my life. The superintendent of a naval training ship, and my idiotic daughter falls overboard chasing a kite. One of the junior ratings had to jump in after her. The first I knew of it was when the officer of the watch brought her back to my office looking like a drowned rat".

"It was thirteen-years ago", protested May.

"You nearly drowned. If I can't keep my own daughter in check, how can I be expected to run a training ship. The Admiralty would have pensioned me off there and then".

"Come dear", said Mrs. Baynham pulling on her husband's arm, "I don't think we need to go over all that again for Harry's sake". She led her husband away whilst given her daughter a knowing look. "I'll put the kettle on for another cup of tea. It's getting cold out here, so don't be long".

Harry and May were on their own. May took a step closer to him, looked around to make sure they were unobserved. They then embraced and kissed one another. Then giggled like children, knowing they were breaking all the rules that polite society imposes on young love.

"I've been waiting all afternoon to do that" whispered May.

"I've been waiting four-months", replied Harry. They both felt giddy with excitement. Without words, they both knew what each other was thinking. This was the first time either of them had fallen in love.

"I have a Christmas present for you". Harry said softly in her ear. He put his hand in his jacket pocket and took out a tiny cardboard box. He opened it. Inside was a solid silver charm, about the size of a farthing. She took it out. On one side was a beautifully engraved, stylised heart, and on the other, the initials 'HJC'.

"It's beautiful", she said. "Harry Jasper Cox, my heart"

"I bought it in London and had it engraved. Perhaps you can wear it on a charm bracelet, or around your neck on a chain".

"I shall wear it around my neck, so it will always be close to my heart".

"When will I see you again?" asked Harry.

"I shall be at the Bainbridges' in Eshott Park the first weekend in January. I could write to Alice and get her to ask Tom to invite you up".

"That sounds like a very good plan indeed. I will have to be back in Greenwich that Sunday evening. It will only add an hour onto my journey if I leave from Eshott".

After one more kiss, May said that they had better rejoin the others. "My father might send out a search party otherwise".

Another cup of tea and slice of cake was had by all, and then Harry took his leave. He was escorted off the ship by the captain who shook his hand warmly and said, "You're a fine young man Harry, I hope we will be seeing you again sometime".

"Thank you, sir, I hope very much that that will be the case". The two officers saluted each other and Harry made his way to the tram terminus. "Well, that couldn't have gone much better". Harry said to himself as he waited for the tram.

A letter arrived from Tom the following Wednesday, inviting him up to Eshott for the weekend. He would take all his luggage with him, and return to London from there. There was another emotional farewell as he left the family home on the Friday afternoon to go to the station. His father walked with him on this occasion, to see him off. It was unlikely he would return at least until Easter, or possibly the summer. As they got to Neville Street, Charlie Cox said to his son, "I'm very proud of you, Harry, you've become a proper gent. I hope everything turns out well with this girl you've taken a fancy to. I was only a bit older than you when I married your mother. Best thing I ever did. Get a good woman behind you son, and you can take on the world".

"Thank you, dad, it's a bit early to talk about things like that, I've only ever seen her three times.

"You'll know here if she's the one", replied Charlie putting his hand on his heart. "It flutters when you see her and it aches when you don't".

With that bit of fatherly advice, Harry got on the carriage with his luggage and stood by the window. He waved to his father as the train pulled away and thought to himself; that was the best description he had heard of the way he felt about May.

Ambrose was waiting for Harry at Chevington station with the carriage. It was a cold afternoon but the roads were dry and they got to Eshott Hall in fifteen minutes. As Harry alighted from the carriage, Tom came out to greet him. "Happy New Year old sport" he said, shaking Harry's gloved hand. "What's all this cloak and dagger stuff with you and my sister? She won't tell me a damn thing, except that it was vitally important you came this weekend. Is there something going on with you two that I should know about?"

Harry replied in a quieter voice in order that he wasn't overheard. "There is something going, but not with your sister". He looked around conspiratorially, and with an even quitter voice said, "It's May Baynham, I think we're in love".

"You sly old dog", said Tom, far too loud for Harrys; liking". "How long has this been going on?".

"I started writing to her when I went to Greenwich. I met her parents on Boxing Day".

"Well, that's great news old chap, she's a lovely girl. And the Captain's daughter, eh? Are you looking for a promotion already? Laughing between themselves, they entered the house.

"It's the lull after the storm here now, thank goodness", explained Tom. "My two elder sisters were here with their husbands and off-spring, absolute chaos. They went home yesterday. Poor old Bradders was run ragged".

They entered the drawing room just as Tom's mother was pouring the tea. "Ah, Harry, how positively delightful to see you again, Happy New year".

"Happy New Year to you Mrs. Bainbridge", he replied, giving her a deferential nod of the head. "I understand from Tom that you have had a busy Christmas".

"Yes", she said with a sigh, "Grandchildren can be so exhausting. I'm pleased to say that it will only be the six of us this weekend". She handed Harry a cup of tea. "Now, come and sit next to me and tell me what you have been doing in London".

An hour or so later, Tom's father came in, followed by Alice and May. All three were dressed in their riding clothes and had just returned from a ride around the estate. "Nice to see you again Harry".

"Thank you, sir, Happy New Year to you".

"Anymore tea in the pot, my dear? Or shall I ring for a fresh one?"

Alice walked up to Harry and gave him a kiss on the cheek. She squeezed his arm and gave him a knowing look. "Hello Harry, I'm glad you could make it at such short notice". He smiled at her, then looked at May and said, "I wouldn't have missed it for the world". May kissed him on the cheek. In Harry's mind, it seemed to linger. He remembered what his father had said at the station. There was definitely a flutter.

Harry felt that he was in a bit of a tricky situation. Tom and Alice knew of his affections towards May, but their parents didn't. If they knew the truth of it, they were bound to do the honourable thing and act as chaperone whenever he and May were together. He really didn't want to offend his hosts by keeping up the charade that they were just passing acquaintances.

When Tom took Harry upstairs to show him his room, Harry shut the door behind them and told Tom of his dilemma.

"Yes, I see what you mean old boy. It just goes to show what an honourable and noble fellow you are. I shall brooch the subject with my mother, and you can take your lead from her".

"Thanks, old man, I'd really appreciate it".

"Right you are, I'll see you downstairs for dinner, usual time".

About twenty-minutes later, there was a knock at the door, and in walked Tom. "I've had a word with mother. She was charmed by your honesty. She suggests that you get down to the drawing room half an hour before dinner.

Harry, dressed in another borrowed dinner jacket, went down to the drawing room at seven-thirty. May sat on a sofa next to the roaring fire. Bradders was standing at the far end of the room. He approached as Harry entered the room and offered May a glass of sherry from a silver tray. He offered the same to Harry. "Will that be all sir?"

"Er, yes, thank you Bradders, the others will be down shortly".

"Very good, Sir". Bradders left the room, closing the door behind him. They were alone.

They kissed, they caressed, they expressed their undying love for one another. Unfortunately, the moment only lasted fifteen minutes before footsteps were heard outside in the hall. In a louder than normal voice, Mrs. Bainbridge said, "Bradders, Mr. Bainbridge would like the 1900 Chateau Margaux served with the main course this evening".

She opened the door to the drawing room and found Harry standing by the fire sipping his sherry and May sitting on a nearby sofa, browsing a copy of the latest 'Ladies Field' Magazine. Both were slightly red in the cheek.

"Good evening you two, sorry I'm late", she said as she swept into the room. "It seems ever so warm in here, I'll ask Bradders to open a window".

Harry and May sat next to each other at dinner, under the watchful eye of their hosts. Harry was encouraged to tell all about his first four-months at Greenwich and his adventures exploring the capital.

Tom told Harry about his latest project at Swan Hunter; "A twin-screw steamer for cargo and passenger. It's for the French, and they're calling it the 'Afrique', it's nothing fancy. In fact, it is a toy compared to the Mauretania.

Harry and Tom started to talk shop, which encouraged the ladies to leave the room. Mr. Bainbridge stayed at the table and lit a cigar. When there was a lull in the conversation, he chirped in; "Have you told Harry about your new toy?"

"Not yet" said Tom, "!'m keeping it a secret until tomorrow, after breakfast, I shall reveal all", he looked at Harry with a schoolboy grin.

"Good show", said his father, "Shall we join the ladies?", he said, standing up.

Harry thought that was a very good idea.

The rest of the evening was spent playing games of chess and draughts, a piano recital by Mrs. Bainbridge, sewing for the ladies and the reading of books, papers and magazines. Harry and May managed to snatch a quick kiss before everyone retired to their rooms.

Harry went to bed that night, his mind made up that he was going to marry May. He loved her, she loved him that is all that was needed for a successful marriage. He wouldn't be able to do anything about it for some time. First, he would have completed his current course at Greenwich, and then wait and see where he was to be posted. He wouldn't talk to her father yet. He'd wait until he was settled in the job, then he'd have no reason to object. Besides, he was an officer, what more could a Captain want for his daughter?

Breakfast was the usual affair of eggs, bacon, kidneys, kippers, tea and toast served buffet style. The ladies were dressed for riding, as was Mr. Bainbridge. When they'd finished eating, Mr. Bainbridge addressed Tom, "Make sure the horses are well away before you start the thing up. Damn horse bolted and nearly had me off the other day".

Harry looked at the pair of them, none the wiser as to what they were talking about.

Off they all went, leaving Tom and Harry at the table.

A quarter of an hour later, Tom got up and said, "Right then, come and have a look at my new toy. Prepare to be amazed". Tom walked them round to the stable block and opened a door to one of the storage rooms. "Wait here", he said, "And close your eyes".

Harry did as he was told. He heard a few indiscernible noises, then Tom said, "Right, open them".

Harry 's eyes lit up as he looked in amazement at the machine before him. "What is it?" he said with enthusiasm.

"It's a motorcycle".

"I can see that, I'm not that naïve. What model is it?"

"It's a Norton, made in Birmingham, with a French Peugeot engine".

"How much power does it have?"

"It's 5-horse power. I've had thirty-miles per hour out of it. It's the same machine that won the International Auto-Cycle Tourist Trophy on the Isle of Man earlier on in the year".

Harry walked around the gleaming machine, stroking it as he went. "When did you get it?

"My father bought it for me as a Christmas present. He knows I like anything with an engine, and faster the better. Let's start her up and I'll show you how to ride it".

By the time lunch was served, Harry was covered in mud. Fortunately, he had been wearing a pair of Tom's old overalls, and had fallen off numerus times. He and the Norton remained relatively unscathed. A quick wash and brush-up were all that was required before rejoining the others.

Saturday evening was very much the same as the previous night. Harry and May met in the drawing room and had fifteen-minutes alone before their hosts arrived. They both thought it was very sweet, and quite progressive of Mrs. Bainbridge to allow it to happen.

The next morning, they all went to church. It was a custom in the family that they would attend the local service on the first Sunday of each month whilst at Eshott. After the service, they went on a good walk. In normal circumstances, Mrs. Bainbridge would have been happy for the children and their friends to go off alone. But not now. May's parents would surely disapprove and put a stop to future visits. As Alice's best friend, she was almost one of the family.

The dreaded time came when after lunch, Harry would have to head back to London and on to Greenwich. Mrs. Bainbridge thought it would be a good idea if Alice, May and herself went to the station to see Harry off, then they could have a little ride in the carriage before it got dark.

Harry said his goodbyes and thankyous to Tom and his father and left for the station accompanied by the ladies. Once at the station, Mrs. Bainbridge suggested that she and Alice would wait in the carriage and May could go to the platform and wave Harry off. They had a few minutes in the waiting room out of sight of the Bainbridges', and were able to kiss each other goodbye. He promised to write to her every week, and she to him. It was going to be months before they would see each other again. Once again, Harry thought about what his father had said only on Friday; the ache in his heart had started.

Harry got on the train and waved frantically as the train pulled away. It had almost disappeared into the distance before May turned, wiped her eyes with a handkerchief and walked back to the waiting carriage. "Let's go back to the house, shall we? Said Mrs. Bainbridge, giving May's hand a motherly squeeze. "We'll have an early cup of tea and a scone".

17 - A Visit to London

Over the next few months, Harry travelled to various naval dockyards; Chatham, Portsmouth, Devonport, Sheerness and Pembroke. It was important to make a good impression at these places, as it might one day be the yard he is posted to. He liked the idea that he could also be posted to Malta, Bermuda or Hong Kong. He'd never been abroad before, and the very idea of it sounded exciting and romantic, especially if he could take May along with him as his wife.

Harry and May wrote to each other every week. In mid-March, he had to give her the news that he would not be home for the Easter long weekend. The intensity of the course he was on went up a notch, and now there was plenty of work to do in the evening and at weekends. May was naturally heart-broken at the thought of not seeing him until the summer. However, a couple of weeks later, May wrote to him with some incredible news.

Mrs. Bainbridge was planning to spend a few days in London in mid-May in order to visit the Franco-British Exhibition at the White City. Alice would be going with her, and they had invited May to accompany them. They would be staying at a newly built hotel called the 'Piccadilly' in London's West End. May's parents had agreed on the understanding that

Mrs. Bainbridge would act as chaperone. This was wonderful news and made up for the earlier disappointment. They would be arriving in London on Wednesday the thirteenth of May, and leaving on the Sunday. Harry was invited to spend the day with them on the Saturday.

The week of May's arrival in London soon came. Harry worked hard all week in order to keep the weekend free. He went to the Piccadilly Hotel on the Saturday morning and spent the day with May and the Bainbridges'. By now, he was quite an expert guide and took them to St, James's Park, Green Park and Hyde Park, where Harry took them out on a boat around the Serpentine. It was a gloriously sunny day and not too hot. Mrs. Bainbridge was the perfect chaperone. She allowed the two of them to have private moments where they could speak to each other freely and snatch the occasional kiss, unobserved.

As they walked down Piccadilly, back to the hotel, with the sun shining on his back, Harry reflected how his life had changed over the last few years. The young dreamer in a cloth-cap who would sit on the banks of the Tyne sketching boats, was now walking along Piccadilly in London with the woman he intended to marry and his future career mapped out in front of him.

Harry escorted the ladies back to their hotel and arranged to return the following afternoon to join them for lunch before they left for Newcastle.

The weekend could not have gone any better as far as Harry was concerned. He was not to know the devastating news that awaited May when she arrived at Newcastle Station. Her father was waiting for her, he looked tired and pale. He put on a brave face in front of Mrs. and Alice Bainbridge but May could see there was something troubling him. Once alone and in the privacy of a Hansom cab, he broke the news to her. Their second eldest son, Henry Hudson Baynham, had died of typhoid fever in South America whilst serving as a purser in the Royal Navy. He was 22-years of age. The news had arrived the day she had gone off to London. Her parents, though distraught, did not want to call her back home, especially as she was seeing Harry. They knew it would be months before another meeting could take place between them, and they wanted to do all they could to encourage the relationship between them. May wrote to Harry the following morning to tell him the news.

18 - Wedding Plans

Harry worked hard all through the summer and completed his course. He was now a qualified member of the Royal Corps of Naval Constructors. He had hoped for an overseas posting, but because he did so well, and impressed the right people, it was decided that he would be posted to the Admiralty in central London. It wasn't exactly what he wanted but it was a feather in his cap. May had also expressed a desire to travel the world like her father and brothers in the Royal Navy. Her mother had also travelled, having been born in Saint Helena in the southern Atlantic.

Now that Harry had the foreseeable future of his career mapped out in front of him, he decided to seek an audience with May's father and ask for his daughter's hand in marriage. May had spent the last eight-months priming her parents for this event and knew there was unlikely to be any objections on their part. Afterall, she was now twenty-six years of age and the eldest daughter. It was time for her to get married and start a family of her own. Harry had written to his own father and told him of his plans. They were met with whole-hearted approval.

Harry was given a weeks' leave at the end of August, before taking up his new position at the

Admiralty. Wasting no time, he got the late afternoon train from London, arriving back in Newcastle close to midnight. May had made arrangements with her father for him to receive Harry Saturday afternoon on board the Wellesley.

"Good afternoon, sir", said Harry, his heart pumping like a steam piston. "Pull yourself together", he said to himself, "He knows exactly why you're here. If he didn't like the idea, he would have told May, and she wouldn't have arranged the meeting. God, I'll be glad when this is over".

"Harry, my boy, it's very good to see you. I hear congratulations are in order. Only the best of the best gets posted to the Admiralty. Under all those watchful eyes, eh?"

"That's very kind of you to say so, sir".

"You deserve every bit of it. You don't get to run a training ship without recognising potential in a man. I could see the first time you came here, that you were a man with ambition and prepared to work for it. Things like that do not go un-noticed. "Now, I understand you want to marry my daughter?"

The sudden change in the conversation and its directness took Harry by surprise.

"Er, well, erm, yes, yes sir, I do" he stammered.

"Good man. I have no reservations or doubt whatsoever, and neither does my wife. As for May, I can see she's in love with you. She never stops talking about you. You will be a very welcomed addition to our family and you have my blessing".

Harry stood there and breathed a sigh of relief. Before he had a chance to say anything, Captain Baynham walked around the desk and shook Harry's had so vigorously, Harry winced in pain. "A celebration is in order", announced the captain.

He turned to a small cupboard in the corner of the room, took out a decanter of port, poured two glasses and gave one to Harry. "To a long and happy future together". They raised their glasses and downed it in one. "Now", continued the captain, "May is waiting for you on our private deck. Go and tell her the good news and then come and join Mrs. Baynham and I in the parlour for some tea".

Harry did as he was told. May stood there in the mid-afternoon sun looking radiant, although slightly nervous. Her face brightened enormously when she saw the look on Harry's face as he approached her.

He gave a verbatim account of the conversation he had just had with her father. When he finished, he said; "There is just one little formality to go through before my mission here is complete". She looked at him questioningly.

Like a conjurer, a small box appeared from nowhere and sat in the palm of his hand. He opened the box and went down on one knee and said, "My darling love, will you do me the honour of becoming my wife?". The thin gold band with diamond centrepiece sparked in the August sun. "Yes, kind sir", she smiled, eyes welling up. "I will".

The rest of the afternoon was spent on the quayside, under the watchful gaze of May's parents, talking and planning for the future. Neither of them would particularly miss Newcastle. The lure of cosmopolitan life in London was compelling. They could find a modest little house to rent in one of the suburbs and raise a family of their own. If a posting abroad was offered, they would face the adventure together. A wedding in the following spring was suggested, which found favour with Captain and Mrs. Baynham and later, Harry's father, when he returned home.

Harry spent the week visiting May, old friends at Swan Hunter and of course, Tom Bainbridge. Tom was utterly delighted with the news and felt that he had played a major part in bringing the couple together. The Sunday afternoon before Harry was to return to London, Mrs. Bainbridge invited the betrothed couple to afternoon tea with their respective parents at Holmwood. During a quiet moment Charlie Cox whispered to Harry, "Bless my soul, how the other half live, eh? I wish your mother was here to see this".

"Do you think she would approve of May?"

"Oh, I do son, I do. She's a delightful young girl. You've done all right for yourself on that score. It's a shame you're both going to be living in London, but I suppose that's where the work is, for now at least".

"I'm sure we'll both be up to visit regularly".

19 - The Admiralty

Harry walked down Whitehall the following morning. He no longer had that first day of school butterflies feeling in his stomach, but the air of a confident man who has shown himself to be competent in his chosen field. No one could ever describe him as arrogant, far from it, it was just he now had a new-found confidence in himself and a belief in his own ability. May's love for him had given him a boost. Everything he was going to do, now and in the future, was for the benefit of both of them.

The Admiralty was not a lot different to Greenwich in terms of discipline and etiquette. There were however, a lot more civil staff working in the labyrinth of corridors that made up the Admiralty building. The other side of the building to which he entered on Whitehall, overlooked the square that the Horse Guards Parade took place on each year for the Trooping of the Colour.

After a tour of the building, he was taken to meet the man in charge of his new department; Sir Philip Watts, Director of Naval Construction. A solidly built man of about sixty-years of age and sporting a fine walrus style moustache. The name of Sir Philip Watts, had recently gone down in naval folklore as the man behind the Dreadnought. Not just the name of a single ship, but a class of its own. If Harry was going to make his mark in this profession, he would do so by emulating the man sitting in front of him. He was in awe of the great man. They shook hands over the large oak desk, piled high with folders, manuals, drawings and all kinds of paperwork.

"It's very good to have you with us", said Sir Philip. "I understand you're from Tyneside?"

"That's correct Sir. I was apprenticed to Swan Hunter at Wallsend before joining the navy".

"I worked for one of their rivals", Sir Philip gave Harry a smile, "Armstrong's, at Elswick. Our yard wasn't as big as yours".

"I believe not sir; the yard was expanded when we got the Mauretania contract".

"Did you work on that?"

"Yes, sir. I was just a trainee draftsman at the time, but it was good experience".

"Oh yes, you can be proud of that, she's a fine vessel".

The two men sat and talked about the north-east, and drank the tea that was brought to them. Despite having what looked like a mountain of work on his desk, Sir Philip gave the impression he had all the time in the world. "The amount of work we have in front of us is really being dictated by the ambitions of Admiral Tirpitz over in Germany. They seem to be building up their fleet in an attempt to match that of our own. We can't let them get ahead of us; in case it gives them ideas. Still, it keeps us on our toes".

Harry enjoyed his new job. He was now at the cutting edge of modern ship design. Where the Royal Navy led, the rest of the world would soon follow. His departmental head was a stubborn Welshman, who had had a meteoric rise in the industry. A protégé of Sir Philip, he wasn't liked by the senior ranks and politicians because of his confrontational approach to authority, but whatever could be said about John Harper Narbeth, there was no denying that he was excellent at his job. His work on the Dreadnought and the new Invincible class of Battlecruiser, had caught the attention of the right people and led him to the elevated position he was now in, at the age of forty-four. Harry liked him, He didn't mince his words and always encouraged people around him to explore new ways of doing things, and if he agreed with you, he would fight your corner to the death.

The commute to Whitehall took a lot longer that Greenwich, but Harry soon got into the routine. A train to Charing Cross, then a walk, or if the weather was bad, an omnibus or tram. The people with whom he worked were originally, from all over the country. Now, they were residing all over the metropolis and beyond, just like him. He didn't venture out much mid-week, but his weekends were often spent in the company of his fellow boarders; Alaistair and Albert.

On one occasion, he went over to Perivale and had a good look at the house he had stayed in on his first visit to London with Tom. It could prove to be an idea place for May and himself to live, should he still be in London when they got married. He would have to have a chat with Tom about that nearer the time.

Christmas came, and Harry spent the week back in Newcastle. His time was divided between his father's house and the Wellesley. The question of a wedding date was mooted. Harry said that he would like to get a full year in the job before he asked for time off to get married. All concerned agreed that this was a sensible course of action and that perhaps a date in late September or early October would be the time to aim for. Between themselves, He and May had decided that if he were to be sent abroad at short notice, a white wedding would have to be cancelled and a ceremony at a register office would have to suffice in order for her to go along with him.

The Bainbridges were having their usual family get-together up at Eshott Hall and never saw Harry at all while he was in Newcastle. Harry did however, get a cryptic note from Tom shortly before he returned to London, saying that he was working on a plan that would get him down to London at the end of January. He would explain more nearer the time.

20 - An Unexpected Visitor

A few weeks later, Harry got a letter from Tom saying that he was coming to London on the evening of the twenty-ninth, and he would like Harry to call on him at the house in Perivale the following day around eleven o'clock in the morning. Harry thought this was a bit of a strange request. Why not meet in the city somewhere? Oh well, Tom must have his reasons, he thought.

Harry made the journey across London to Perivale on the Saturday morning to Tom's place as per the letter. He hadn't seen him for a few months and was looking forward to catching up with him. He arrived at the house in Perivale Gardens a little after eleven. Tom answered the door and there was a good deal of handshaking and back slapping. He showed Harry into the parlour at the front of the house, where a pot of tea was set out on a small table in the centre of the room. Harry noticed that four cups were laid out. "Do you have other guests?" he enquired.

"Yes, we do old chap", said Tom with his trademark boyish grin on his face, looking like a secret was about to burst out of him at any moment.

"You can come in now", said Tom in a loud voice as if calling to someone at the other end of the house. Harry heard the sounds of footsteps walking along the hall. The door slowly opened and Alice walked into the room. "Alice", said Harry, looking a little surprised. "I had no idea you were here with Tom. It's lovely to see you, how are you? Is your mother here with you as well?".

Alice suddenly adopted the same grin as her brother. "Mother is otherwise engaged, so she won't be here this weekend", she sniggered. "But somebody else is". She turned back towards the door and said "Come in, then".

Harry thought his legs were going to give way beneath him. He couldn't believe his eyes. May slowly walked through the door, beaming with the most radiant smile, then rushed towards him with her arms outstretched. "My darling", she cried as she threw her arms around him and kissed his face repeatedly.

Over tea, Alice explained their little deception. "Mother and father were coming down to London to get the boat-train to Paris. I asked if I could come to London with them and bring May with me. And do some shopping. Mother said it would be fine as long as Tom came along as well to accompany us back to Newcastle. Which of course, he was pleased to do, weren't you, big brother?".

"To be a wet-nurse for my baby sibling, is what I live for",

"Anyway, we stayed in the Piccadilly last night and had dinner. This morning, after an early breakfast, we all parted company. Mother and father went off to

Paris, thinking we would be off shopping for the day and getting the train back up north this evening. The truth is, we're staying here for the night and going back tomorrow afternoon".

"What on earth will you parents say if they ever found out?" said Harry to May.

"They are hardly likely to", said May defiantly. "They think I'm here with Mr. and Mrs. Bainbridge".

"When in fact", interrupted Tom, "You are here with Mr. and Miss Bainbridge".

They spent the afternoon walking around town. Harry showed them Whitehall and where his new office was, and all the other places of interest he had discovered on his many walks.

After an early dinner, they returned to the house in Perivale. It was cold and dark when they arrived, but Harry soon had the fire in the hearth roaring in the parlour, where they sat and talked and drank wine until it was late. Tom and Alice retired to their respective rooms, knowing full well that Harry and May would very much like to be left on their own.

For the first time since they had met, they were truly alone. No chaperone keeping a discreet distance, making sure the social conventions of the day were upheld. No parents to impress. It was just the two of them. This is how it would be when they were married. Sitting in front of the fire on a cold evening, holding each other, kissing, caressing, their actions speaking volumes without a word being said. This was pure and unadulterated love. There was no doubt in either of their minds that this was very real, and together, they could face whatever challenges life was to place before them. This was undoubtedly, the best night of their lives.

Tom came downstairs the following morning, looking slightly hungover. The smell of breakfast wafted from the kitchen. He stood in the doorway and surveyed the scene before him. "A picture of domestic bliss", he said trying to sound his usual jolly self.

Harry and May were in the kitchen preparing a breakfast of eggs, bacon, toast and tea.

"Good morning my happy pair of lovebirds". They both looked at him with a slightly embarrassed and nervous look on their faces. "Good morning, Tom", they said in unison.

"I say, you two, you could come and live here once you've tied the old knot. Assuming you're still working in London".

"Oh, Tom, could we really?", it's such a lovely house", said May enthusiastically. She looked at Harry, "It wouldn't be too far for you to travel, would it?".

"Not at all", replied Harry, "It's almost the same distance as I'm doing now. He turned to Tom, "Perhaps we could rent it from you?"

"I won't hear of it old chap. You can have it rent free for as long as you like. It will be my wedding present to you both".

After breakfast, they went for a brisk walk around Pitshanger Park and then back to the house to pack their things. Harry went to King's Cross Station to see them off. May was in tears as the train drew out of the station. She waved her handkerchief out of the window until she was out of sight. Harry made his way back to Lewisham with a noticeable spring in his step, all the while wondering what he was going to say to Mrs. Dickenson.

A few days later, Harry was relieved to receive a letter from May, saying that she had returned home on Sunday and there had been no awkward questions or concern about her trip to London. The last thing he wanted, was to get on the wrong side of Captain Baynham.

The arms race that Sir Philip alluded to the previous year had begun in earnest. The liberal government of the day introduced new taxes to increase the defence budget and ships of every description were now on order. As far as Harry was concerned, it couldn't have been a better time to work in the field of naval construction. In the few months he had been there, he felt that he was honing his craft and getting experience that could not be found anywhere else. The work was demanding and challenging in equal measure but at the same time, enjoyable and rewarding. He only saw daylight at the weekends during those winter months. Starting work in the morning before the sun had risen over the London skyline, he didn't leave until it was dark again. He settled into a routine. The commute home allowed him to clear his mind of the day's activities and leave him in a more relaxed mood for when he got home. He loved his work, but he also realised the importance of getting the balance right. The sentiment of the proverb; 'All work and no play, makes Jack a dull boy', was not lost on him. It would be good training for when I'm married, he thought to himself. My father never brought his work home with him. I shall do the same.

Harry continued to write to May every weekend. He didn't do a lot during the week other than work, so there wasn't much to say. Besides, his work was covered by the Official Secrets Act that had come into force twenty-years previous. May's grandfather had been the governor of Saint Helena, born and bred on the island. However, his father had been a German. Even now, after all this time, and the service he had given to the empire, the authorities would take a dim view if Harry was found to be talking about his classified work with his fiancé.

21 - Unexpected News

At the end of March, Harry received an unexpected letter from May. He'd had his usual one which was always waiting for him when he returned home on Monday evening, but this latest one arrived on the Thursday. Intrigued to know what could be so important that it could wait a few days, he was surprised and delighted to hear that sha was coming down to London at the weekend with the Bainbridges' and would see him at the house in Perivale on Saturday morning. He noted sub-conscientiously the letter was matter-of-fact and not filled with the gushing sentiment he was used to. Saturday morning couldn't come around quick enough.

As he walked along the garden path that led to the front door, he noticed the curtains twitch. As he reached out to use the door knocker, the door swung open and May was standing there. She looked pale and had obviously been crying, a damp handkerchief clutched in her right hand. Before Harry had a chance to say anything, she threw her arms around him. He could feel her sobs transfer through her body into his He half lifted and half dragged her over the threshold in order to shut the door and away from any prying eyes. She clung to him as if her life depended on it. The sobs grew louder. "There, there, my angel, what is it, what has happened?". As he said it, he clasped her face in his hands and put his forehead against hers so that their noses touched. Tears were streaming down her face and making his hands wet. Once again, in a soft voice he said, "My poor darling, what has happened?". When the answer came, it nearly knocked him off his feet. If he had not been holding onto May, he would surely have ended up on the floor. "I'm going to have a baby", she cried.

He sat on the sofa in the parlour next to May, holding her hand. He knew it was a stupid question, but he thought he'd better ask it anyway, "Are you sure?".

"Of course I am, I've been examined by a doctor. It will start to show in about a months' time. Oh Harry, what are we going to do?".

He kissed her hand and thought for a moment. "We'll do what we've always planned to do, get married of course".

"I don't know how my parents will react when they find out. They'll disown me. I've brought shame on the family. Oh God Harry, I'm so scared".

"I'm sure we can find a way to deal with this".

"But how?".

"We always said, that if I was offered a post abroad, we would get married strait away and go together".

"Yes?".

"Well, what if we say I have been offered a job abroad and need to get married quickly, but then after the wedding we decide not to go or say it has been cancelled, or something like that. You could stay with me here in London, and we could announce the news of a baby a few months later".

"My mother has had nine-children, she'll see straight through it".

"Yes, but hopefully by the time she does, we'll be a happily married couple living in London".

"I'm prepared to do anything than tell my parents the truth. I know that sounds terrible, but I just don't have the courage to tell them and break their hearts".

"We love each other, we were going to get married and have children anyway. It's just going to happen a bit sooner, that's all". He tried to sound reassuring but there was nervousness in his tone.

"Can we really do this?

"I don't think we have much choice, do we?".

Harry would have been prepared to break the news to his own family, certain in the knowledge that his father would be philosophical about it, but May's parents were another matter altogether. Captain Baynham had contacts at the Admiralty and could make life difficult for Harry if he so wished. The trouble with Harry's plan, is that it could easily fall apart if there were any communication between the captain and anyone at the Admiralty. They would just have to chance it.

They sat there in silence, playing out the various scenarios in their minds. Slowly the door opened, and a sheepish Alice and Tom Bainbridge entered. They had gone for a walk just prior to Harrys' arrival, in order to give them time alone. Alice sat beside May, who turned and gently started sobbing on her shoulder. Harry stood to greet Tom.

"Hello old man" he said, without his usual jovial air. "If there is anything we can do to help, just ask. Our mother knows all about it, she organised the visit to the doctor. The old thing is quite a modern thinker".

"Thank you, both of you. We were planning to get married sometime this year, we'll just have to bring it forward, that's all". Harry tried to put a positive spin on it but it didn't really convince anyone.

"That's the spirit", said Tom. "I said, coming down on the train, Harry will sort things out, he's an honourable chap, he won't let anyone down".

"Oh, for heavens' sake", interrupted Alice, crossly. "Getting married isn't the issue, May is going to have a baby. That's not something you can brush under the carpet and ignore, or hide away until the time is right".

Tom looked crestfallen, "I wasn't trying to make light of the situation, I was just trying to be reassuring with regards the predicament that faces us".

"I understand you Tom, and I'm sure May does as well. Thank you. We've got a plan of sorts. Not sure how it will play out but it's the only thing we have at this moment in time".

Harry talked through what they proposed to do. Saying it out loud to an audience, seemed to make it more believable. He began to think it was possible after all. A lot would have to depend on May being able to carry on as normal over the next few weeks until he could arrange things, such as a register office for the marriage ceremony and some time off work.

Alice, Tom and May were in London on the pretext that they were shopping with Mrs. Bainbridge. This time, Mrs. Bainbridge was in on the deception and the only people that were really in the dark were May's parents. Harry and May spent an emotional weekend together. He saw them off at King's Cross Station on Sunday afternoon and made his way back to Lewisham. He decided to tell Alastair and Albert at his lodgings the full story. He was sure that they would not judge him too harshly. He was right, they offered him their full support and offered to be witnesses at the register office if required. The plan was starting to fall into place.

22 - Arrangements Made

Harry went to work the following morning and discreetly asked his longer serving colleagues around the office, about the likelihood of being posted abroad. The general consensus was that although it wasn't unheard of, those positions were more likely to be given to those working at the shipyards. It wasn't exactly what he wanted to hear, but one person did tell him that Lloyds Register of Shipping in London were regularly looking for people trained in naval construction and had offices all over the globe. It could be an option worth considering for the future.

Harry booked the register office in Lewisham, just down the road from his lodgings, for the last Wednesday afternoon in April, along with a few days off work. Alistair and Albert confirmed they would be able to attend and act as witnesses if required. He booked it mid-week in the hope that it would put off people wanting to travel down to London from the north-east to attend the ceremony. He knew that May would have loved a white wedding, with both families in attendance, but that was no longer possible in the circumstances. He wrote to May and told her of everything he had done since he saw her last. He suggested that he should write to her one-week before the wedding and break the news of his impending post abroad. This will give May plenty of time to prepare herself, and too little time for others to make arrangements to attend. He awaited her reply.

He didn't like the idea of deceiving his father, nor May's parents. What should have been a wonderful occasion, uniting two families, was going to go by almost un-noticed. It wouldn't take a genius to work out that their child was going to be born about six-months after they had married. He felt that he had let himself down and all those around him that he cared for. It was going to be a bit awkward, to say the least, when he would have to go and tell his supervising officer of his marriage to a Captain's daughter at a register office. It would certainly raise a few eyebrows when he notified them later of a birth in the family. Perhaps, he thought to himself, I should write to Lloyd's and see if they have anything to offer.

Harry returned home from work the following Monday, Unusually, there was no letter from May sitting on the hall table. Perhaps the winter weather has caused a delay with the post, he thought. He waited a further two-days before one finally came. He took it upstairs to his room and sat at the desk which was lit by a gas lamp. Once again, he got that sinking feeling and a sense of hopelessness as he started to read the letter. The cat was out of the bag. Since May had returned home from their last meeting, she had been suffering from terrible morning sickness, probably as a result of the stress of the situation she was facing. There could be no hiding place in their private quarters on board the ship where they lived, so, confronted by her mother, she had decided to tell the truth of what had happened. Fearing the worst, her mother displayed a totally unexpected acceptance of the situation and a desire to make things right. She fully understood the course of action that May and Harry were about to undertake, and suggested that they continue with the scheme purely to save face with their respective families and acquaintances. May's mother insisted that they went to see Mrs. Bainbridge in order for May to apologise to her for the trouble she had caused and so that Mrs. Baynham could thank Mrs. Bainbridge for the motherly care and help she had afforded her daughter. The only fly in the ointment was going to be Captain Baynham. His wife was going to have to approach that problem with a good deal of tact and diplomacy.

By the time Harry got to the end of the letter, he had experienced a rollercoaster of emotions. The one that now sat with him was relief. Relief that May had found the strength to tell her mother the truth without jeopardising their relationship. May's mother had said to her, that she had already lost three-children, she didn't want to lose anymore. The relief that Harry felt was still tinged with apprehension. He felt he would never be able to look either of his parents-in-law to-be, in the eye ever again. Would a disgruntled father-in-law do or say anything to ruin his son-in-law's career? He didn't know the answer to that one yet.

The situation was slightly better than it was before he opened the letter especially from May's point of view. She had her mother on side. That was definitely a bonus. In the moments that followed, he decided to tell his father the truth. If Mrs. Baynham could accept the situation, then so could his father. His father would be able to break the news to his brothers and sisters. They would bound to be disappointed about missing out on a family wedding, but he could make it up to them another time. He pulled out a sheet of notepaper and began to write. By the time he went down to dinner, he was feeling a bit happier about the situation. Over dinner, he broached the subject with Mrs. Dickenson, whose final words on the subject were; "These things happen my dear. You love each other and are doing the right thing. That's all that matters".

Harry received a reply from his father a few days later. It was everything he thought it would be. His father expressed disappointment about the wedding arrangements and the family occasion they were all hoping it would be, but he fully understood the need for discretion and to get the matter resolved as quickly as possible. He said that Harry was doing the honourable thing and that he was looking forward to becoming a grandfather. That brought a smile to Harry's face. With all the upset of hastily organising a wedding, he had forgot the reason why he was actually doing it. He was going to be a father. He'd never really thought about it before, the actual practicalities of it.

He'd soon be going out to work to provide for his wife and family. That was a whole new responsibility. Everything that he did from now on would have to be carefully considered, every decision he had to make will be made with the family in mind, not just himself. Surely it can't be that difficult, he said to himself. Most people get married and have children, lots of them. He had no doubt that May would be an excellent mother. She was loving, caring and tender, and had the experience of being the eldest daughter in a family of nine siblings. She was almost a mother now to the younger ones.

He had a good job with good prospects to further his career, he even had the offer of rent-free accommodation, thanks to Tom. For the first time since hearing the news of imminent fatherhood, he felt a certain calm. It may turn out to be the calm before the storm, but he realised then and there that this was no longer a thing to dread, but to look-forward to. He had risen to every other challenge in his life, this was yet another on the long road ahead of him. A journey that he would share with his May and however many children they decided to have.

23 - Mr. & Mrs. Cox

A few days before the marriage ceremony, Harry received a letter from May, saying she would be arriving on the mid-afternoon train on the Tuesday. It had been arranged that May would spend the night in Mrs. Dickenson's apartment on the top floor of the house. There seemed little point of having a chaperone now, but Mrs. Dickenson insisted on keeping up appearances.

After the marriage, they would set up home at number 1, Perivale Gardens, Ealing. All thanks to Tom Bainbridge, who was adamant that no rent money was to be paid. He had told Harry, that it was a wedding present. He had gone as far to say that should Harry wish to buy the place, he would let him have it at a favourable price. Harry spent the weekend before the marriage, at the house, cleaning, tidying up the garden, getting in supplies for the kitchen. He opened up accounts at all the local shops; butcher, baker, dairy, greengrocer, drapers and hardware store. His final touch, was to cut some fresh daffodils growing in the garden and put them in a vase in the front window. The house started to looked lived-in again.

The day of May's arrival in London, Harry went to work as usual but left at lunchtime. He wasn't expected back until the following Monday, by which time, he would be married. His colleagues in the office knew he was planning to get married at some time, but none had any idea it was the following day. It was going to be quite a surprise to them when they hear the news on his return. He had some lunch in a Charing Cross tea room and then took a slow walk up to Kings Cross Station.

The Newcastle train arrived more or less on time. Harry stood on the platform. It was difficult to see very far along the line of carriages due to the steam issuing from the locomotive. As it drifted away, he thought he caught a glimpse of May's silhouette. He stared hard. The woman was holding the arm of a tall man. Surely, that couldn't be her. Another cloud of steam obscured his view. A few seconds later, it cleared and he saw his May walking towards him, with her father.

Harry wanted the ground to open up and swallow him. He had no idea May would be travelling with anyone, let alone her father. His mind raced. He stood there, rooted to the spot, not knowing what to do or say. He'd never been so terrified in his life. As the two of them approached, May let go of her father's arm and ran the last few steps and enveloped Harry with her outstretched arms. All the time he was looking over her shoulder at the huge figure of her father, now just standing in front of him, no more than a yard away. Harry broke free from May's embrace and somehow managed to get out the words; "Good afternoon, sir".

His throat was dry, his voice was shaky and his hand trembled slightly as he held it out to Captain Baynham.

The captain looked him in the eye as he shook his hand with a strong grip. "I won't beat around the bush, Harry. This isn't what I had planned for my eldest daughter. I am very disappointed in the way things have turned out. I realise that we cannot undo past events, so we'll just have to accept what has happened and try and make the best out of a bad situation. Go and get married, and make her happy. When the baby is born, I'll expect you'll want to come back up north to visit us and your own family. You'll both be welcomed".

May had started to cry. Harry wanted to join her out of sheer relief. Instead, he quietly said, "Thank you, sir. I am very sorry for all the distress I have caused. I love May very much and I will do everything within my power to make her happy".

"Right", said the captain, "I have to catch a train to Portsmouth in an hour, let's go and have a quick drink".

They walked around the corner to the Midland Grand Hotel, where a sherry and two whisky and sodas were ordered. Harry learned enroute, that Captain Baynham was attending a reunion in Portsmouth with some of his former shipmates from his time spent during the Egypt Expedition.

The drink helped Harry to calm his nerves. Perhaps the old fellow wasn't so bad after all, he thought. The two men spoke about the Admiralty, and Harry's role there. A few names were mentioned that caused the captain to laugh out loud and say something along the lines of; "I remember him when he was a First Lieutenant, never thought he'd make it to Rear Admiral".

As the time came for the captain to depart, he leaned in towards the two of them and raised his glass. Not wanting to be overheard, he lowered his voice, and said, "Here's to the two of you. He looked at his daughter, "The next time I see you, my dear, you will be a married woman and a mother. God bless you all".

May started to cry again. She had been doing a lot of that lately and so had a handkerchief at the ready. It was hard to see any emotion on her father's face because of the thick brown beard he sported, but Harry could see it in his eyes, he was holding back the tears.

Final goodbyes were said and the captain strode off, leaving Harry and May standing outside the hotel with three small cases containing her worldly possessions. Harry hailed a Hansom cab and they made their way to Lewisham.

Mrs. Dickenson introduced herself as soon as they arrived at the boarding house, and straight away, began to make a fuss of May. She was sat down in the most comfortable chair in the house, with extra cushions, and given endless cups of tea with slices of cake. She was introduced to Alastair and Albert when they came home from work and quite a pleasant soiree ensued. Over dinner, Mrs. Dickenson commented how nice it had been having Harry around and that she would miss him like a son. They drank a toast to Harry's last night in Lewisham. As from tomorrow afternoon, he would be a resident of Perivale, on the diagonally opposite side of London.

In the morning, Alastair Campbell went off to work at the hospital, assuring Harry that he would be at the register office just before one-o'clock. The rest of the household had a leisurely breakfast. Mrs. Dickenson had been given a bit of extra money by Harry in order to purchase some nice things from the grocer's shop. After breakfast, she started to prepare the sandwiches and cakes. She had offered to make a small wedding cake but Harry had thought it would look out of place at such a small reception. He had made a promise to May, that on their first wedding anniversary, they would throw a big family party to make up for it. As for a honeymoon, that would be a bit difficult as the baby May was carrying, had begun to show.

May had a bath after breakfast and was periodically attended to by Mrs. Dickenson, who helped with her hair and the pressing of her wedding outfit. When it was time to leave for the register office, she swept down the staircase to face Harry and Albert waiting in the hallway. Harry thought she looked stunning.

She wore a lavender blue full-length skirt and matching jacket, piped in black velvet, to match the ankle boots she wore. A white blouse with a cameo broach at the neck, all crowned with a straw boater decorated with dried flowers of complimentary colours. Harry had never seen her look so beautiful. He stood there, in his best suit and bow tie, mouth wide-open in amazement. She joined him at the bottom of the stairs. No words were uttered, none were needed. The look on his face said it all.

Wednesday, 28th April 1909, was just an ordinary day to most of the inhabitants of Lewisham. But for two of them, it was the most special day of their lives and would be etched into their memories for ever. Alaistair arrived on time and along with Albert, they carried out their duties as witnesses. The ceremony was short and perfunctory, and over in the blink of an eye. Albert had acted as best man, and produced the gold band from his waistcoat pocket when required. The Registrar conducting the ceremony duly wrote out the marriage certificate and handed it to Harry. They walked out of the municipal building as husband and wife, Mr. and Mrs. Cox. A short stroll up the road and they were back at Mrs. Dickenson's, who had laid out a most impressive spread on the dining room table. A bottle of champagne was opened and everyone drank to the happy couple. Harry gave a little speech, in which he thanked Alaistair and Albert for their services that afternoon and for their friendship since he arrived at the house. He thanked Mrs. Dickenson for everything she had done for him and for May, and for being like a mother to him. This brought tears of joy to her face. Lastly, he thanked May, for being his wife and apologised for not giving her the wedding of her dreams.

A carriage had been booked for three-o'clock, which duly arrived. Between them, they had five cases, so travelling on the tram or trains would have been awkward. It would be considerably more expensive, but it was their wedding day, so why not arrive at their new home, together for the first time, in style?

Farewells were said, and off they went, heading west with the sun shining in their eyes all the way.

The sun was low in the sky as they drew up outside the house in Perivale Gardens. The luggage was unloaded and the driver paid off with a generous tip, Harry opened the door with the key and proceeded to pick May up in his arms and carry her over the threshold.

They both crashed down onto the sofa and laughed. Harry looked at May and stroked her face. "Well, Mrs. Cox, this is it. The first day of the rest of our lives".

She smiled sweetly back at him, "Thank you, Harry, it's been a wonderful day".

24 - Life in Perivale

After a very pleasant few days off, Harry returned to work at the Admiralty. His new route to work took him along the Metropolitan & District Railway from Ealing Broadway to Charing Cross Station, with a short walk at either end.

The first thing he did was to go to the personnel and records office to notify them of his marriage. He was told that he would have to fill in a form and have it signed by his department head. This was something he was hoping to avoid. He didn't want to have to explain to everyone in the office why he had decided to get married quietly. That was going to be a bit awkward.

He kept his head down during the morning in the hope that no-one would ask what he got up to on his week off. At lunchtime, he waited until most people were out of the office before going in to see Mr. Narbeth.

"Excuse me, Sir, would you sign this for me please?".

Without looking up from his desk, Mr. Narbeth said, "What is it?"

"I have to fill in a form for records, to notify them about my marriage".

Mr. Narbeth looked up with a quizzical expression on his face, "When did you get married?"

"Er, last Wednesday, during my week off", replied Harry, now feeling a little embarrassed.

"You kept that a bit quiet, didn't you?"

"Yes, er, well, you see, it was all a bit of a last-minute thing".

Mr. Narbeth gave Harry a knowing look. "Yes, I think I do see". He smiled and then said "Leave it on the desk, I'll sort it out later".

"Thank you very much, sir", Harry turned to go out of the room.

"Harry".

"Yes sir".

"Congratulations".

"Thank you, sir".

25 - Lloyd's Register of Shipping

A few days later, Harry came home from work to find a letter addressed to him on the kitchen table. "This came for you today, darling. It was sent to Lewisham and has been redirected here" said May, pouring out a cup of tea.

Harry examined the envelope. Printed on the back of it was; 'Lloyd's Register of Shipping – London',

He opened the letter and read it. "They would like me to go in and have a chat with them".

"Who are, they", enquired May.

"Lloyds, they keep a register of ships, all over the world".

"It doesn't sound very exciting. Besides, I thought you liked it in the navy".

"I do, but there will be little chance of travel while I'm working at the Admiralty".

"Even less working in a register office I would have thought".

"I wouldn't be doing the boring paperwork side of it. It's all to do with the design, construction and maintenance of ships and making sure they comply to a certain standard.   Apparently, they employ people like me, all over the world. Wouldn't you like to live abroad?".

"You know I would. We've spoken about it often enough. As long as we are together, I don't mind where we go".

"Well, I shall go along and see what they have to say. Nothing ventured, nothing gained".

A week later, Harry found himself standing outside the offices of Lloyd's in Fenchurch Street.

He went into the reception and asked to see Mr. Buchanan, of the Ships Surveyors Staff.

He was duly met and taken around the office. Harry noticed almost immediately, that the office environment was a lot less formal. Everybody seemed to be on first name terms with each other and there was a good atmosphere about the place. He also noticed that all the furniture and drawing equipment was new. There was nothing stuffy about the place whatsoever.

He asked lots of questions about the work they did, and they in turn asked him of his training and experience. They asked him about his current work at the Admiralty, but understood that he was unable to talk about it in any detail. He asked about being stationed abroad, and was told that there was a good possibility as they had offices in every continent.

After giving them his new address, he went back home and told May everything he had learned. She realised now, that it wasn't a boring office job he was after, but to be part of something prestigious. "They always have openings for the right kind of man", he said as they ate their dinner. "They said they would be in touch, so I'll just have to wait and see, I suppose".

He didn't have to wait long. One week later, he received a letter from Lloyds, inviting him to a formal interview with the Senior Ship Surveyor, Mr. Cornish. Harry wrote back immediately, to say he would attend. May began to share Harry's excitement about the prosect of a new job. "At least you will be able to talk to me about what you are doing each day. My father will be disappointed if you leave the navy. I think he likes the idea of having a son-in-law working at the Admiralty. Anyway, he is due to retire soon, so I don't think he'll mind that much".

Harry attended the interview the following week. Mr. Cornish, along with two other senior surveyors from the department, questioned him on all manner of technical issues. He answered the questions put to him in a clear and unambiguous way. The atmosphere in the room was very pleasant, and Harry got the impression that they were looking for reasons to employ him rather than reasons not to. He brought up the subject of overseas postings, and they gave him the impression that willingness to travel would be looked upon favourably. He left feeling that he could not have done more to show them of his suitability. He went home and told May all about it and that he was quietly confident. He always had confidence in his own ability, but the decision wasn't up to him. He hoped, very much, that they had seen in him, what they were looking for.

Harry received a letter three-days later telling him he had impressed the interview panel and they would like him to join the organisation at his earliest convenience. As he read the letter, May looked at him and smiled. She could tell by the look on his face, it was good news. "Good grief". He exclaimed, "They're going to start me on two-hundred pounds a year. That's considerably more than I'm getting now".

"Oh, darling, how wonderful, you deserve every penny of it".

"We shall need it, with a baby on the way. I shall write out my resignation letter tonight and hand it in tomorrow. When I've done that, I shall write to my father and tell him".

"And I shall write to my parents as well", said May, brimming with pride.

26 - New Job and the New Arrival

The next couple of months flew by. Harry worked his notice at the Admiralty and in late July, he started his new job at the offices of Lloyds Register of Shipping, 71 Fenchurch Street, London.

May was now six-months pregnant and proudly displaying a neat little bump. Being the height of summer, Harry would often come home to find her sitting in the shade of the rear garden, with her feet in a bowl of cool water. She had written many letters to her mother in recent weeks, asking for advice and recipes. Despite what her father had said about visiting after the baby was born, May's mother said she would come to London at the appropriate time to help with the birth. This pleased May no end. She would much rather her mother, than an unknown mid-wife be there. Shortly after moving into the house, Harry had registered with a local doctor in preparation. Everything was in readiness for the arrival of the baby.

The baby duly arrived at the end of October. A healthy baby boy that looked more like May's side of the family than Harry's. May's mother had come down the week before and had been an invaluable help. The doctor had been called just after the event and had given mother and child a clean bill of health.

"Have you thought about a name for the child?" inquired Mrs. Baynham. She and Harry were having dinner together. May had been advised to stay in bed for a few days to recover her strength.

"Yes, we talked about it yesterday", said Harry, "We thought; Charles, after my father, and Hudson, after your father, May's grandfather. And we thought we would throw a Baynham in there for good measure".

"Charles Hudson Baynham Cox, yes, that has a very nice ring to it. What will you do about a christening?"

"We thought we'd leave it for now", Harry looked around the room guiltily. "Perhaps if we are lucky enough to have any more children, we could do a job lot".

Mrs. Baynham smiled, "You're a very practical man Harry, I like that".

Once May was up and about and had settled into her new routine, her mother returned to Newcastle. The three of them would be travelling up north themselves at Christmas to see both families. They would stay at Harry's father's house, where there was more room.

Harry settled into his new job. The atmosphere in the office was relaxed and he was making plenty of new friends. The Friday after the baby was born, all the staff in the surveyors' department took him to a nearby pub to wet the baby's head. All the drinks were paid for by Mr. Cornish, who was also in attendance.

His work took him out of the city on a regular basis. Being based in London, the staff there were responsible for work being carried out at the south-east ports dotted around the coast from Norfolk to West Sussex. If ever he needed to stay away, a generous expense account allowed him to stay in a pleasant hotel. The work itself was varied and yet again, he found himself on a learning curve that was both challenging and rewarding. With a new wife, new job and a new baby, he was enjoying life and all it had to offer a young man in his twenties.

Two weeks before Christmas, tragedy struck the Baynham family once again. May's second youngest brother Arthur died of a complication arising from a bout of influenza. He was fifteen years old, and was studying to go into holy orders. He passed away quite suddenly onboard his father's ship.

May was distraught. She had lost three brothers in the last six-years. When Harry explained the circumstances to his employers, they allowed him to start his Christmas holiday a week early and give him extra time to be with his wife's family. Travelling up earlier than planned, had the added bonus of not being caught in the Christmas rush. They had a train compartment to themselves for most of the journey.

Christmas was a strange mix of emotions. The Baynham household was in a state of mourning, whilst the Cox household were celebrating the festive season and the new addition to their number. Harry and May spent a great deal of time with both families and had many visits from friends and well-wishers. They had gone to Eshott for the day to visit the Bainbridges. In a quiet moment, Harry had thanked Mrs. Bainbridge for all she had done with regards to his courtship with May and intervention when may needed a doctor. Tom was delighted to be asked if he would consent to being Godfather to little Charles at some future date, yet to be decided.

The following summer, May's father retired, signalling the end of a naval career of forty-four-years. Originally from London, he decided to return to the city of his birth. Having visited his daughter on a number of occasions in the intervening months, he had grown fond of the area in which they lived, so much so, that he decided to take a vacant house that was just three houses along from Harry and May. Travelling south with their parents, came May's three younger sisters and her only surviving brother, twelve-year old William.

Harry and May would still have to travel to the north-east to visit Harry's side of the family, but they would no longer have to divide their time between the two families.

May was very happy to be close to her parents again. There was now plenty of help on hand with regards to little Charles, who could now see his grandparents, aunts and uncle every day. Having May happy at home meant that Harry could really throw himself into his work again.

Harry kept in touch with all his former work colleagues at Swan Hunter and at the Admiralty. He had heard that the naval arms race between Great Britain and Germany was at an end, with the British maintaining its naval supremacy. Germany however, had decided to concentrate its efforts on building up its land forces. It seemed every country in Europe was either sabre rattling or building alliances with one another. Britain, France and Russia being on one side, Germany, Austria-Hungary and Italy on the other. Tensions were rising in Europe.

On Monday 15th April 1912, Harry went off to work oblivious of the unfolding events going on in the North Atlantic. When he arrived at the office, there was a buzz of excitement going around the place. News was coming in of a catastrophic event concerning the White Star Line's RMS Titanic, which had left Southampton the previous Wednesday, on her maiden voyage to New York. She was the largest vessel afloat and was a hundred feet longer than the Mauretania. The eyes of the world were watching and praying for a favourable outcome. Initial reports in the newspapers had said that the ship had struck an iceberg but was still afloat and that all lives were saved. It was believed that she was being towed to Halifax, Nova Scotia. Harry returned home that evening visibly shaken. He already knew what the headlines in the next mornings' newspapers would be. He glossed over the details when he told May what had happened. Later that evening, he spoke to his father-in-law and told him that the Titanic had sunk and that fifteen to seventeen hundred crew and passengers were missing, feared dead. The effects of the tragedy and subsequent investigation rippled around the world, leading to far more emphasis on maritime safety and new design principles were implemented almost immediately. As far as Harry was concerned, lessons had been learnt, and the industry vowed that something like that would never be allowed to happen again.

In November, Harry and May both received letters from Tom and Alice Bainbridge, telling them of their fathers' death. May had known the Bainbridges for such a long time, she was almost one of the family, and took the news very hard. Although they were planning to go up to Newcastle at Christmas, May decided that she should attend the funeral. So, she travelled up with her father, who had arranged to meet some of his former colleagues on the Wellesley.

27 – Cecily

In the summer of 1913, May announced that she was expecting another child. The news was met with sheer delight by Harry and the extended family. The circumstances surrounding the birth of this child were not going to be as traumatic as when Charles was born. When Harry wrote to his family in the north, his father replied that Harry's younger sister Laura, was also expecting. A few months later, May's sister Pauline, also announced that she had a second child on the way. It looked like 1914 was going to be a good year.

On the twenty-sixth of March, young Charles got a baby sister. After a lengthy discussion, they decided to call her Cecily Pauline. She had been born in the same house and the same bed as her brother, with May's mother acting as midwife. During the Easter holiday, Harry and May went to visit Harry's family in Newcastle. Whilst in the north, he was able to visit his old friend, Tom Bainbridge, who had recently become an officer in a signalling unit, in the special reserve. They met in the pub that was their regular haunt when they both worked at Swan Hunter. "There's going to be a war Harry, mark my words" said Tom, earnestly.

"I'm not so sure, there is plenty of talk about it in the papers, but nothing seems to be actually happening".

"The Kaiser is spoiling for a fight, with the least provocation, he'll start something".

"Our navy is bigger and better equipped; we have the best army in the world. I can't see him starting anything with us. What would be in it for him?".

"Who knows how the mind of a madman works. Anyway, you haven't come all the way up here to talk politics". Raising his glass, Tom said, "Here's to young Cecily, I trust she will grow up to be as beautiful as her mother".

"We might have her christened with Charles in the summer", said Harry. "Perhaps you can come down and stay with us for a while, in your house",

Tom laughed, "You'd better be careful, I might give it to my future godson. If you don't buy him enough toys, he'll kick you out"

28 - Early Casualties

On the twenty-eighth of June, came the spark that lit a fire across Europe. Heir to the Austro-Hungarian empire, Franz Ferdinand and his wife were assassinated in Sarajevo by a Serbian backed terrorist group. Over the following five-weeks, one by one, the nations of Europe went to war. Britain declared war on Germany at eleven-o'clock on the evening of the fourth of August, when it failed to respect the neutrality of Belgium. Harry's work was now on a war footing. Major changes were to come as he, along with everyone in the industry, took stock of the situation and their new obligations to assist in the war effort.

Everyone was keen to do their bit. May's father offered his services to the Admiralty, and his youngest son William, enlisted in the Royal Navy as a midshipman. Harry's two brothers' Cecil and Reginald volunteered, one going into the Royal Fusiliers, the other into the Rhodesian Regiment. Tom Bainbridge was called up and was soon to go to France.

The Lloyd's surveyors' staff were seconded to the Admiralty. They continued to work at their office in Fenchurch Street, but under supervision from Harry's old colleagues in Whitehall. Harry was in a favourable position. Having worked at the Admiralty, he knew exactly what was expected. Once the war began in earnest, it was obvious to everyone that the British ship builders were not going to keep up with the supply of vessels that were needed in a war that was to fought far beyond the shores of Europe. Ships of all classes were going to be needed from the Canadian ship yards and those in the United States of America. The Admiralty would need the best men they had access to, in order to oversee the construction of such ships and act as a liaison. Harry was put on the short list.

"How long would you be away for?" asked May, on hearing Harry's news

"I have no idea, for the duration of the war presumably".

"It doesn't feel right abandoning our country in its time of need".

"We won't be abandoning anything. I'll be working for the Admiralty, doing essential war work. This could be the start of a new life for us, all of us".

"What if we don't like it? Could we come back?

"Yes, of course. I don't want to go anywhere without you and the children".

"When do you think you will find out whether they want you to go or not?"

"Quite soon I expect.

"I shall hate to leave my family behind".

"Yes, I know darling, it won't be easy for any of us. Just give the idea some thought, so we are ready to make a decision if the time comes".

It wasn't long before tragedy struck. Harry returned home one evening to find May sitting with her parents, tears cascading down her face. Her mother was also in tears. He looked at Captain Baynham, who stood next to his wife and said, "What has happened?"

He handed Harry a crumpled letter; "It came in the second post this afternoon; it's from Miss Alice Bainbridge".

Harry sank into an armchair and started to read the letter that was addressed to May and himself. His initial thought was that it must be some bad news about her mother, a wonderful, warm-hearted woman he admired very much.

As he read the letter, his eyes welled up which made it difficult to read. By the time he got to the end, he too had tears running down the cheeks of his face. Tom, had been killed in action in Flanders. His body buried in a field near where he fell. Harry got up and knelt down on the floor in front of May. He held her tightly, and they cried together.

The war had suddenly got very personal. Now, it was real. It could happen to any family at any time. No-one was going to be immune. It was one thing to lose a close friend or family member to illness or an accident, but this was wholesale slaughter that could never be justified. The only way to stop this war, was to win it. Only by defeating the enemy, could a lasting peace return. Harry changed that night. He had been hard-working and patriotic as the next man, but now he was angry. How dare they take away from him such a good man, his best friend. He went to work the next day with a fire in his belly and a commitment to redouble his effort in feeding the British war machine and seeing the job through to the end.

29 - Atlantic Crossing

In June, Harry came home with the news he had been officially requested to go to New York on behalf of the Admiralty, to check and approve the plans of American shipbuilders constructing vessels for the Royal Navy.

"They are raising my salary to three-hundred and fifteen pounds a year, with an annual bonus of three-hundred. This is an incredible opportunity. It may only last a year or two, but I really think we should do it".

Harry was sitting on a stool in the kitchen. May had her back to him and was putting together a cold meat salad for their evening meal. She turned, "Whatever I say, you are going to go. You're going to do it for Tom".

"I'm going to do it for Tom, I am going to do it for us, I am going to do it to help put an end to this bloody war".

"I have had plenty of time to think about this. I've discussed it with my mother and father. Whilst I am loathed to leave my home and family, I fully understand that this is a once in a lifetime opportunity for us as a family. As long as we are together, the four of us, I think we can make it work. Whatever situation we find ourselves in".

Harry stood, walked towards May and cuddled her. If I was in any doubt, I wouldn't jeopardise our future happiness, not for one-minute".

"I know", she said, "You have my full support. Go to work tomorrow and tell them you accept. No looking back".

"No looking back", he echoed.

It was later decided that Harry would go to America first, and once he had found a place to rent, May and the children would follow on. In the weeks before his departure, he went up to Newcastle with May and the children to see his family. They also went to visit Mrs. Bainbridge and Alice, who were still in a state of mourning. Tom's death had hit them hard. During the emotional reunion, Mrs. Bainbridge told Harry that Tom had bequeathed him something in his will. She didn't know what it was but that the solicitor acting as executor to the estate would be contacting him at some point. May said that she would write to Mrs. Bainbridge as soon as they had an address in the United States for correspondence.

The morning of his departure, Harry walked Charles to school. When they reached the gates, he went down on one knee and gave his son a hug. "I won't see you for a little while", he said.

"I know daddy, you're going to America".

"That's right, and before you know it, you'll be coming to join me. You must promise me one thing. You must look after mummy and Cecily for me".

"Yes, I promise". There was one last hug and Harry kissed him on the forehead. Charles turned and skipped off into the playground and into school.

By the time he had returned home, May had taken Cecily round to her parents and was now getting ready to go to the station to see Harry off on his Atlantic crossing.

Two months ago, the RMS Lusitania had been torpedoed by a German submarine off the coast of Ireland, travelling back from New York. Twelve-hundred people had been killed, so understandably, there was still a lot of nervousness about such a journey, in the minds of both May and Harry. Lloyds had booked him a passage on an American ship, the SS Saint Paul, as it would be free from German aggression, being from a neutral country.

They stood on the platform at Euston Station, holding each other. Both had tears in their eyes. "Write to me as soon as you get there", sniffed May.

"I'll send you a telegram, it will be quicker".

The guard of the Liverpool train shouted out that the train was to depart and for all passengers to get aboard.

There was time for another warm embrace and a kiss, then Harry got on board the train. He stood by the closed door with the widow fully down and held May's hand. As the train lunged forward and started to get traction, she let go. She waved her damp handkerchief and he leant out of the window. They waved and blew kisses until they were out of sight of one another.

Harry arrived, without incident, in New York on the third of July. The first thing he did, was to go to a telegraph office and send a telegram home; 'ARRIVED NY. WILL WRITE SOON. H.'

Harry hailed a taxicab and asked the driver to take him to the Belmont Hotel on Park Avenue and forty-second Street. Once his luggage was loaded, the motorcar set off, weaving its way through the busy streets of lower Manhattan. This was Harry's first time abroad. He peered out of the open window and took in all the sights, sounds and smells of the city like an excited school boy. It was a hot summers afternoon but due to the high buildings all around, there were plenty of pockets of shade. The first thing he had noticed, even before getting off the ship, was the size and height of the place. The roads were long and straight, the buildings higher than anything even London had to offer. There seemed to be construction work going on all over and the skyline positively bristled with cranes carrying their heavy loads to the workman high above the ground who looked like ants in the distance. He was very impressed with what he saw. This was industry going at full pace. His job would be getting them to build the ships needed in Europe for the war effort. The sinking of the Lusitania and the killing of many American passengers, had galvanised opinion in favour of Britain and her allies. He felt he would be among friends.

He noticed that there was an awful lot of flags flying about and bunting tied to almost everything.

How very patriotic he thought, before realising that today was the third of July and that tomorrow would be the fourth. That should prove to be quite a spectacle.

The cab driver shouted out something unintelligible. Harry, not realising it was directed at him, continued to stare, wide-eyed out the window. The driver turned to face him and said, a lot more clearly, "Where're ya from?".

Harry leant forward to speak, "Just off the boat from England, Great Britain".

"Aahh, gee, are things as bad as they make out in the newspapers? It sounds like you guys are having a tough time over there".

"Yes, I think it's fair to say it's pretty bad. The newspapers are censored, so I don't think we're getting the full story".

"That's too bad. I don't think you're gonna get much help from Wilson".

"As long as he is prepared to sell us some ships, I'll be happy".

The cab pulled up outside the Belmont Hotel. It was, thought Harry, enormous. It had in actual fact, been the tallest hotel in the world when it was completed some seven-years earlier. He paid off the driver while a porter loaded his cases onto a trolley and took them into reception. Harry followed behind. He gazed in awe at the large red-marble space before him. It was the size of a booking hall at one of the main

London stations. It was refreshingly cool after being in the cab.

The hotel had been booked by Lloyds. He had a room booked for two-weeks, after which time, he would be expected to find an apartment to rent and would then receive an allowance. The exchange rate was very much in his favour, with nearly five-dollars to the pound. He was duly shown to his room by the porter up on the eleventh floor. The view from his room looked south down Park Avenue and over the lavish mansions of Manhattans wealthier class. I am going to be quite comfortable here for a few weeks, he thought to himself.

After he unpacked, he went out for a stroll in order to get his bearings and find out where the nearest subway station was. Tomorrow was going to be a busy day. He would report to his boss, even though he wasn't actually expected to start work there until the following week. He would use the time wisely and waste no time in looking for an apartment to live in when May and the children arrive.

After his walk, he returned to his room and changed for dinner. Like everything in this hotel, the dining room was vast. Enormous cut-glass chandeliers hung from the high ceiling. It was a wonder they didn't pull it down. After a light meal, he retired to his room for an early night. As he lay on the bed, he could still feel the roll of the ocean. He hadn't quite got his land-legs back.

After a hearty breakfast, he left the hotel and made his way to the Grand Central Station. He travelled four-miles south on the subway and got off at Bowling Green, the closest station to Battery Place, where his new office was to found at number seventeen. It was a handsome building of about twenty-floors high, overlooking the harbour. The lower section was built of limestone in the Georgian-style of architecture as often seen in London, with the rest of it constructed from three different shades of red brick.

He was surprised to find the building open, it was after all, a Sunday. He made enquires with the doorman and discovered that the offices of Lloyds were currently open seven-days a week, due to the extra workload caused by the situation in Europe.

He made his way up to the seventh floor, where the offices of Lloyds were located.

Harry introduced himself to a clerk in the front office and was then escorted to an office along the corridor, the door of which had 'James H. Mancor – Chief Surveyor' written in gold letters upon it. Harry was shown in and announced by the clerk.

James Henry Mancor was a man of fifty-six, tall, well dressed with a balding head and thin moustache. When he spoke, it was it was with a soft Scottish accent with a slight hint of American thrown in for good measure. "Hello Harry", he said, rising from his chair, walking around his desk with an outstretched hand.

"Welcome to New York. Did you have a good crossing?"

Harry shook his hand. "Yes, thank you sir, a very pleasant voyage, I got in yesterday afternoon".

"Excellent", Mr. Mancor put his arm on Harry's shoulder and ushered him to a chair. "First things first, we'll have none of that 'yes sir', "no sir' business. We're all on first name terms here, so you can call me Jim from now on. The Americans don't like all that formal stuff. You'll soon learn that when you start dealing with them. The people running the shipyards and good enough fellows, it's the unions you have to watch out for. You're lucky to find us all in the office. We've been doing half days at the weekend to keep up with demand. Hopefully, when you get up to speed, we can finish doing the Sundays. Now tell me, how are things looking in Europe?"

The two men spoke at length about the war and its effects on their industry. "I took on this job", said Jim, "as a prelude to my retirement. Thanks to this damn war, I'm working harder than ever. I've been here for twenty-one years now; I'm part of the furniture. We have another fourteen offices around this country and seven in Canada, for which I am responsible".

"That's a huge responsibility for one man",

"You're damn right it is. The only way I can do it, is to have good people around me. People like you".

"Thank you, Jim, hopefully it won't take me too long to learn the ropes here".

"With your training and experience, you'll pick it up easily enough".

They finished the tea that had been brought into them. Getting to his feet, Jim said, "Right, I'll introduce you to the others.

As they walked down the corridor, Jim said, "At the moment, we have two principals and two ship surveyors. On the engineering side we have five engineer surveyors. All of them good men".

They entered a large office. Clean, bright and modern, it had five drawing boards set up with a large desk beside each of them. The three men in the room looked up from their work as Jim and Harry entered the room. "Good morning gentlemen, I'd like you to meet Harry Cox, your new surveyor", announced Jim. Then walking around the room, he introduced Harry to them individually. "This is my number two, Neville McClelland. The other principal is currently in Scotland visiting his family. He'll be back on the seventeenth of July. And these two reprobates", he said jokingly, "Are the ship surveyors, Anthony Allen and Edward Evans".

They all shook hands with Harry and welcomed him to the office. Jim went back to his office and left Harry with Neville.

Harry spent the rest of the morning talking to Neville and the others about the work they were doing and plans for the future.

"They've put me in the Belmont Hotel for a couple of weeks. I shall need to find a place to rent. My wife and children plan to join ne as soon as they can. Any suggestions?"

"Most of us live about ten-miles up on the west side. Transportation links are good and the rent is a lot cheaper than living in this end of town. You should be able to find something quite comfortable for about forty or fifty dollars a month".

"That sounds promising", replied Harry.

"What have you got planned for tonight? The city goes a bit hysterical on Independence Day".

"The hotel is having a party on the roof I believe. I should get quite a view of all the fireworks from up there".

Harry left the office around lunchtime just before the office closed for the day. He headed off in the direction of the subway but rather than go underground, he decided that as it was such a nice day, he would take the elevated section along Ninth Avenue along the west side on Manhattan. It was a pleasant ride that took him past Central Park and the Natural History Museum. He made a mental note to come back one day with young Charles, he'd gone to the one in London and thought it was wonderful. He got off the train at 155th Street, and armed with a map they had given him at the office, went exploring.

Harry watched the fireworks light up the Manhattan sky. Around him, people dressed in their dinner jackets and party gowns, sipped champagne and danced. It seemed a million miles away from where he'd been just a week ago. He thought of May and the children, and their extended family. His contribution to the war effort would be made from the safety of America. Anti-German sentiment was on the rise. The papers had been full of the attempted murder of the American financier, J. P. Morgan, by a German sympathiser. If only the might of this industrial powerhouse entered the war on the side of the allies.

He returned to his room and wrote a long letter to May.

After breakfast, he returned to the area he had visited the previous day for further exploration. Being Monday, there seemed to be a lot less people on the street. Apart from a good selection of local shops, his main priority was to find a suitable school for Charles. Once he was happy with what he saw of the area, he made his way down to Central Park on the subway, getting off at 72nd Street. He found the offices of Pease & Elliman, a reputable realtor and made enquires. They didn't have anything on their books in the locale that Harry specified that would be suitable for a small family, but that it was only a matter of time before they did. He left his details and they would contact him as soon as something suitable came up.

He wasn't due to start work for another week. Feeling guilty about all the work they had on, he spent the afternoon back at the office. After talking to Jim, it was decided that he would take up his position as from tomorrow. He would be given time off to view any apartments as and when required. Once he had got up to speed, they could possibly give up working at weekends. Everyone would be happy about that.

Although Harry was the youngest in the office, his training and experience, especially his recent work at the head office in London, soon propelled his standing amongst his colleagues. His quiet efficiency and good humour, was appreciated by everyone he met, in or out of the office. Two-weeks after he started, the other principal, Andrew McNab, returned from leave in Scotland and made up the full compliment. The office was now firing on all cylinders.

As promised, the realtor called Harry one afternoon to say a family-sized apartment had just become available in his preferred area – Washington Heights. Wasting no time, he arranged to meet the agent outside the apartment later that day. He made his way on the subway to 157th Street and walked round to number 400, West 160th Street.

The building was newly constructed. Internal work on some of the lower floors was still in progress but in a few months, it would all be complete. The temporary sign hanging outside identified the building as; 'Roger Morris Apartments'. It looked beautiful and just what he was looking for. "Who was Roger Morris?" enquired Harry

"He was one of your fellow countrymen", replied the agent. "He was a British army officer who bought the estate back in 1765. The area was evacuated by the British in 1783. Now they're back". He smiled at Harry.

"Yes, we're back, and all because of another war. You'd have thought we would have learnt our lesson by now".

It was fourteen-floors high and elegantly proportioned with a limestone base and the rest of pale brick and terracotta. The marble hallway led into a magnificent lobby with a highly styled art-nouveau flower motif on the ceiling. Two elevators led to the upper floors.

"There will be just over a hundred apartments when it's finished, with eight apartments to a floor. Each apartment has a bathroom and there are servant's quarters at the top of the building you can rent separately, as and when required. All the work will be complete by January We are getting a lot of enquires, as I'm sure you can imagine. If you're quick, you can have your pick. Personally speaking, I would go for something high up. The views are great and it'll be cooler in the summer. If you choose one that is already complete, you can move in straight away".

Harry had already made his mind up, without even going into one of the apartments. He was certain May would love it as well. Going inside only reinforced his belief that this was the right place. Deciding to strike while the iron was hot, he went back to the realtor's office with the agent and signed up.

Harry wrote a long letter to May that evening, describing as best he could, everything about the apartment. He suggested that it was now time to book a passage across to New York. The correspondence between them took longer than it would normally do because of the war. British ships were at danger of attack by German U-Boats going across the Atlantic, this sometimes meant a delay in the mail. Over the next month, it was decided that she would come out on her own, leaving the children with her parents. There would still be plenty for her to do once she got there and doing it without two young children would make life easier. Charles and Cecily would come over later, possibly with their grandparents or an aunt. Like Harry, May was to sail on an American registered ship. She was booked on the SS New York, which would depart from Liverpool and arrive on the twenty-ninth of September.

30 - A Close Call

One night in early September, Harry was kept wake by the heat. It had reached ninety-degrees during the day, and it didn't feel much cooler in the evening. He tossed and turned for most of the night. As the sun began to rise, he gave up the fight and decided to get up and go to work early. At least it would be a bit cooler down by the harbour.

It was quiet around Battery Place. The only sound was coming from the docks as stevedores on the night shift loaded and unloaded cargo. He entered the building. It was ghostly quiet. He thought it strange that there was no doorman on duty, but in this heat, he'd probably gone off to get a drink or have a nap somewhere.

He went up to the seventh-floor. He got his office key out and went to unlock the door. Strangely, it was already unlocked. His initial thought was, somebody else couldn't sleep last night and had the same idea as himself.

As he opened the door, he was met with a scene of disarray. The clerk's office looked like a bomb had gone off. Papers were strewn all over the floor, drawers to desks were forced into. "Christ", exclaimed Harry, "We've been burgled".

No sooner had the words left his mouth, he heard the unmistakable sound of wood splintering under force, coming from Jim's office along the corridor. Harry's heart started to race. He quietly put down his briefcase and glanced around the office, looking for something to arm himself with. In the corner of the office was wooden pole with a brass hook on the end for opening and closing the highest windows in the office. With that, he slowly crept down the corridor to Jim's office. Inside, he could hear the frantic rustle of papers and draws being open and slammed closed. It sounded like the work of one individual. He gently pushed the office door open. A muscular looking man dressed like the many dock-workers in the area was stood by the desk rummaging through a pile of paperwork and books. He looked up and saw Harry standing in the doorway. Quick as a flash, he pulled out a knife and slowly went towards Harry.

Harry entered the room and closed the distance between them. He held the pole as would a Masi warrior hold a spear to keep a ferocious animal at bay. In broken English, the man said, "Let me go, or I will kill you". Harry was horrified and scared, but most of all, he was angry. A sense of outrage took over him. He glared at the man, "How dare you come here and try to steal from us".

The man tried to make for the door. Harry ducked as the man lashed out towards his face with the knife. As the man pushed past, Harry thrust the wooden pole forwards knocking the man over into the corridor. As he landed, the knife fell from his hand. There was no room for Harry to take a swing with the pole, so he just jabbed it as hard as he could, repeatedly into the man's back and shoulder. All the same time he was doing it, he was shouting out for help. He had no idea if he was alone in the building or whether anyone could hear him.

Harry's arms grew tired very quickly. He wasn't use to such physical activity. As he thrust the pole into the man's back, he turned and deflected it with his arm. The man was powerful, he manged to take the pole off Harry and get to his feet. Harry tried to get down the corridor to the reception area but was tripped and landed flat on his face. He rolled over. The man had thrown aside the pole and now had the knife back in his hand. Harry tried to scrabble backwards but it was no use, he couldn't get away. He was terrified. The man had murder in his eyes as he stood over Harry. The man changed his grip on the knife so he was now holding it as a dagger. He lent down over Harry and raised his right arm. Just as he started his downward thrust towards Harry's chest, the shot rang out. The man jerked backwards, dropping the knife. He had been shot in the shoulder by a police officer.

Harry feinted.

The next few hours were a blur. The place was crawling with police. The injured man had been taken to hospital under armed guard. Harry was checked over by a doctor and given some pain-killers. The full complement of staff were now in the office and once the police had finished taking Harry's statement, the clear-up could begin. It was suggested that Harry should go home and get some rest and come back tomorrow if he felt up to it. He ached all over, so he didn't take much persuading.

The pain-killers were strong and he slept for twelve-hours. He returned to work the following morning to find a new man on the front door. He went up to the office and as he entered, all the clerks started clapping him and cheering as if welcoming a hero. He stood there for a moment looking bemused and a little embarrassed. Jim Mancor appeared at his side and the noise subsided. "Good morning, Harry", he said with a smile, "There's a chap in my office who would like to have a chat with you, a sort of policeman".

"Yes, of course".

They went to Jim's office. A well-dressed man of average height and average build sat in one of the chairs in front of Jim's desk. He got up as Harry approached and shook his hand. "Good morning, Mr. Cox, my name is Richard Finch, I am an agent from the Bureau of Investigation, part of our Justice Department".

The three men sat down. "I expect you'd like to know what yesterday's caper was all about?"

"Well, yes", said Harry, "I thought I had caught a burglar red-handed, but after he tried to kill me, I began to wonder if it was something else".

"The man that attacked you works on the docks here; his name is Otto Muller and is of German descent.

He has been passing ship movements onto his contacts ever since the war in Europe began. Unfortunately, because we are neutral, that doesn't constitute illegal activity. However, yesterday he crossed the line".

"I'd say he did", said Jim. "Ransacks my office and tries to kill one of my men".

"What was he looking for?", inquired Harry.

He was told by his contact to come to this office and steal your registers of shipping. They would be very useful to an enemy".

"But the registers here would only have the details of ships built in the states", replied Harry. "It only contains details of commercial vessels, nothing military".

"Well, whichever way you look at it, it's a sinister turn of events that we will have to keep a very watchful eye on. Muller obviously never found them?"

"No, he didn't. They are locked up in my safe every night, company policy".

"Can I suggest you notify all your other offices worldwide, and tell them what's happened here?".

"Certainly, I'll cable our head office in London straight away", said Jim.

"Do we know how he got in the office? When I arrived in the morning, the office door was unlocked".

"Yes, Muller came into reception on the ground floor and asked where the Lloyds's office was. He then coshed the doorman and took his keys. He probably thought he'd knocked him out cold, but the poor feller was only dazed. He went round the block to look for a cop. Fortunately for you, he found one".

"Yes, just in the nick of time". Harry shook his head slowly, "I really thought my number was up".

"You're a brave man Mr. Cox. Muller is a strong man. He's been a dock worker most of his life, not many would take him on in a fight".

"What will happen to him now?"

"Oh, he'll be charged with assault and battery, attempted murder, burglary, criminal damage and anything else we can throw at him. Hopefully, when he realises how much trouble he's in, he will tell us about the people he's been working for".

As Harry walked back to the surveyor's office, he stopped and looked at the blood-stained carpet that was yet to be replaced. A little shiver went through his body. He decided not to tell May of yesterday's events. It would only upset her and make her worry. He'd give her an edited version of the story once she was safely here, in their new home.

Muller never did talk. Harry found out after a visit from agent Finch a couple of weeks later, that whist in a prison hospital, Muller had his throat cut as he lay in his bed. The man that did it, was another German sympathiser who was already on death row for blowing up a train in Pittsburgh which had killed a dozen people. Harry was relieved that that was the end of the matter and he wouldn't be called to give evidence in court. He wanted to forget the whole unsavoury affair and get on with his life.

31 - Reunited

May's ship arrived on a warm, sunny Wednesday afternoon on the twenty-ninth of September. Harry had been given the rest of the week off, and now stood on the jetty watching the passengers coming down the gangplank. As always when a ship lands, there is a seemingly chaotic surge of people coming and going in all directions. Above the noise of the crowd and machinery, he heard the faint call of his name. It was quite likely that there was more than one Harry in the crowd, but the tone of the voice told him it was his May. His eyes darted up and down the gangplank and along the deck, where the passengers were queuing to get off. His eye was caught by a hand frantically waving from the deck. It was May. He waved enthusiastically back. Their eyes met for the first time in nearly three-months.

She stepped off the gangplank and threw herself into his outstretched arms. She squeezed him tightly, "Oh, darling, darling, darling, I've missed you so much", she cried.

"I can't believe you're here; you get more beautiful as time goes by, my angel". Harry's eyes were full of the tears of joy. They stood there, in an embrace that neither of them wanted to release. People milled around them, going about their business. For Harry and May, time stood still for a few moments.

They talked non-stop as May went through immigration control and customs. Harry wanted to hear everything about the children and May asking about his work, his new friends and of course, their new home.

Within an hour of getting through customs, they were standing outside the apartment block. "Oh, Harry, It's wonderful. I can't wait to see inside".

They left the dusty ground floor and went up to the eighth, where everything was sparkling like new and the sound of workmen barely noticeable. May walked into the large apartment and gasped at its splendour. "It's enormous", she said, walking from room to room. Harry stood and smiled as he watched her gliding from one room to the other, her eyes wide with excitement. "It lacks a woman's touch of course", he called out as May entered the master bedroom at the end of the passage. "That's your job. I've opened an account at a reputable store downtown where we should be able to get all the furniture and things, we need to make it a home".

"Oh, Harry, this is perfect, I can't wait to get started".

"Well, you're going to have to wait, at least until tomorrow. I will give you a guided tour of the city".

May settled quickly into her new life. Within a couple of weeks, they had all the furniture they needed, curtains were hung and the decorations complete. The apartment looked fresh, modern and homely. As the weeks went by, they got more and more neighbours and soon, all the apartments on the eighth-floor were occupied.

Towards the end of October, Harry returned home from work one Saturday lunchtime. Jim Mancor had put a stop to Sunday working once Harry had got up to speed, but there was still the need to work a half-day Saturday.

As was his usual routine before getting the elevator, he took a key from his waistcoat pocket and checked the mailbox. There was one letter addressed to him, from England. As he ascended, he opened the envelope and started to read the letter therein.

The door opened at the eighth floor. Harry stood there with his mouth open, staring at the letter, looking dumbfounded. "I don't believe it", he said in words barely audible, "I don't believe it", he repeated. The doors stated to shut with him still standing in the elevator. He pressed the button quickly to open them again and then hurried along the passage to the apartment.

He opened the door, and started to call out excitedly, "May, May, where are you?"

May came running from the lounge into the hallway, where Harry stood, still staring at the letter. "What is it darling?" she cried; her brow furrowed with worry. "What has happened? Has something terrible happened? Tell me"

Harry regained his composure. "Do you remember when we last saw Mrs. Bainbridge?"

"Oh no", cried May, "Nothing awful has happened to her, has it?"

"No, not at all. Do you remember she said that Tom had left me something in his will and that his solicitor would write once they had sorted out his estate?"

"Yes, I remember it very well. Is that a letter from the solicitor?"

"Yes, it is. I just can't believe it".

"What? What does it say?"

"He's given me the house in Perivale".

In March of the following year, Harry had his appointment confirmed as a permanent position. He wouldn't be returning back to England after the war. With that in mind, he put up for sale the house he had inherited from Tom and started to make arrangements for the children to come over and join their parents.

Captain Baynham had returned to the navy and his wife did not want to leave the country during a time of war. It was agreed that May's nineteen-year old sister Lucie, who had done such a great job of helping her mother take care of Charles and Cecily, would travel to America with them.

32 - All Together

On Wednesday the fifth of April, the same ship that had brought Harry to New York, docked with his children on board. There was a great deal of hugging, kissing and crying by all concerned. Charles was now six-years old and Cecily, two. Harry hadn't seen them for nearly a year. He was so relieved to see that Charles hadn't forgotten what he looked like. He had worried about that. Cecily was too young to remember and barely recognised her mother. She was quite content to be carried in the arms of Lucie as they went through all the immigration and customs checks.

As they drove back to the apartment, Charles stared out the window in wonder at all the skyscrapers, the like of which he had never seen. At the apartment, he ran around and explored all the rooms. When he found his room, he jumped up and down on the bed like a trampoline. It was clear to all, that he was going to like it here. The adults sat in the lounge and drank tea, whilst Cecily played with a toy on the rug in the middle of the room. The family were reunited. Harry didn't want to be without them ever again.

Charles started at a local school after the Easter holiday. Things were now much the same as they were back in England, with Lucie around to help look after Cecily May enjoyed having her around. It made her feel less isolated and closer to her family. She really missed her parents, and between Lucie and May, there was a never-ending stream of correspondence going across the Atlantic.

Harry continued to work hard. At the end of May, Jim Mancor had announced his retirement, and there was to be a reorganisation of the staff. Much to his surprise, Harry was promoted to Assistant Chief Surveyor for the United States and Canada. His new boss was going to be James French, who had been Jim Mancor's assistant just prior to the outbreak of war and who had been the principal surveyor in Glasgow, Scotland for the last twelve-months. Andrew McNab was being sent to San Francisco to head-up things on the west coast, and Neville McClelland was going to Boston on the east coast. Of the surveyors; Edward Evans would be transferred to Detroit but Anthony Allen would be staying along with two new members of staff; Albert Chisholm and Joseph Gardiner.

Harry's salary would be increased to one-thousand-pounds sterling per annum. The same week that the announcement was made, he had heard from his solicitor in London, that the sale of the house in Perivale had gone through. On the way home, he stopped off at a wine merchant and purchased a couple of bottles of Champagne. This was most definitely something to celebrate.

The war in Europe went on relentlessly. President Wilson's government was committed to remaining neutral, despite a growing concern about attacks on its shipping fleet. In October, Harry received terrible news in a letter from his father. His elder brother Cecil, had been killed in France during the Somme offensive. He was thirty-four-years of age and had attained the rank of Captain in the Royal Fusiliers. Two years into this war and he had lost his best friend and a brother. If he was in England and not in a reserved occupation, then he too may be called to the front. Conscription had originally been for single men, but now it was married men as well. He felt guilty that he wasn't doing more and that he lived in the safety of a neutral country, far removed from the battle fields, where his fellow countrymen were making the ultimate sacrifice in the name of peace.

On the 4th April 1917, the United States of America declared war on Germany. This was a huge relief to the allied forces that had been engaged in a war of attrition for nearly three-years. The industrial might of America would break the stalemate and lead to a swift conclusion of hostilities. Harry's work stepped up a notch. Everything was now on a military footing. Within one-year, the shipyards of America were launching nearly one-hundred ships per day and the size of the workforce had increased by sixty-percent of its pre-war number. There was no way Germany and its allies could compete against those numbers. As a mark of appreciation from his company with regards to the work he had done, Harry received an increase of five-hundred-pounds in his annual salary.

On a cold damp Monday morning in November of the following year, Harry got out of bed and went into the bathroom to wash and shave in preparation for his commute to work. Through the bathroom vent, he could hear a persistent din like foghorns coming from the direction of the Hudson River. Perhaps it was foggy out there, thought Harry.

He kissed May and the children goodbye and left the apartment.

When he got down to street level, he sensed that something was going on, but he didn't know what. People were walking in all directions, more hurriedly than usual. There was a sense of excitement in the air. The sound of the foghorns in the distance seem to grow louder. Motorcars on the street were randomly sounding their horns. He could even hear church bells ringing out. By the time he had got to the subway, he had heard passersby saying that the war was over. There was only one way to find out for sure. He would go to the office and check the overnight messages from London. As the train got further downtown, more and more people were getting on and talking about the news. When he finally made it out of the subway at the Battery, he was hit by a cacophony of noise. Every ship in New York harbour was sounding its foghorn and factories were blowing their steam whistles. It was the sound of celebration, not alarm. Harry walked to the office as fast as his legs could carry him. He was met by signs of jubilation as he walked through the office door. The clerks were singing 'The Star-Spangled Banner' at the tops or their voice, whist tearing up pieces of scrap paper and launching it out of the window so it fell like snow onto the gathering crowds below. He ran down the passageway to Jim French's office. All the surveyors were there. "Is it true?" gasped Harry, now totally out of breath. "Is it over?"

Joe Gardiner handed him a telegram; he had tears in his eyes. It was from head office in London, and read; '11th November 1918 - Compiegne, France - Armistice signed by allies and Germany - Effective 1100hrs – God Save the King'.

There was a lot of hugging and back-slapping and, as if not to be out sung by the clerks, a hearty rendition of 'God Save the King' was sung. Harry walked over to Jim and said something in his ear. Jim nodded, and said in a loud voice to be heard over the hubbub; "Gentlemen, gentlemen, your attention please". He waited until the din subsided. "I think it's fair to say that no-one will be doing any work today. So, I think you may as well all go home and celebrate this glorious news with your loved ones. See you all tomorrow, we still have plenty of work to do". There was cheering all round and slowly the office emptied.

Harry made it home in about an hour. It seemed as if the total population of the city were out on the streets. He found May, Charles and Cecily standing in the street outside the apartment block talking to their neighbours. He ran up to them. "Oh Harry, is it true? Is it really true?", cried May.

"Yes, darling it is. I've just seen the telegram from London. The fighting stopped at five-o'clock this morning. It's finally over". They hugged and they cried. The relief and the joy were overwhelming.

Harry laid in bed that night emotionally exhausted, it was hard to believe that, after four-years of war, life was going to get back to normal. He couldn't actually remember what normal was. He certainly didn't know what the new normal would be. The world had changed, he had changed. For the first time in his life, he didn't have a plan, or a goal or a target. He had no idea of what was coming next. He knew that he had May by his side and two-wonderful children. He had a well-paid job and money in the bank. He would work hard, just like he had always done, and he would wait and see what came round the corner. His homeland was battered and bruised, and would take years to recover, if at all. He felt he was in the right place. This was his home now. America would soon recover, and he would play his part. He reflected on the friends and family he had lost, and that others had lost more, a lot more. He considered himself one of the lucky ones. He would strive to help re-build a new world, hopefully one in which his children would never have to fight for their very existence.

The new year saw much celebrating in the Cox household. May's father; Captain Baynham became an Officer of the Order of the British Empire (OBE), for his military service. He had been officially notified two-years ago, that he was the oldest serving officer in the Royal Navy. It was a fitting end to a life-long career of service.

Harry and May, after much discussion, decided that Charles would receive a better education in England. So, in the Summer, May Charles and Cecily went to Egland for a lengthy visit and to get Charles settled into a boarding school in the quiet, rolling countryside of Hereford. May was able to spend a lot of time with her family in London, and visit Harry's family in the north. Whilst she was in Newcastle, she was able to meet with Mrs. Bainbridge and Alice for a very tearful reunion.

Tragedy never seemed to be too far away. Towards the end of December, Harry received a distressing letter from his eldest sister Lucia. Their father lay in a sanitorium suffering from the influenza that was claiming the lives of young and old around the world. Apparently, his father had been asking for Harry. He wanted to see his son before it was too late. Thinking he would have time to arrange a trip home after the Christmas and New Year holiday, he received a telegram on the twenty-ninth December, saying that his father had died. Adamant that he was not going to miss the funeral, he booked a passage on the

Mauretania, arriving in Southampton on the sixth of January.

His father's funeral in Newcastle was a quiet family affair, attended only by his children and two sons-in-law'. Like May earlier in the year, he was able to see Mrs. Bainbridge, and at last, offer her his condolences in person for the loss of Tom.

He was also able to see Charles at his boarding school. According to the headmaster, he was doing very well in all academic subjects and was a popular lad. Prior to going back to America, he stayed with Captain and Mrs. Baynham and visited his old colleagues at Lloyds in Fenchurch Street. He returned home at the end of January.

33 - New Horizons

Prior to the war, Japanese ship-builders sent their plans to the London office of Lloyds for approval and inclusion in the registers. When hostilities broke out in Europe, it dramatically slowed down the process. One way around this problem, was to get the plans to New York, where Harry and his team could maintain the process without lengthy delays. They after all, were also supplying vessels to assist the allied forces having entered the theatre of war in 1914. During and after the war, Harry had suggested to head office, that as Japan had the biggest ship-building industry outside of Europe and America, it would be beneficial to all, to set up a national committee of Lloyds in Japan, whereby they would have a vested interest in the management of the society's work.

In the summer of 1920, the board of directors in London, came round to Harry's way of thinking. One afternoon, he was called into the chief's office.

"Well, Harry, I think you've finally made them see sense. They want to run with your idea". James sat at his desk, puffing at a cigar, a stack of papers in front of him. Harry sat down in a chair by the window and gave him an inquisitive look.

"Japan, Harry. they want you to go to Japan", He handed him a letter. "This came today from London.

You are to go to Japan as a special representative, and with the assistance of our man over there; Arthur Llewelyn Jones, set up an office that mirrors exactly what we do here and in London. Well done, Harry. This could be the start of a great adventure for you and your family".

"Japan?", May didn't know how to react. Harry stood there looking at her while she mulled the idea over in her mind. "I have absolutely no idea what life would be like in Japan. Mind you, I didn't have much of an idea about how life would be here when I first came".

"From my limited experience in dealing with anyone from Japan, they seem to me to be honest, honourable, hard-working and industrious people. What I am being asked to do, has never been done by one man before. It will be a huge feather in my cap if I can pull it off. It's quite an honour to be asked. I know it means more upheaval for you, but if the children are in boarding school, it shouldn't have a detrimental effect on them. They will always have family near them, wherever they go, we can make sure of that".

May put her arms around her husband. "I said I'd follow you to the ends of the earth. I didn't think I'd be doing it literally. When do you have to let them know?"

"Well,", Harry looked a bit sheepish.

"You've already told them, haven't you?"

"It wasn't so much as a request, but more of a command. I've been suggesting the idea of it to them for some time now".

"So how long do I have to pack?"

"Six-weeks".

"It's a good job you have such an understanding and loving wife Mr. Cox".

"And a beautiful one".

A hectic six-weeks followed, in which letters were sent out to all the family. Charles's boarding school was notified, the apartment was vacated and all their person effects that wouldn't be going to Japan with them, put into storage. Cecily was only six-years old and had been attending a local kindergarten. Her parents would find something suitable in Japan until she was ready for boarding school. Harry was given a good send-off by his colleagues from the office and wished every success in his new role.

Harry, May and Cecily arrived at Yokohama in Japan on a sunny autumnal afternoon. The journey from San Francisco had taken fifteen-days. They were met at the harbour by the resident principal surveyor, Arthur Jones. "Welcome to Japan", he said with an outstretched hand. "It's so nice to meet you at long last, Harry. And welcome to you as well, Mrs. Cox, I am quite sure you will love it here, just as my wife and I do. She'll take you under her wing and show you the ropes. We've been here for over twenty-years now. There's quite a community of us foreigners here, it will be like a home from home".

"Thank you. Please call me, May. And, this is our daughter, Cecily". Cecily was very tired after the long journey and was hiding behind her mother. She poked her head out and looked shyly at Arthur. "Well, hello, young lady", he said, "Tell me, do you like cats and dogs?"

Cecily's face lit up, "Yes", she said, "I do".

"Well, that's good. My wife has two of each, and they would love another friend to take them for walks. Do you think you'd be able to be their friend and take them for walks?"

"Oh, yes, she replied excitedly, looking up at her mother, "Can I really, mummy?"

"If Mrs. Jones says it's all right, then it is all right with me".

After the usual bureaucracy at customs and immigration, the party made their way to the railway station and boarded the west-bound train to Kobe.

"You'll find it a bit of a culture shock, after living in New York. Everything runs smoothly and quietly out here. It reminds me of what England was like about twenty or thirty-years ago. You'll soon learn the Japanese way. They're fiercely patriotic and are the most polite people you will ever meet".

"Yes, I know. I've had a fair bit of dealing with them in the New York office during the war. When I studied at Greenwich, one of the chaps on my course was in the Japanese Navy. I learnt a lot from him about the social hierarchy of this country". Harry looked out of the window as the train moved off. "The thing that I find most striking, is how small the buildings are. Compared to New York, and London for that matter, they're tiny. I notice that a lot of them are still made from wood in the traditional style".

"Yes, well you see, this is an earthquake zone, so I suppose they can't go too high".

May gave Harry a worried look, which didn't go un-noticed by Arthur. "Oh, don't worry May. We get the odd tremor, but there hasn't been a big one for nearly twenty-five-years, and that was at the other end of the country".

The train trundled through the countryside. To Harry, May and Cecily, everything looked different. The trees, the plants and crops, the wildlife. Cecily sat there in wonderment. Out of the left-hand window, she could see the coast speckled with fishing boats and small cargo ships. Out of the right-had window, she could see the mountains of the interior.

It was dark when the train arrived at Sannomiya station. Of what they could see of it, it was like a long open-sided shed. There was no platform to speak of. They just climbed down the carriage steps onto the flat ground, which acted as the road when no trains were running. An army of rickshaw drivers were on hand to take the four of them plus the Coxs' luggage to the Oriental Hotel. "It's a very nice place", said Arthur. "Probably the best Kobe has to offer. I have an estate agent lined up for when you've got your land-legs back, to show May and yourself the rental accommodation that's available. Most of us Europeans seem to congregate at one particular part of town they call the Foreign Settlement. How original".

The following morning after breakfast, Harry went out for an exploratory walk with Cecily, leaving May to un-pack their things without distractions.

The whole area around the harbour looked very modern and western in style. The hotel was on the waterfront, on a stretch of road called 'The Bund'. As with any harbour town, anywhere in the world, it was busy with people to-ing and fro-ing, ships large and small docking and casting-off, loading and unloading. It reminded Harry of Tyneside. The building next to the hotel was the offices of the Osaka Shosen Kabushiki Kaisha, which had one of the biggest shipping fleets in the far-east, a company whose ship designs Harry had signed off on many occasions during his time at Lloyds.

They turned right, into a street called Akashi-Machi and quickly found the Lloyd's office, which was on the third-floor of the Meikai Building at number thirty-two.

"Hello Harry and hello young Cecily", said Arthur Jones as they were shown into his office. "I'm surprised to see you up and about so early after your long voyage".

"It was long, but quite relaxing, anyway, I'm not really one for sitting around and doing nothing. I'm quite keen to get started".

"Would you like me to introduce you to the team? They're all here this morning. We have three ship surveyors and an assistant. The engineering boys have their own office and tend to keep out of our way".

"Yes, that's a good idea. I already know one of them; Henry Buchanan, he was in New York for a while".

Arthur led the way to the ship surveyor's office, followed by Harry and Cecily.

It was very similar in style and layout to the New York office. The view wasn't as good, with only the building opposite to look at.

"This is Simon Preston, Herbert House and, someone you already know; Henry Buchanan".

Harry shook them all by the hand as they each welcomed him.

"It'll be just like old times", said Henry.

"Yes, it will", smiled Harry, "But without the added pressure of a damn war". They all laughed.

As they chatted away, a young Japanese man walked into the office. Immaculately dressed, and when he spoke, it was with a perfect English accent. "Ah", said Arthur, "This is our assistant surveyor; Jo".

"I am very honoured to make your acquaintance Mr. Cox", he said, giving a little bow of the head.

"Likewise, I'm sure", replied Harry, shaking Jo's hand. "But please, call me Harry".

"Thank you, Mr. Harry-san".

"Tell me, Jo, how many Japanese nationals do we have working for Lloyds here at the moment?"

"I am only one of two working for the company in Japan".

"I see. Hopefully, when I've set up what I have been tasked to do, we can train-up more of you local chaps who will one day, run the whole show".

Jo looked very excited at this prospect and gave Harry another deferential bow of the head.

Harry asked Arthur if he could arrange for the estate agent to visit him the following morning at the hotel, but not before Cecily had plucked up the courage to ask when she could see the cats and dogs Arthur had talked about. "When you have settled into your new house, then we'll invite you round for tea", was the answer.

The following morning, the estate agent picked up Harry, May and Cecily, and took them up to the residential area of Kitano Cho, about two-miles out of town towards the mountains. The air was clean, it was quiet and the houses were a hybrid mix of European and Japanese architectural styles. They were shown three properties, all of which were spacious, airy and came in good decorative order with suitable furniture and furnishings. The agent had obviously saved the best for last. Harry and May looked at each other on several occasions whilst being shown around it, and nodded to signify their approval. It was also Cecily's choice, on account of it having the biggest garden they had seen.

Not wanting to miss the opportunity, Harry went back to the agent's office to sign a contract for the first year. His housing allowance from the company was going to pay for most of it. The three of them strolled back to the hotel for lunch, happy in the knowledge that in a week's time, they would all be in their new home. "This will be our third home together", observed May.

"Yes, I know. You don't mind, do you?" Harry gave her hand a gentle squeeze.

"Not at all, darling. It's all been quite an adventure. I wouldn't change it for the world.

Harry went back to work the following week, leaving May to once again, create a home for the three of them. She made friends with Albert's wife, Laura, Herbert's wife; Winnifred, and Simon's wife; Jane, and was absorbed into the community of the British contingent. There was plenty of children to play with, of her own age, for Cecily to play with.

At a meeting in Tokyo, In April 1921, the representatives of Japan's leading shipyards, Shipowners and underwriters, agreed to the proposals laid out by Harry, regarding the formation of a committee, working to specifications and class, as laid out by the Lloyds Register of Shipping. In less than six-months, Harry had won the trust of the Japanese ship building fraternity and was given the authority to approve every vessel of over one-hundred tonnes, built in Japan.

The following year, Arthur Jones retired. Harry had been the Principal Surveyor of Japan in waiting, and in November, he was officially appointed to the position. He was told, that the job was his, for as long as he wanted it. Despite having good friends and work colleagues around them, Harry and May had always known that the possibility of being transferred somewhere else, hung over them. Now, they finally felt as though this really was going to be a permanent home for them. Harry was invited to join the Kobe Yacht Club by Henry, and soon after, received an invitation to become a member of the local Masonic Lodge, both of which he accepted. Most of their friends were British and resided in the Foreign Settlement. Most, if not all of Harry's work contacts were Japanese. In the office, Jo did all the translation, but Harry did pick up the basics of the language as time went by.

34 - New Beginnings

The first of September 1923, started off as any other Saturday. Just before lunch, Harry was in the garden doing a little pruning and tidying up. May was in the kitchen preparing lunch and Cecily was trying to entice their next-door neighbour's cat to jump over the fence so she could play with it. The only sounds that filled the air was birdsong and the occasional chirping of crickets.

Harry stood up, and slowly moved his head from side to side, as if to try and pin point a sound. May looked out of the kitchen window and noticed Harry standing there, looking perplexed. She wiped her hands on a tea towel and went out into the garden. "What is it?" she said quietly.

"Listen", replied Harry.

After a moment or two, May said, "I can't hear anything".

Exactly. The birds have stopped, there's nothing".

Before May could reply, there was the distant sound of rumbling. Suddenly, the silence was filled by the sound of screeching birds and insects going berserk. In a matter of seconds, the rumbling turned into a roar and the ground beneath them started to vibrate. May called out to Cecily, but she could not be heard over the noise, which now sounded like ocean waves crashing onto rocks. The ground started to shake from side to side. May screamed, "Cecily". This time she was heard. Cecily came running and threw herself at her mother and father who were now standing together. The ground was shaking so violently, they found it difficult to stand. Harry led them to the middle of the lawn where they laid down. For what seemed like minutes but was only seconds, they lay huddled together on the grass until the shaking stopped.

Cecily was crying and May looked terrified. "Stay here", said Harry, getting to his feet. "You'll be quite safe here out in the open. Nothing can fall on you. I'll go in the house and check for damage".

"Be very careful darling", said May, putting on a brave face for Cecily's benefit.

Apart from a few tiles that had slipped off the roof and smashed on the floor, the house seemed to be free from any serious damage. Back outside in the garden, he could hear the sounds of ship's foghorns tooting away in the harbour about two-miles away.

"I'm going to have to go into town and check the office. Being a taller building, it might be more prone to damage. Will you be alright without me?".

"Yes, we'll be alright. But please be careful, and don't take any chances".

"Of course I won't. I'll be back as quick as I can.

Harry walked into town. Everybody was out on the streets surveying their properties. Some of the smaller Japanese wooden houses had taken a bit of a bashing but he was amazed at how little damage there was after what felt like a powerful quake. He was relieved to see his office building still standing. He ran up the stairs and went through each office. Apart from a few books that had fallen off their shelves, there was nothing to worry about. As he left the building, he met Simon Preston outside. "Are you and Jane all right?"

"Yes, we're fine. That was quite a shake. The biggest one I've ever experienced. It must have caused a lot of damage somewhere".

"Thankfully, not here. Can you go and see the others from the office and make sure they are all right? I'd like to get back to May and Cecily. They're a bit shaken by the whole experience. It's the first one for all of us".

"Yes, of course. I'll see you on Monday. Take care Harry".

Word reached Kobe later in the afternoon that the earthquake had struck Yokohama and Tokyo. There was severe damage to both places. A fire-storm had swept across the two cities, killing tens of thousands of people. Ships anchored in the harbour at Yokohama were forced to head out to sea. Burning oil was floating on the water and presented a danger to all shipping. Before heading out, the P & O liner; SS Dongola, successfully managed to pick up five-hundred survivors from the largely destroyed harbour and made its way to Kobe. With the shipyards of

Yokohama out of action, Kobe now became the centre of the Japanese ship-building industry. It would take a number of years for production to return to normal.

The country was in shock and in mourning. It would be Harry's job to help get things moving in order for the country to re-build itself.

Japan changed after the destruction it had suffered. The devout declared that it was divine intervention, to warn them of the self-centred, decadent, western-liberal lifestyles they had been adopting ever since the Perry Expedition of 1853. The people of Japan saw it as an opportunity to rebuild the physical and moral structure of their country, and a return to the traditional Japanese of values of old. This new patriotic fervour that was to sweep the nation would also bring with it a fanatical militarism. For now, Japan would accept all offers of financial and material help from the outside world. She would build herself back up again, stronger than before.

In 1927, Charles finished attending boarding school in England and decided he wanted to go to College in the United States. It was arranged for him to attend Whittier College in southern California. May's sister Lucie, had married an American by the name of George Foley, a senior figure in the Murphy Oil Corporation, and had settled there. Charles would spend the summers in Japan, and the rest of his college holidays, with the Foleys'.

With the rebuilding of Tokyo and the surrounding area most affected by the Great Kanto Earthquake, as it was now called, Harry saw a business opportunity. Setting up a company with his son and brother-in-law; George, they started to import timber from California. Hardwood for construction was in short supply, so with Harry's shipping contacts on both sides of the Pacific, they were able to negotiate good terms and build a profitable business.

At the same time, Cecily was sent to St. Margaret's, a boarding school in Victoria, British Columbia. She too, would return to Japan in the summer, with the longer holidays spent at the Foleys'.

Having their two children in easy reach of the west coast of America and Canada, meant that the travelling distance would be kept to a minimum by going straight across the Pacific Ocean. It was a far better option than going to school in their native England, which could take upwards of three-weeks as opposed to the one-week it was now going to take.

35 - Old Friend

In the summer of 1930, Harry travelled to Tokyo by train. It was a journey he had made frequently since being in Japan. The journey had been reduced to nine-hours, thanks to the new Swallow Express, pulled by the first Japanese-made high-speed locomotive.

Tokyo had changed beyond all recognition since the re-building program had begun. The new streets were wide and modern, with most buildings being built of brick, concrete and stone, rather than the timber-frames of old.

Arriving at the Imperial Hotel, he had an early dinner and went to bed.

The following morning, he made his way to the offices of the Nippon Yusen Kabushiki Kaisha (NYK), to see his old friend; Noboru Otani, the company's managing director.

They had first met in London, shortly after Harry had started with the company, and then again in New York. NYK had the largest fleet of ships in Japan and the far-east. Harry liked the man. He was a pleasure to do business with, and Harry considered him a good friend.

Harry had received a letter from Noboru, asking him to come to the office that day, as he would like him to meet someone. He didn't elaborate any further than that, so as he went up in the elevator to the top floor of the Yusen Building, Harry was intrigued.

He was greeted by Noboru, who had come to the reception area. "Harry, my dear friend, I am very honoured to see you. How is your charming wife; May, and your two lovely children?"

They shook hands. "It's always a pleasure to see you Noboru. May is just fine, she sends her love, and the children are spending the summer with us. Charles is still at Stanford, studying law and Cecily starts at a new college in California when she returns".

"Such a charming family". Noboru walked slowly along the corridor with Harry to his office.

"I have someone here that I would like you to meet", Noboru looked at Harry, "He doesn't need an introduction".

Harry looked back at him, with an eyebrow raised and followed him into the office.

With a grin on his face, Noboru said, "I think the two of you have met before?"

"Good lord", exclaimed Harry, stepping forward with an outstretched hand. "My dear old friend; Yuzuru Hiraga, how the devil are you? It must be over twenty-years".

"I am very well my old friend; it is so nice to see you after all this time. You have made quite a reputation for yourself. You are the most respected surveyor, and I am very pleased that you are working for the benefit of our great nation".

"You are too kind, Yuzuru. If anyone has achieved great things, it is you, my friend. The last I heard; you were a Vice-Admiral in the Imperial Japanese Navy and the greatest designer of military vessels they ever had".

"It is true, I have had an honourable career, but now, I have retired and am now an advisor to the Mitsubishi shipyards in Kobe and Nagasaki where, as you know, the majority of our naval fleet is constructed. We also build vessels for Mr. Otani and the NYL line".

"Well, that is superb news. I am based in Kobe myself. Hopefully we will be able to see more of each other".

"I would find that most enjoyable".

Tea was served, and the three men sat down and talked. Harry told the story of how he had met Yuzuru as a fellow student and the Royal Naval College in London, and Yuzuru told them of the occasion of being introduced to King Edward VII at a diplomatic reception at St Jame's Palace in 1907. He had soon risen through the ranks, and in 1923, had been appointed the head of the technical department of the Imperial Japanese Navy, with the rank of Rear-Admiral, becoming Vice-Admiral in 1926.

During lunch, which was had back at the Imperial Hotel, Harry asked Yuzuru about the emperor, who had been on the throne four-years now.

"He is a good man. He is thoughtful and measured and will instil confidence in the public, as well as respect. I pray that he does not surrender too much authority to the army".

36 - Love at First Sight

Cecily was in the grounds of the vicarage helping her mother and the other ladies of the Foreign Settlement in Kobe, set-up for the church fete. All Saints, was the only Anglican church in the area, and was a hub of activity for the British residents. As she unpacked the crates of crockery, she noticed a young man setting out tables on the far side of the lawn. Crikey, she thought, I've never seen him before.

She turned to her mother, but she was busily discussing with Winnifred House, the age-old conundrum of whether to put the cream on first or the jam, with regards to scones. Jane Preston was nearby, so she asked her; "Mrs. Preston, do you know who that chap is over there?" indicating with a look across the lawn. "I don't think I've seen him before".

Jane Preston followed her gaze. "Oh, that's Mr, and Mrs. Ibbotson's son. He's been at school in South Africa. He doesn't come home very often. Nice looking lad, isn't he?" She gave Cecily a knowing look, which made her blush a little.

"Yes, yes he is".

Perhaps you could go and ask him if we can have another table over here, we could do with one". Again, the knowing look.

"Yes, I think I will". Cecily put the plates down, pulled her shoulders back, lifted her head up and with forced confidence, marched across the lawn.

"Hello", she said, "I'm Cecily. I haven't seen you here before".

"Hello, I'm Peter, Peter Ibbotson. This is my first time actually. I normally spend summers with my grandparents in England. I'm at school in South Africa".

"That's interesting. I've just finished school in Canada. After the summer, I will be going to college in California".

"What part of California? It's a big place".

"The Dominican College in San Refael. It's near San Francisco".

"Well., how's that for a coincidence. My mother is from San Francisco".

"Gosh, it's such a small world, isn't it?"

"Perhaps we could meet for a cup of tea together sometime".

"Yes, that would be nice". Cecily turned to walk away, "Oh, I nearly forgot. Could we have another table over there please?"

The following afternoon, Cecily met Peter at the nearby Tor Hotel. A large, imposing building at the foot of the hills overlooking the harbour.

"I like a girl who's punctual", beamed Peter, as she approached the terrace.

"They say it's fashionable to be late these days, but I think it is quite rude", replied Cecily, removing her sun-glasses.

"Who is this little fellow?" Peter bent down to stroke the dog Cecily had on a long lead.

"That's d'Artagnan, he's an Airedale, and quite a good one. I enter him in shows".

"Good boy, d'Artagnan". The dog rolled onto its back and was enjoying having his belly rubbed. "If this is d'Artagnan, what are you going to call me? Porthos, Aramis or Athos?".

"I think Peter will suffice. Now then, are you going to pour the tea, or shall I?"

They talked well into the afternoon. Cecily had got Peter's life story and told him hers. He had been born in Yokohama, to an English father and an American mother. His father ran an engineering company that specialised in Mond gas engines. His mother's family were in the silk trade, exporting mainly to America. Peter was seven-months younger than Cecily and had two half-brothers he rarely saw. When he finishes his education, he plans to go to England and train as a civil engineer.

"What does the future hold for you?" he asked.

"Oh, I don't know. I shall probably come back here to live. I'd like to train as a veterinary nurse and look after dogs. I like dogs more than people sometimes. And then I'll get married I expect".

"God help the man that comes between you and d'Artagnan", he laughed.

"You know where you are with dogs", she retorted.

"What does your brother Charles do?"

"He's at Stanford in California, studying law. He likes America".

"I think I prefer England. My father's family live on the Isle of Wight. It's lovely there"

After another cup of tea, they headed off in the direction of home. Outside Cecily's house, Peter said, "I've really enjoyed this afternoon. Perhaps we could do it again some time?"

"Yes, I'd like that. It will have to be sooner rather than later though. I'm off to my new college in three-weeks' time".

"How about Tuesday then? Same time, same place?"

"Perfect. I'll see you then". She kissed him on the cheek, turned and walked down the garden path with d'Artagnan following behind.

Cecily finished her schooling in the summer of 1932, at the age of eighteen and returned to the family home in Kobe. Her brother; Charles, graduated from Stanford, with a distinction, and was offered a place at the Harvard Law School in Boston, Massachusetts, and would start the following year.

37 - A Visit to England

In April of 1933, Harry, May and Cecily returned to England for an extended holiday. May's parents had moved from London and were now living in Ferndown, a small village in the southern county of Dorset. They were quite elderly now and in poor health. Cecily stayed with her father's sister; aunt Lucia, in Brockham, Surrey.

She had enrolled on a course of practical kennel management, run by Captain M. J. Holdsworth, at his kennels in Abinger Hammer, seven-miles away. Quite by chance, Cecily's friend; Peter Ibbotson, was also in England. Having finished college in South Africa, he had started to work as an assistant for a firm of engineers, headed by Frank Palemon Dyson, the son of Sir Frank Watson Dyson, Astronomer Royal. They had become very good friends since their first meeting. They spent the summers together in Kobe, and wrote to each other regularly until they finished college. He now lived in Notting Hill.

Heartache came in early June, when May's father died at the age of eighty-six. They barely had time to bury him when, twenty-three days later, her mother died, aged seventy-two. They were the last of their generation. All that was left of May's family now, were her three sisters and one brother.

Cecily finished her kennel management course, and decided, on the advice of Captain Holdsworth, to do a months' training with a qualified veterinary surgeon and get experience as a canine nurse. The advice made good sense, as she had hoped that one day she could open a kennels in Japan, looking after the many dogs that couldn't travel with their owners. Just such experience was on offer from a Major William Hamilton Jepps Kirk MRCVS, at his practice in Golders Green, London. She could stay with her mother's sister; Pauline, who still lived in Perivale, having married a Mr. Ducket. This would allow her to see Peter at the weekends.

Peter stood outside Piccadilly Circus station, on the steps of the Shaftesbury Memorial Fountain, smoking a cigarette. As he watched the traffic go by, he became aware that someone had, very quietly, walked up behind him and was only inches away. As he slowly turned his head, to see who it was, he felt something press into the small of his back. Before he had time to react, a voice behind him said, "Stick 'em up"

He smiled, and said, "Hello old thing".

"Hey, not so much of the old. We're the same age. Well, almost".

He turned, and saw Cecily's beaming face. He put his arms around her and they hugged and kissed. He lifted her off her feet as he swirled her around and put her down on the pavement. "It's wonderful to see you again. I'm sorry to hear about your grandparents. It must have been awful to lose them both in quick succession like that".

"Yes, it was pretty grim. But let's talk of happy things tonight. I want to hear all about your new job. Where shall we go to eat, I'm famished?"

"A chap at work recommended a place down Lower Regent Street. It's called the Hungaria".

"Is it Hungarian, by any chance?" Or do you only go there when you are hungry?"

Peter shook his head, "That's the worst joke I have ever heard.

Cecily put her arm through his and they walked off in the direction of the restaurant.

At a quiet, candle lit table for two, they sipped their cocktails. "So", enquired Cecily, "Tell me about this job of yours".

Well, I got it through a contact of my fathers. We are a small civil engineering firm and we sub-contract out to larger ones. We build bridges, roads and anything people want really. The good thing about it, is that I will get to go back to South Africa from time to time because we have a few projects going on over there".

"You like South Africa, don't you?"

"Yes, I do. I miss it a lot more than I thought I would. The great outdoors doesn't get any greater than Africa. I miss the sun as well. It's always so grey in England".

"Yes, I know what you mean. I quite enjoyed myself in California. I don't think I would want to live there forever though. I'm quite happy in Japan for the moment. My father has just been appointed as the principal surveyor for all of the far-east. I expect we'll spend the rest of our lives out there one way or another".

With the waiter helping them to choose, they ordered; Toltott Tojas, a Chicken Ppaprikash for Cecily and a Goulash for Peter, and finished with the Dobos Torta. All washed down with a bottle of Tokaji.

As the last mouthful went down, Peter sat back in his chair and put his hand on his stomach. He patted it gently and said, "I think that was the best meal I have ever had. I shall definitely be coming here again".

"Yes, it was delicious. Quite spicy, but I don't mind that".

Peter took out a cigarette from a silver case, "You don't mind, do you?"

"Of course not. Let me". She took the cigarette from out of his mouth, and the lighter from his hand and proceeded to light it herself. She took a small puff. Coughing and grimacing, she passed it back to him. "I never could get the hang of it".

"It's covered in lipstick now", said Peter.

"Consider it a kiss".

"Thank you. How sweet of you", he smiled. "I shall treasure it forever".

Peter paid the bill, and they walked back up towards Piccadilly Circus, arm in arm.

"So, how long will you stay in England?" asked Cecily.

"Another six-years I expect. If everything works out, I'll be able to take my exams in 39' and become a member of the Institute of Civil Engineers, and then I can go anywhere the fancy takes me".

"How serious are you about this kennel business you want to set up?"

"Very. Now that I know we're going to be in Japan for quite a while, it makes sense. I couldn't think of a better job really. It will keep me occupied until a handsome man asks me to marry him". She smiled at Peter. He took a long draw of his cigarette and said;

"Could you wait six-years for something like that to happen?"

"Oh yes", she said, "If it's the right man".

They parted company at the station, with the promise that they would see each other at least one more time before she had to go back to Japan with her mother and father.

Once again, they met at the same time and same place. It was a mild, dry evening, and Peter was sitting on the same steps reading a newspaper. Cecily dropped down beside him and kissed him on the cheek. "Hello my sweet, anything interesting in the paper?"

"Hello, love of my life. I was just reading an article about that new man in Germany. He seems to be a man of action. He's building up the German economy and putting a lot of money into modernising the country. It's certainly going to be good for us civil engineers".

"Is he the man Mr. Churchill doesn't seem to like very much?".

"That's right. Herr Hitler. Mr. MacDonald seems to think he is a good man".

"So, you might go to Germany instead of South Africa now?"

"Anything's possible. Who knows what will happen between now and 1939, when I pass my 'Civils'".

"Civils?"

"My civil engineering exam, they're called 'Civils'".

"Oh, I see. Come on, I'm not spending all night talking about politics. Are we going to the Hungaria again, or have you discovered somewhere new?"

I rather fancy the Hungaria again. Do you mind?"

"Of course not. Only, I think I will pass on the egg hors d'oeuvres this time".

Over dinner, they talked of the things they had done since their last meeting. Cecily had finished her basic veterinary nursing course and was preparing for her return to Japan.

"Oh, I forgot to tell you, my brother Charles is going to become an American citizen".

"What on earth for?" Peter looked somewhat taken aback.

"He's decided to stay there. When he finishes at Harvard, he'll probably join a law firm, or start his own practice. It'll make things easier if he's a proper citizen".

"What do your parents think of that?"

"They don't mind. They like America. Aunt Lucie lives there and loves the place. I suppose it makes sense really".

"Mmm, I think I would rather be British than American. What would happen if we went to war with America. He'd be fighting his own kind. It doesn't seem right to me".

"Don't be silly, the Americans are our allies. We won't go to war." Cecily shook her head in dismay. "Besides, you should be more worried about me. The Japanese are always attacking China for some reason. Anyway, the last war has put a stop to that nonsense. Why are we even talking about it?"

"Sorry, old girl. My fault".

"Honestly, men. Why can't people be more like dogs. The world would be a much happier place. All one would need is a drink and a biscuit from time to time".

"Yes, if only it were that simple". Peter looked her in the eye and held her hand. "When do you think we'll see each other again?"

"I don't know. My father comes over for business occasionally, I could probably come with him some time, but I have no idea when. I'll definitely come when you get your 'Civils', if you make it worth my while".

"You're on". Peter took a small silver case out of his pocket. Inside, were some small cards with his name printed on. He took out a pen and wrote on the back; 'I promise to give Cecily Pauline Cox a bottle of Champagne and a biscuit at 11am, when I get my Civils'.

He handed her the card.

"A biscuit? I'm not coming all the way here for a biscuit".

You just said that that was all you would need in life".

Ha-ha, Mr. Ibbotson, it's going to cost you a lot more than that". They smiled at each other. As the smiles faded away, Cecily suddenly looked a little forlorn. "You will write to me. Won't you?"

"Haven't I always, since the day we met?"

"Yes, you have, and I don't want you to stop. Promise me you'll keep writing".

"! promise".

38 - Life in Japan

Harry sat in his office, pondering over a typewriter. He had been made Commodore of the Kobe Yacht Club and was working on a speech, to be given at the annual dinner and dance. The telephone on his desk started to ring. He answered it, and heard the voice of his good friend Yuzuru Hiraga. After pleasantries were exchanged, Yuzuru asked; "Would you and your charming wife be able to attend a dinner party on the twenty-fourth of March?"

"Thank you Yuzuru, we wouldn't miss it for the world. It's my daughter's birthday two-days after, but we have nothing planned".

"Well, in that case, please bring her with you. I am sure there will some people of her own age she can talk to".

That's splendid, thank you. Is it a special occasion, a birthday or something?"

"No, no, I just wanted to talk to some of my old friends".

"Thanks again, Yuzuru, we will see you next Saturday. Goodbye".

"Oh father, do I really have to go?"
"I'm not going to make you go if you don't want to, but if you stay here, you'll be on your own.".

"I don't mind. I'll have D'Artagnan to keep me company".

May tried to reason with her; "Mr. Hiraga is a very important man. It would be very disrespectful if you don't go, especially after he invited you when he heard it was your birthday weekend. Besides", she continued, "I've heard that he has a very handsome son. Winnifred saw him in the bank the other day with his mother. She said, she wished she was thirty-year younger".

Harry, May and Cecily arrived at the Hiraga's house, a short cab ride away, at the appointed hour. The house was a large, traditional Japanese style, timber-framed building but with a nod to the western aesthetic. Paper lanterns illuminated the garden path, leading to the front door. Two men, armed with rifles, stood to attention either side of the porch. Harry noticed that they wore the uniform of the Imperial Japanese Navy. As they approached the door, it opened. A young junior naval officer greeted them with a smile and a very pronounced bow. He took the clipboard from under his arm and said "Good evening, sir. May I take your names please?"

"I say, this is all very official, isn't it? We are Mr. and Mrs. Harry Cox, and daughter Cecily".

The officer looked down at the clipboard and made a tick with his pen against their names. "Thank you, sir, please follow me".

He led them across the spacious hall towards a closed double-door, from behind which the hubbub of conversation could be heard. With a single, well-practised manoeuvre, he opened the doors. Stepping to one side, he announced the Cox family and ushered them into the room.

"Good grief", gasped Cecily, looking around, taking in all the splendour of the occasion. "This isn't a dinner party, it's a military convention", she whispered to her mother.

On first glance, the room appeared to be filled with high-ranking military personnel from all branches of the services. It wasn't long before the eye started to pick out the women in their evening dresses, younger people not in uniform at all and the occasional child running around.

From out of the throng stepped Yuzuru and his wife Kazuko and greeted them warmly. A waiter offered them a glass of Champagne, and they made their way into the room and joined the other guests.

"I thought you had retired from the navy", said Harry

"Ah, that is not quite so. They have allowed me to do other things, but I will always be at their beck and call. The privileges of my rank would be very difficult to surrender, and besides, I know too much, they will want to keep me on a short leash. The people in this room are those that I consider true friends, made during a long career. Times are changing Harry; we must all have friends that we can rely on".

"You make it all sound rather sinister".

"I'm sorry, I do not mean to. After dinner, there is something I would like to discuss with you in private".

"Yes, of course, only too glad to help".

Harry didn't know any of the military men in the room, but he did know some of the others. Many of them were senior figures in the shipping world and he had met them in the course of his work.

As her parents made small talk with some of the other guests, Cecily sipped at her Champagne and looked around the room. As her eyes scanned the room, she stopped and with a gulp, she nearly choked on her drink. Standing near the back of the room by the doors to the garden was an incredibly attractive man. Her pupils dilated and her heart began to beat a little faster. He wore the crispest, white naval uniform she had ever seen, it almost glowed. His jet-black hair and tanned skin stood out in contrast against it. Tall, and athletic, she thought he was the most handsome man she had ever seen. Without taking her eyes off him, as though in some kind of trance, she reached out her arm and tapped her mother on the shoulder. "Who is that?" she asked, almost dreamily.

Her mother followed her gaze, "I expect that is the son I was telling you about. Why don't you go and introduce yourself, while he's not talking to anyone?"

Without a second's thought, Cecily negotiated a path through the crowd and homed in on the young man, like a moth to a flame. "Hello", she said, going slightly red in the cheeks.

"I'm Cecily Cox. You must be Mr. and Mrs. Hiraga's son?" She held out a hand.

The young man stiffened, took the fingers of her outstretched hand, and gave a courteous bow.

"Good evening, Miss Cox", he said with a polished English accent. "My name is Akira Hiraga. It is a pleasure to meet you. I believe our fathers are old friends?"

"Yes, they met at Greenwich, while my father was in the Royal Navy".

"My father speaks very highly of him. He has done a lot for the ship-building industry in Japan".

"I see you are in the navy as well",

"I am a Lieutenant in the Imperial Japanese Navy. A lowly junior officer, but I hope to have as distinguished a career as my honourable father".

"I'm sure you will". Cecily put her glass down on a nearby table. "You speak frightfully good English. Where did you learn?"

"I went to school in England, Harrow".

"That's interesting. I was born near there, a place called Perivale, near Ealing. That's where we lived until my father took us all off to America".

A gong sounded in the hall, and people started to make their way into the adjacent dining room. "Do you wish to sit near your parents at dinner?" enquired Akira.

"Not really, I'd rather sit with someone my own age".

"Would you do me the honour of sitting next to me at the table?"

"That would be absolutely perfect".

The dining room was larger than the reception room from which they had just come. A series of beautifully laid and decorated tables were arranged to fill the space. It looked more like a banquet than a dinner party. Harry and May sat with Mr. and Mrs. Otani and other notables from the shipping world. Cecily sat opposite Akira.

An army of near invisible waiters served the Kaiseki and accompanying drinks, while a Hogaku orchestra played traditional Japanese music in the background. When the meal was finished, a number of the guests, mainly the women, retired to the reception room for coffee. Akira asked Cecily if she would like to go for a walk in the garden. She was very happy to do so.

Harry sat at the dinner table smoking a cigar, talking to Mr. Hori of the OSK shipping company, when he was joined by their host. "Do you mind if I drag you away Harry? I would like your opinion on a little matter. Would you come to my study?"

Harry excused himself from the table and followed Yuzuru to his office. He sat down at the offered chair and Yuzuru sat at the desk.

Yuzuru put his elbows on the desk and rested his chin on his hands. The smile had left his face and he was now looking grave. In a quiet voice, he said; "What I am about to tell you Harry, is officially secret, and must not be discussed with anyone else". Harry lent forward, stubbed out his cigar in the ashtray on the desk, and waited for Yuzuru to continue.

"A few weeks ago, one of our new torpedo boats, the Tomozuru, capsized during its first sea trials. One-hundred hands were lost. It was a vessel that I designed, Harry. I have been told that there will be a board of enquiry into the incident and that the integrity of my design will also be under scrutiny".

"My dear chap, that is awful. I can't believe that they will call into question the integrity of your design. You're one of the best naval architects in the world".

"Thank you, my dear friend, for your words. The loss of life is enough to haunt a man, but to think I may be dishonoured in this way, I cannot comprehend such a thing".

"There must be something I can do to help. I assume the navy will be keeping the enquiry in-house as it were?".

"That is correct. The architects that will examine my designs, will be those that I have trained myself over the years. The pupils are now expected to examine and cast judgement on work of the teacher".

"What would you like me to do to help? I'm not sure what to suggest, there must be something".

"Would you be prepared to act as my independent advisor? I will have to get it cleared by Admiral Hiroyasu. With his agreement, I would like you to examine my designs and give testimony at any future board of enquiry. I know it is a lot to ask of a busy man such as yourself. Everything would have to be done in secret. Can I ask that of you?"

"Of course you can. I will do everything in my power to help".

"Thank you, Harry, I will sleep a little easier tonight knowing I have you on my side. Come, let us go back and join the others. They will wonder where we are".

On the way home, May said, "Well, that was a thoroughly enjoyable evening. What wonderful hosts the Hiraga family are. You seemed to be getting on well with the son. He was by your side all night. What did you say his name was?"

"Akira". Replied Cecily with a note of a sigh in her voice. Yes, he was very attentive. I like him very much. He's offered to take me out in his car next weekend"

"That's nice, dear" Turning to Harry, she said; "And what did Yuzuru want to talk to you about?"

"Oh", said Harry, rather non-committedly, "He just wanted to ask my advice on a little project of his. Nothing important".

Akira picked up Cecily the following Saturday. It was a sunny morning, and every inch of his beige Datsun Phaeton, two-door sedan, gleamed in the sunlight. The roof was down and on the back seat was a small wicker hamper. Akira looked completely different out of his uniform, but just as handsome, thought Cecily.

He opened the door for her and then turned to give a respectful bow to Harry and May, who had come out to wave them off.

They headed north, over the hills, and by lunchtime, they had found a place to have their picnic. Overlooking the harbour, they sat on a blanket in the shade of a tree. It was a beautiful spot. A selection of sushi was on offer, and a flask of cold oolong tea.

"D'Artagnan would love it here", said Cecily.

"Who is D'Artagnan?"

"He is my dog. An Airedale terrier. He would love running around here, chasing the squirrels".

Akira smiled, "You English, you love your dogs. Sometimes, I think they are your best friends".

"We have a saying; 'A man's best friend is his dog'. They are loyal and obedient, sometimes more than humans".

"Ah, but can a dog have honour? I think only humans can have that".

"You Japanese", said Cecily, grinning at Akira, "You love your honour".

"Tuchez" he replied, and they both laughed.

After lunch, they went for a walk along the Yura river.

"Did you say you work near here?"

"Yes", Akira turned to and pointed to the right. "Just beyond those hills. I am stationed at the Maizuru Naval Arsenal".

"It's beautiful".

"It is very beautiful here, but not at the dockyard".

"What exactly do you do there?" Oh, I'm sorry. I shouldn't have asked". For a moment, there was an awkward silence, which Cecily felt compelled to fill; "My father was in the navy, as you know. I expect he did things that he wasn't allowed to talk about. It was before I was born".

"He is an honourable man. My father has the greatest respect for him".

"What a lovely thing to say, thank you".

They got back to Kobe early evening, after a leisurely drive home. Cecily kissed Akira goodbye and skipped off into the house. She flopped down into a chair with a long dreamy sigh.

"Did you have a nice day, dear"? enquired May.

"Oh, yes. It was wonderful. He is such a gentleman. He has invited me out next weekend".

"I liked his car", said Harry. "The Japanese have started to produce some good models".

"He's a very good driver. The navy taught him apparently, which is strange, I thought they taught people to do things on water".

"His father told me that the boy is in the Tokkeitai, which is the navy's version of the military police".

"No wonder he wouldn't talk about it when I asked what he did. He did say however, that his father thought you were a good man. Wasn't that nice of him?"

Harry smiled. "We go back a long way".

"I had better take D'Artagnan out for his walk before dinner. Has he been a good boy?"

"Yes, of course. He's always a good boy. You have him well trained".

A few weeks later, Yuzuru Hiraga phoned Harry and invited him to lunch. The two met at the Imperial Hotel in Kobe.

"Thank you for coming, Harry. I have some news about the delicate matter we talked of. Admiral Hiroyasu has agreed to let you be an independent examiner. I would like you to scrutinise every aspect of my work, my drawings, plans, calculations, and report your findings to the board of enquiry. If I have made a mistake, I will need to know what errors I have made and how to rectify them. My honour and my future career are in your hands, Harry".

"Knowing your reputation and the years of experience you have; I doubt if I'll be able to find anything amiss with your designs".

"Perhaps I am getting too old for this kind of work".

"Nonsense, you're only a few years older than me. This tragedy could have simply been an unfortunate accident. They do happen from time to time".

"I appreciate your efforts in trying to relieve my anxiety, I pray that this will not be the way I end my service to Japan".

After a light lunch, Yuzuru handed Harry a large box file containing folded blueprints and other paperwork. "This is going to take some considerable time. I'm sorry for all the extra work I am burdening you with, I know you are a very busy man"

"Please don't worry, Yuzuru. I am honoured that you have come to me and asked for help. That's what friends are for".

The Tomozuru has been towed to the naval base at Sasebo, near Nagasaki. Let me know if you want to examine the vessel, I can arrange access for you. If you need anything else, just ask".

"I'll make a start on it this week".

"Father?"

"Yes, my dear?"

"Can I talk to you about a business proposition?"

Harry sat behind the desk in his study, pouring over a stack of architectural drawings of the Tomozuru. It was a Saturday afternoon, and he would have liked to have been at the yacht club, but the inspection he was doing for Yuzuru was taking far longer than he had envisaged.

"Does it involve me giving you a pile of cash that I will probably never see again?"

Cecily looked offended. "Good heavens, no", she said. "I want to start my own business. It will be a loan, that I fully intend to pay back".

Without lifting his head from his work, Harry asked; "Is this about the kennels you want to open?"

"Yes, that's it".

"Remind me how you are going to make any money from this venture?"

"It's quite simple really. Everybody round here, especially the Europeans, have dogs and cats. When they go back to England, or wherever it is they come from, they need to leave the pet with someone they can trust. That's where I come in. Board and lodgings all provided. If anyone has a new dog and wants it trained, they can bring it to me and, if it has any medical requirements, I can do that too. I will also be breeding animals as well to sell on. A dog with a good pedigree will command a good price".

"You seem to have thought it through, I must say. What do you need to get it up and running?"

"Well, a small plot of land, about the size of our garden, and someone to build the kennels. I shall design them myself. They will be like the ones I used at Captain Holdsworth's place last year".

"Do you have anywhere in mind for these kennels?"

"Not yet. Akira is picking me up in the car shortly. We're going to go look for somewhere suitable".

"Well, you seem to have it all in hand. What could possibly go wrong?" Harry said the last part with the air of someone who knows it is going to be futile voicing any objections. "Let me know how you get on".

"Thank you, father". She leant over the desk and kissed him on the top of the head. "I'm sure it won't be expensive".

39 - That's What Friends Are For

Later in the year, before Harry had completed the work Yuzuru had asked him to undertake, there was a catastrophe. The Imperial Japanese Navy's entire Fourth Fleet was on exercise 250-miles off the Sanriku coast. A typhoon hit the fleet, causing severe damage and great loss of life. Once again, Yuzuru, who had designed most of the vessels, found his designs under the microscope.

Yuzuru told Harry of the latest incidence, once again in the strictest confidence. This was another incident that was never going to be made public knowledge. He looked like a broken man, when Harry had visited him at his house. Harry reassured him, that as yet, he had found no glaring errors in any of the work he had inspected thus far. The typhoon that had caused the latest damage had been more powerful than most, and in Harry's opinion, not many vessels would have been able to survive such a battering unscathed.

The day after his meeting, Harry was notified by his head office in London, that he was going to receive a visitor by the name of William Penrose. It didn't say when, but every assistance was to be afforded him. He thought it strange that the telegram didn't elaborate. He had no idea what the visit was about. Oh well, he thought, I will soon find out.

When he returned home that evening, Cecily was waiting at the door, anxious to tell him the good news; "I've got it", she said with great enthusiasm. "I've got it on a five-year lease".

"That's wonderful sweetheart. That's the plot of land you found with Akira, is it?"

"Yes. He's even found me a local man to build the actual kennels. I should be up and running within a month".

"Where is it exactly?"

It's on the road to Osaka, about six-miles from here, at a place called Okamoto".

"Ah, yes, I know it. Well, you'd better start advertising yourself. Start getting some money coming in. What are you going to call the place?"

"Well, I've been thinking about that. Last year, when I was in England, I entered one of Captain Holdsworth's dogs in a show. It did very well. It was called Dainsley D'Artagnan. As I already have a dog called D'Artagnan, I thought I'd call the kennels; Dainsley. It has a certain style, don't you think?"

"Sounds good to me. Well done".

The following day, Harry was sitting in his office when there was a knock on the door. The receptionist said that a Mr. Penrose was here to see him. Harry looked blank for a moment, and then the penny dropped. "Oh, yes. Show him in".

"Hello", said Harry as the man was shown into his office. "I'm Harry Jasper Cox, Principal Surveyor". They shook hands.

"It's very nice to meet you Mr. Cox. I am William Penrose. Please excuse my grubby appearance, I've just arrived on the ship from Shanghai. Bit of a rough ride I'm afraid. I thought I'd catch you now, before I go in search of the hotel".

William Penrose was a very average looking man of about forty-years. The only thing about him that stood out, were his pale blue eyes. They seemed very alert, almost intense. Harry formed the impression that he had been a military man.

"Please, sit down, and tell me how I may be of assistance".

Surprisingly, the first thing Penrose said was; "I understand you were a navy man?"

"Yes, that's right. Not for very long though. I did my training at Greenwich and then worked under Sir Philip Platt at the Admiralty".

Penrose nodded, as if Harry had just confirmed what he already knew. He put his hand inside his jacket pocket and pulled out a wallet. He took out a card and handed it to Harry. It was a Royal Navy identity card, similar to one he had himself many years ago. It read; Commander William Penrose.

"Mr. Cox".

"Please, call me Harry", he interrupted.

"Thank you. Harry, I am with naval intelligence, and we have a favour to ask".

"Yes, of course. I'll do anything I can".

"We understand that you are good friends with Vice-Admiral Hiraga, and that you are helping him with regards to a bit of a sticky situation he has found himself in".

"How on earth did you know about that? It's supposed to be highly confidential".

"What happened to the Tomozuru and, more recently with the Fourth Fleet, would be difficult for anyone to keep quiet. Suffice to say, we have people on the inside that feed us information from time to time. When we found out that you were helping him, well, it was too good an opportunity to ignore".

"What is it you want me to do exactly?"

"For some time now, we have suspected that the Imperial Japanese Navy have been feeding us false information about the specifications of the ships they have been building. We strongly suspect that they are not compliant with the treaty obligations. As you know, they have given notice to withdraw from the Washington Naval Treaty. It will take effect from the end of next year. It would be nice to know, if they have any advantage over us in the event of a future conflict. All we are asking you to do, is tell us your findings and provide us with evidence if you find any breach of treaty obligations. That's all".

Harry thought for a moment. "It's going to put me in a very difficult situation if it ever gets back to Yuzuru Hiraga that I have collaborated with British intelligence. My position here would be untenable".

"I understand your concern, Harry. As I have already alluded to, we already have assets in place. We can make it look as if the information came from elsewhere, rather than you. You have my word on it".

"Well, to tell you the truth, I have been working on this project for about a year now, and so far, I have found nothing that is amiss. The designs are sound, the calculations are correct. At this moment in time, I am of the opinion that the Tomozuru was the victim of a freak accident. Whether that will be the same for the ships of the Forth Fleet, I cannot say, I've yet to see any of them, but again, the drawings look sound".

"We thank you for your co-operation".

"Who's in charge of Naval Construction these days? I've lost touch with my old navy crowd".

"Sir Arthur Johns, he's been running things for a few years now".

"I recognise the name, but I don't think I ever met him".

Penrose stood up. "I'd better be on my way now; I've taken up enough of your valuable time. Thanks for everything. How far away is the Imperial Hotel?"

"Oh, it's just around the corner. Turn right out of the building, then left, you can't miss it. How long are you in town for?"

"Just two nights, then I'm off to Hong Kong. No rest for the wicked".

"Perhaps we could have lunch before you go, or dinner?"

"Thanks for the offer, but it's probably not a good idea to be seen in public with me. I wouldn't want to put you in an awkward position should we bump into someone you're acquainted with".

"Ah, yes, I see".

"If you ever have anything for us, post it to you London head office, marked for my attention. They will see that it gets to me".

Penrose left. Harry sat at his desk deep in thought. He hoped that he would never have to betray the confidence of an old friend.

The Dainsley Kennels duly opened for business. Cecily was interviewed for a local English-language newspaper, organised by an acquaintance from Harry's masonic lodge.

It was unusual to see a young European woman running a business. The article served as a good advertisement for her services, which were taken up by the local community. Business was soon booming, and it was clear to all, that this was her passion, something she excelled at. Akira would come round to see her and help out where he could, but his heart wasn't in it. He couldn't understand the love for animals that many foreigners seem to have.

One late afternoon, as they were walking some of the dogs, he asked her about the future.

"Oh, I don't know", she said, "I used to think that I would get married one day, have children and live the kind of life like my mother. I'm not so sure I want that anymore. I've found something that I'm good at. I love my work here at the kennels, I don't want anything to change".

"I think I am the opposite". Akira's voice had a note of melancholy in it. "I wanted to travel the world and have an honourable career in the navy and work my way to the top, like my father. Falling in love was not a thing I had even contemplated. Now, I think I will need the love of a good woman to help me through the next stage of my life. Just like my mother has done for my father". They arrived back at the kennels. The dogs slipped their leads and ran off into the compound. Akira stood in front of Cecily and put his hands gently on her shoulders, and looking her in the eye, he said. "I think I am in love with you". They kissed.

News arrived from Charles in America. Not only had he passed his course at Harvard and become a member of the State Bar of California, but had also become a naturalised citizen of the United States of America.

"Well, well, well", said Harry, reading the letter from Charles. "We have an American in the family. I never thought that would happen".

"Well, I think it is a perfectly reasonable thing to do. Besides, George Foley was the first American in the family", replied May.

"I know, but he was born there. Charles was born in England. His parents are English, his grandparents were English. I'm not saying I don't approve. It will take some time for it to sink in. We now have a son that is an American and a daughter that is English. It's strange, that's all. I shall go and write him a reply, and tell him how proud we all are".

Sitting together in the lounge, Cecily said to her mother. "Akira said he loved me today".

"Oh, darling, how wonderful. He's a very charming boy".

"Man, mother, he's a man, not a boy".

"Yes, you know what I mean". There was a brief silence, and then May continued, "Does that mean you're not interested in Peter Ibbotson anymore?"

"I love Peter dearly, but we want different things. He has his heart set on living in South Africa, I want to stay in Japan or live in England. We still write to each other regularly".

"And what does Akira want to do?"

"His career in the navy. To make his parents proud. To have a wife to take care of him and any children that come along".

"Isn't that what you want?"

It used to be, but I'm not so sure now. I want to live my own life for a while. Now that I've found something that could be my life's work. I'm not sure I want to be a man's surrogate mother. Not even for Akira".

"Well, my advice would be to wait and see. You're still young. You both might change your minds in due course. The secret is to enjoy it. Don't let it worry you. Your father and I just want you to be happy in life.

Neither of us are saying you ought to get married and have children. I'm sure you'll make the right decision when the time comes".

The final part of Harry's investigation for Yuzuru, took him on a trip to the naval base in Sasebo, near Nagasaki, three-hundred-miles to the west. It was a long journey on the train. The following morning, he was picked up from his hotel by a subaltern of the base commander. On arrival at the shipyard, he was shown into the office.

Vice-Admiral Gengo Hyakutake, greeted Harry; "Good morning, Mr. Cox, I am delighted to meet you. Your reputation precedes you".

"That is very kind of you Vice-Admiral, I hope I will not take up too much of your valuable time".

"It is no trouble at all. You are, after all, here to help out mutual friend".

"Yes, indeed. Yuzuru sends his regards and thanks you for your co-operation in this matter".

"He is an honourable man. A good friend and colleague. It saddens me to think that there are people in this navy that have called into question his honour and his technical brilliance. This navy would not be the third greatest in the world, without him".

"Well, I'm pleased to say that so far, I have found nothing in my investigations that would cast any shadow of doubt on the integrity of Yuzuru's work".

"It lifts my spirit to hear you say that".

Harry drank the tea that was offered to him by an orderly, and the two men talked about the latest developments in ship design.

The Vice-Admiral got up and suggested Harry make a start on his examination of the Tomozuru. "There is one thing I respectfully ask of you Mr. Cox; that is, we would like you to wear a blindfold until you are below deck. This is a very busy military installation and secrecy is of the utmost importance. My superiors have ordered that non-service personnel will be escorted at all times and only be able to view what they need to, in order to do their job. I hope you understand?"

"Yes, of course. I fully understand".

"Thank you. We are becoming very militaristic in this country; I am not sure I approve. There is a constant battle between the army and the navy as to who can best control the government. I pray that the wisdom of our beloved emperor prevails, and holds us both in check".

A young officer appeared at the door carrying a silk blindfold. Harry was shown to the waiting car. He got in and put on the blindfold. It was a strange sensation. Unable to use his eyes, his hearing and sense of smell took over. He was definitely in a shipyard. The sounds and smell were unmistakeable. He could hear the noise of heavy industry being carried on. The clanging of steel on steel, pneumatic rivetters firing away like a machine gun. The smell of burning metal caused by the welding torches and red-hot rivets. He formed the impression that there was a lot of work going on here. Out of professional curiosity, he would have loved to have seen it all. It remined him of his early days at Swan Hunter when he'd sit on the quayside eating his lunch with Tom. Those days, and the subsequent war that took his best friend away, seemed so far away now.

After a few minutes the car stopped, and Harry was escorted along what felt like a gang plank and onto the deck of a ship. He was then positioned so that he could descend into the lower decks on the steel ladders. Finally, he got to where he needed to be and the blindfold was removed. Being fairly dark, it didn't take long for his eyes to adjust to the light. He was handed his case, and he set to work.

After a couple of hours, Harry sat there in his overalls and made notes. The place was a complete mess. The ship had capsized at sea and fuel and oil had escaped coating everything in a sludge. After he made his notes, he realised that his escort was nowhere to be seen. He called out, but no-one was there. He thought it would be a good idea to go up to the main deck to get some fresh air. He climbed the ladder and took a deep breath of fresh, clean, salty air as he reached the hatch. He could hear a conversation in Japanese taking place on the other side of the deck, towards the bow, and the smell of cigarettes. Treading quietly, he passed through the hatch and looked around him.

He couldn't believe his eyes. There were ships of all types and sizes being worked on. He had never seen such a busy shipyard in his entire career. Ships being re-furbished, ships under construction, some under repair, the amount of work that was going on was on an enormous scale. No wonder they didn't want me to see any of this, thought Harry. This is only one of many such places the Imperial Japanese Navy had. The last time he had seen anything like this much activity, was during the war when Britain and America were on a war footing.

The voices he had heard had stopped, and he could hear footsteps heading his way. As quickly and as quietly as he could, he slipped back through the hatch and down the ladder to where he had left his notebook. When the Japanese officer returned from his cigarette break, Harry was where he had left him, scribbling his notes.

When Harry had finished his examination of the vessel, he told the officer who placed the blindfold back on him before guiding him up the ladder. The car stopped outside the office and the blindfold was removed. Another officer came out and told Harry that the Vice-Admiral had been called away and to pass on his apologies. The officer gave instructions to the driver to take him back to his hotel.

Harry was glad that he didn't have to do any socialising that night. Instead, he had a long soak in a hot bath and scrubbed his fingernails to remove the grime.

Harry got back to Kobe the following afternoon and went to the office. Before he left for the night, he typed out a company envelope, addressed to Mr. William Penrose, at the head office address in London. In it, he put a brief handwritten note that simple read; 'Looks like our friends are preparing for war.' signed HJC.

He popped it in the mailbag on his way out and said goodnight to everyone.

After Christmas, Harry finished his report for Yuzuru. At a lunchtime meeting at the Imperial Hotel, he handed it over.

"I told you", said Harry, with a hint of self-satisfaction in his voice, absolutely nothing to worry about".

Yuzuru looked overjoyed, there were tears in his eyes. "I cannot thank you enough for what you have done for me, Harry. I will be forever in your debt. You have restored by honour and my self-belief. I am truly thankful old friend".

"With regards to the Fourth Fleet incident, I have made some suggestions for your people to consider if they don't want any more accidents in freak weather. There was nothing you could have done about it, with the information you had at the time of construction. What you did was standard practice the world over.

Now we have a better understanding of what such weather like a typhoon can do to a vessel, we can make the necessary adjustments".

They drank a toast to old friends.

"What will you do with your spare time, now that you have your life back", said Yuzuru guiltily.

"I shall get back to the sailing club and spend more time on my boat. Avoiding, of course, any typhoons in the area".

"A wise move, Harry".

40 - Storm Clouds Gathering

In the spring of 1937, Harry travelled to Shanghai on business. After a couple of days there, he went on to Hong Kong. In the company's office in Alexandra Buildings, he met Charles Rowcliffe; Lloyds' surveyor in Hong Kong, and John Sim; the surveyor in Manchuria.

In 1931, the Japanese had annexed the Manchurian region of north-east China. Tensions had been growing, and skirmishes between the occupying authorities and the local Chinese resistance, intensified.

As the man in charge, Harry made the decision to scale down the activities of the Manchurian office in Dairen, so that it could shut down business and relocate to Hong Kong, if things escalated and the threat of aggression was too dangerous to ignore.

"The Japanese are becoming very militaristic", said Harry. The meeting was over, and he was chatting to Charles Rowcliffe in his office over a cup of tea. "Wherever you go, there are men in uniforms everywhere. Military and police alike".

"The news coming out of Manchuria isn't good. The Japanese are brutal to the indigenous population. They crack down on any kind of dissent with a rod of iron. Something has got to give. The Nationalists and the Communists have joined forces. There's going to be one almighty power struggle between those two if they ever get the Japs out".

"I think I've made the right decision. If a fire starts in Manchuria, it is likely to spread to the rest of the country. It will be best to get out of China altogether, and come here".

"Yes, it's a good idea. In fact, the whole Chinese operation could come here, if need be, there's plenty of room".

"Hopefully, it won't come to that". Harry stood up, "Right, I promised May I would pick up a few things while I'm here".

"When are you back to Kobe?"

"In the morning. I'm booked on the Rio de Janeiro Maru to Yokohama".

"Nice ship, Margaret and I went to Singapore on it for out last holiday",

"Mr Hori, the president of the OSK line is a friend of mine. If you ever decide to go anywhere on it again, let me know. He's a very obliging chap".

"Perks of the job, eh?"

Harry said his goodbyes to everyone in the office, and went shopping.

The next morning, Harry checked out of the hotel and got a rickshaw down to the Queen's Pier. He looked for the Dojima Maru, a tender belonging to the OSK line, that ferried passengers out to the Rio de Janeiro Maru, anchored in the bay. As always, when one of the larger vessels were in, there was a multitude of people going backwards and forwards. Harry fought his way through the throng, following a local porter who seemed to know which way to go. Eventually the Dojima Maru was found. He paid off the porter, who scuttled off to look for another customer, and got out his ticket for inspection. As he neared the front of the queue, he began to wonder if he would get on. There was standing room only on the main deck. Just when he thought he was going to make it on, a rope was pulled across the gangplank by a very grubby, local individual, who quite forcefully told Harry in broken English, "No more room, no more room, you wait, another boat come".

The man shouted something to the crew onboard the Dojima Maru, and they cast off, and headed towards the Rio de Janeiro Maru, about five-hundred yards out in the harbour Feeling slightly offended at the way he was shouted at by the grubby man, he turned to give him a piece of his mind. The man was gone. Harry looked over the heads of the crowd and saw him, pushing through the crowd, looking over his shoulder as if pursued. He looked like a man running for his life. What on earth is wrong with the man, he thought.

He sat down on his suitcase, and prepared to wait, and estimated that it would be back in about fifteen-minutes. It was already a warm morning. Ladies with coiffured hair carried parasols, some made use of an umbrella to shield themselves from the sun. The vast majority of people wore the traditional cone-shaped straw hat. It always amazed Harry, how they managed to keep them on their heads. He tried one on once. It just wobbled about and fell off. Hundreds of people were milling about, all with a sense of purpose. Commerce was taking place like this in every port or harbour in the world. He thought it was fascinating to watch.

Suddenly, there was an enormous bang. A deafening explosion, the shockwave of which knocked Harry backwards, off the case he was sitting on. As the sound echoed around the harbour, it was quickly superseded by the sounds of shouting and screaming.

Harry got to his feet, there was chaos all around him, people were injured, some seriously. He looked around to see if there was any indication as to what had exploded. Out on the water, there was a huge plume of black smoke. It was the Dojima Maru. It was about half way between the pier and its destination. It was barely afloat. Other small vessels around it look shattered and broken, people in the water were frantically waving their arms and calling for help. As he watched, the Dojima Maru disappeared under the water, which created a loud hissing sound as the funnels filled with water. It was gone.

The smoke dissipated and he could see wreckage and bodies floating on the water, where once was a ship carrying passengers. A flotilla of small boats soon congregated around the site of the explosion and stated to recover whatever they could.

Harry decided to make his way back to the hotel he had been staying in the last couple of nights. Some sort of investigation would have to be carried out, which would affect the departure of the Rio de Janeiro Maru. In the bar of the hotel, all the conversation was about the tragedy that had unfolded. Harry was talking to a fellow Englishman who had been on the same pier. "Did you notice the smell in the air after the explosion?" said the man.

"No, I can't say I did", replied Harry.

"It had the distinctive aroma of Trinitrotoluene".

"TNT?" Harry almost choked on his whiskey and soda.

"I'd recognise it anywhere. I've heard a rumour that the authorities are saying it was a boiler explosion. Poppycock, there's no way an exploding boiler could cause that much damage. Mark my words, that was no accident".

Harry departed Hong Kong twelve-hours later than scheduled. He'd had time to go back to the Lloyd's office, to tell them he was alright and asked them to send a message to Kobe.

On the journey home, he found out that all but one of the thirty-four dead were Japanese nationals. He thought about the man who had stopped him getting on the boat, who had run away just before the explosion. It seemed to him like a deliberate attack on the Japanese. He had no doubt that if this was proved to be anything other than an accident, there would consequences.

In the weeks that followed, Harry read with interest, reports of the ongoing enquiry into the explosion. It was concluded that the vessel's boiler had ruptured under pressure. He found it hard to believe that a ship's boiler could cause so much damage.

Tensions between the Japanese and Chinese continued to grow. It wasn't long before Harry's prediction of war proved to be correct. On the seventh of July, an incident at the Lugou Bridge near Beijing, sparked a full-scale invasion of China. As discussed with his colleagues in Honk Kong, all the staff at five Lloyd's offices in China, relocated to the island until further notice.

Back in Kobe, life carried on, much as usual. Cecily's kennel venture was going from strength to strength. She wasn't able to see Akira as much as she would have liked, owing to the current state of affairs in China. She continued to write to Peter in England, who was still set on starting his own business in South Africa, once he had qualified as a civil engineer.

Yuzuru Hiraga had been re-called back to full duty with the Imperial Japanese Navy and set to work on a new class of battleship; the Yamato. Along with her sister ship, the Musashi, they were to be the biggest and most heavily armed ships the Japanese had ever built.

They were being constructed in secrecy, at the Kure Naval Arsenal near Hiroshima. In an unguarded moment, Yuzuru had told Harry a rough outline of their specifications. He was quite shocked with what he heard. He knew they didn't need anything like that for their skirmishes with the Chinese. What was being built, could take on anything the British and Americans had. Once again, he felt compelled to write to his head office in London. Marking the envelope for the attention of William Penrose, his note simply said; Things are getting bigger and better than ours. I still think the same as my last'. He didn't want to spell it out, just in case the note fell into the wrong hands. Penrose would understand it. He probably already knew if he had people on the inside.

Sabre rattling wasn't just going on in the far-east. The events going on all across Europe were being closely followed by all the European residents of the foreign quarter everywhere in the world. Kobe was no different. Harry knew that in the event of a war involving the British, he could be recalled to London. May and Cecily didn't want to think about such awful things. They knew, that if ever the time came for such a move, they would be ready to follow Harry's lead. In the meantime, things could go on nicely as they were.

May received tragic news from her sister Lucie in America during the summer of 1938. Her husband George had died. He had been ill for some time. "Poor,

poor Lucie. Those three beautiful girls of hers, are going to have to grow up without their father. Charles will be very upset, George treated him like the son he never had".

"Would you like to go and visit her?" asked Harry.

"I would love to, but it's such a long way. And besides, you're too busy to come with me, so is Cecily, and I really don't want to go on my own".

Perhaps we can go for an extended visit next year".

"Oh, I hope so. I feel completely useless here. This is the first time since we arrived, that I have ever thought that I'd like to be back in America. I suppose it's only natural in the circumstances".

"We've never really discussed what we'll do when I retire. We ought to start thinking about it, it'll be here before we know it".

"Do you have any preferences?"

"I think I'm inclined to favour America. I love the climate in California, I think we both do".

"I shall give it some thought. Now, I must write to Lucie".

41 - It's War

In the evening of the third of September 1939, Harry, May and Cecily sat in the lounge, and listened to the BBC Home Service. At a quarter past seven, the British Prime Minister, Neville Chamberlain, made the announcement they were all dreading; they were now at war with Germany. Harry put his arm around May, who had started to quietly weep. Cecily was sitting on the floor, stroking D'Artagnan. "There wasn't supposed to be any more wars", she said to herself. "Why do men always want to fight? I shall never understand them".

"Don't worry", Harry said to May, trying to reassure her. "The company want me to stay here. We'll be quite safe".

"Didn't anyone learn anything from the last one?" said May. "Those damn Germans".

After the initial shock, the European community in Kobe carried on as normal. Some, including most of the German residents returned to their homeland. It was mostly the younger members that left. The older ones had seen it all before. A few weeks after the announcement, Cecily received a letter from Peter. He had passed his final exams and was now an associate member of the Institute of Civil Engineers. He had planned to go to South Africa, but in light of recent events, he had decided to stay in England and enlist. He was about to start officer training in the Royal Engineers.

She wrote back that same day. She congratulated him on his achievement, and reminded him that he now owed her a bottle of Champagne and a biscuit. She would collect it the next time she was in London, assuming he was still there. She signed the letter off, and then added a post-script; 'Take good care of yourself AND, don't do anything stupid'.

Harry and May sat at the breakfast table one morning. "Just think", she said, "If Charles was still a British subject, he might have enlisted into one of the services. I am so glad he's an American, living in California. He's as far from the war in Europe as it's possible to be".

"Yes, I think he's in the best place. Roosevelt has made it quite clear that they don't want any part of it, and rightly so. As long as they keep to their side of the bargain and keep us supplied with the hardware we need, I don't think it will take long to see off the Hun once and for all. Chamberlain was too soft. Appeasement was never going to work with man like Hitler. Thank heavens Churchill is in charge. He seems to be the only one who talks any sense". He got up from the table. "Right, I'd better be off, my dear. "I'll see you this evening. Has Cecily already gone off to the kennels, or is she having a lie-in?"

She went to work early. Akira picked her up. He was in his new uniform. He's been promoted to

Lieutenant-Commander. You know, I still don't know what he actually does in the navy, do you?"

"He's in some internal investigation, intelligence type of role. He probably isn't allowed to tell anyone what he really does. Have a good day my sweet".

"Goodbye, darling".

A year after the war had begun in Europe, Japan, capitalising on the recent fall of Frace, invaded French Indochina. As if that wasn't enough of a shock for the people living in the region, five-days later, Japan formed an alliance with Germany and Italy. This meant that British interests in the far-east, along with those of its allies, were now targets for Japanese aggression.

Liaising with London, Harry sent out a message to all the staff operating in his region, that in the event of any hostile action, they were to make their way to the Americas. Apart from Canada, they were all neutral. Harry spoke to his good friend; Noboru Otani, president of the NYK line. "If my staff and I have to abandon our offices in Japan, will you be able to offer us safe passage across the Pacific".

"Of course, Harry. I really do not think you need to worry. I am certain that you will stay and continue your good work. You have many good friends here, that respect you. You are a very honourable man and a good friend. I will do everything in my power to assist you, but I think you will be quite safe here".

"Thank you, Otani, I hope you are right. There have been rumours going around that suggest foreigners may be interned if things escalate".

"I cannot foresee such things happening in Japan. If the authorities want you to leave, they will deport you, not lock you up. You worry needlessly my friend".

Cecily began to feel a sense of isolation. She was not seeing Akira anywhere near as often as she had. She noticed that his attitude had changed somewhat. He had become more arrogant, big-headed. She'd thought that his promotion had gone to his head. He gave her a filthy look when she told him so. He had definitely become more distant. She hadn't heard from Peter in an age. She had written to him at his flat in London, but who knows if the letters ever arrived. He could be training and living in a barracks somewhere of had even been sent abroad. The kennels were quiet, as many of her regulars had returned home, possibly for good, and those that stayed in Kobe, were not travelling as often.

Harry's last meeting at the Masonic Lodge he belonged to, had been interrupted by a visit from the local Kempeitai, demanding the name and address of all its members. Foreigners were no longer allowed to be a member of any secret organisation, such as the Masons. Attitudes towards Europeans were definitely changing. Officials were becoming openly hostile towards them and when on the streets, they would be frequently asked for some form of identity, which usually took an age to verify.

Each week, Harry's office would compile a list of ships sailing for the west-coast of America, should things escalate. If any member of staff wanted to leave, they would have Harry's blessing, and a ticket on the next available ship. Apart from Oburu Otani, he had talked in private to all his contacts at the shipping lines he dealt with and had received assurances that there would always be a space for them.

It was a very anxious time. The Battle of Britain was raging and fighting for its very survival. The occasional letter arrived from their family. May's younger and only surviving brother had been given a commission in one of the northern regiments. Her sister had talked about the bombing raids on London while Harry's family talked of the same in Newcastle. Closer to home, talk of internment camps for foreign civilians were on the increase. Stories of the brutal way in which the Japanese army dealt with its prisoners, military and civilian alike, in China circulated, putting fear into the hearts of most.

42 - The Summons

One Sunday afternoon in late November, a surly junior officer of the Imperial Japanese Navy arrived at the Cox residence, under orders from Vice-Admiral Hiraga. They were told that a car would return to pick them up at six-o'clock that evening and that they would have dinner with the Vice-Admiral. All three of them are to be ready and there must be no delay.

"Well, I thought he was very rude", said May, after the officer had left.

"I don't suppose he meant it", replied Harry. Yuzuru normally calls me himself when he wants to see me. I don't understand why he sent someone round with a message. To be honest, I haven't seen Yuzuru for some time now, not since he's been working on a big project over near Hiroshima".

"Well, I didn't like the way he tried to order us about. He sounded just like Akira. I wonder if he'll be there tonight. I haven't seen him for ages either", said Cecily.

"I think they're all paranoid about seeing to collaborate with us foreigners", said May.

"I must say, it does all seem a bit out of character".

"I've half a mind not to go", said Cecily.

"I don't think we ought to provoke anyone", replied Harry. "Yuzuru is an old friend and has invited us to dinner. Let's just leave it at that".

As the clock struck six, there was a heavy rapping on the door. "Good grief", cried May, "I nearly jumped out of my skin. I'm surprised the door is still on its hinges".

The same officer as before was standing on the doorstep. Harry and May were standing in the hall, Cecily was in the lounge trying to calm down D'Artagnan, who had been rudely awakened by the knocking on the door. "Bring the dog with you", shouted the officer, "Bring it now, and everybody get in the car. We must go, now".

Harry, May and Cecily looked at each other in astonishment. Harry took D'Artagnan's lead from off its hook and passed it to Cecily. "Better do what he says".

They followed the officer to the waiting car. There was another one parked behind it, containing four men in uniform. Behind that was a truck with a number of men in overalls standing around. Harry got into the front of the car, May, Cecily and D'Artagnan got in the back. As they drove off, with the other car following, Cecily looked out the rear window. "Those men by the truck are going into our house. What do they think they are doing?"

May looked back as well, and came to the same conclusion. She squeezed Cecily's hand, and in her best reassuring, motherly voice said, "Don't let it worry you dear. I'm sure we'll find out what is going on quite soon"

Harry's mind started to race. Was there anything in the house that would give rise to concern with the Japanese authorities? He had papers from his office, but nothing contentious in any way. He had nothing referring to the name of William Penrose. They could never connect the two of them. Unless of course, they had intercepted his mail. The only thing that Harry was particularly perturbed about, was the packet of cash he had in his wardrobe. It was in yen, dollars and sterling, and was to be used to help buy an escape for any of his staff as well as himself. He might have trouble explaining its existence.

The cars arrived at Yuzuru's house. It was quiet and lit by only a few lanterns. The officer who had driven them, stood to one side as they reached the front door and instructed them to go in. As they did so, he turned to the officers in the other car, barked some orders at them, and they all disappeared.

A servant showed the Cox family to the dining room, where they found Yuzuru sitting at the head of the table, on his own. There was a look of sadness on his face which he tried, unconvincingly to hide.

"My wife sends her apologies; she is visiting family in Tokyo. Please sit down and I will have dinner served". As Harry, May and Cecily sat, he rang a little bell that was on the table. Two servants appeared, one with drinks, the other with food.

There was an awkward silence in the room. Harry and may looked at each other, wondering what was going on. This was not the Yuzuru they knew. The man they knew was a convivial host and was expert in making one feel relaxed. The man they saw in front of them looked tired and withdrawn, and clearly didn't want to be entertaining friends.

"Is everything alright Yuzuru?" asked Harry, a note of concern in his voice.

There was a pause, Yuzuru looked into the distance, as if trying to formulate a response. Eventually he replied; "I am sorry Harry, but the country I have loyally served", his voice became softer, as if he didn't want anyone outside the room to overhear, "has been corrupted by those that would, for their own vainglorious desires and hedonistic pleasure, see it go down the path of potential destruction. The element that I refer to, has persuaded our glorious emperor to take the path of treachery, a place where only darkness prevails. No honour will be gained from what is about to come. I am sorry to say, that I am ashamed to be Japanese". As he said this, tears welled up in his eyes.

Harry, May and Cecily looked at each other in dismay. If they were worried before they arrived, they were positively frightened now. Even Harry was lost for words.

Yuzuru rang the bell again when they had finished the course in front of them. More drinks were served and more food arrived, but nobody was in the mood to eat it.

Harry tried to make conversation with banal observations about the weather, but it was clear Yuzuru's mind was elsewhere. Near the end of the meal, he addressed Cecily; "I am sorry my child, but you will have noticed that my son, Akira, has of late, not paid you the attention you deserve. It is not of his doing, but of mine. You see, my wife comes from a noble, aristocratic family, and it is her desire that our son marries into a Japanese family of a similar or higher social position. I must respect her wishes, and in turn, so must Akira. He is very fond of you but his duty to his parents must come first. I hope you understand".

Cecily didn't know what to say. She could feel herself holding back tears. She simply said; "Oh, I see".

Yuzuru looked at his watch and then rang the bell again. The servants came in and cleared the plates. Before they left, Yuzuru whispered something to one of them, and they left the room.

A few moments later, the sound of footsteps could be heard in the hallway outside. The door to the dining room opened and two officers stood in the doorway.

Yuzuru stood up. The tracks of tears could be seen running down his face, reflecting in the light of the dimly lit room. He looked Harry in the eye and then bowed. "I am sorry my friend, that we have to part in this manner. This will be the last time we see each other. Please go with these officers. They are carrying out my orders". He turned to May and Cecily and gave a silent bow to them. He turned, and without looking back, walked out of the room.

Immediately after he had gone, one of the officers said, "Come, come now, quickly", and beckoned them out of the room.

The three of them slowly walked along the hallway towards the door. "Wait", cried Cecily, "Where is D'Artagnan? I left him here in the hall".

The officer that they were following turned, "You see dog later, not now, come quickly". There was a menacing sense of urgency about the way he spoke and the way he looked at her, that made her fearful of what was happening to them. The other officer, who was walking behind the group, started to push Cecily forward in an effort to get the group to start moving again. None of them considered it wise to aggravate the two officers. They were after all, both carrying a pistol in the holster on their belt. Feeling like lambs to the slaughter, they got into the car. Once again, there was another car behind, which followed them as they set off.

They were not going in the direction of home. They were heading south, towards the coast. Only the main roads in Kobe were lit by lamps. The back roads they were travelling along were pitch black. They had no idea where they were being taken. Cecily and May sat in the back, trying to comfort each other, tears streaming down their face. "May said, "It's all right darling, we are all together, we will be all right".

The two cars were driven in convoy, at speed through the dark streets. After what seemed like an age, they turned a corner, and suddenly Harry recognised where they were. It was the Mitsubishi shipyard, on the west side of town.

They approached the main gatehouse, and with a toot of the horn from the lead car, the gates opened and they entered unopposed. The cars thundered along the quayside and finally stopped next to a small tender moored there. Everything was happening so fast. Harry, May and Cecily were almost manhandled onto the waiting boat by the officers from the car behind. No sooner had they got aboard, the boat cast off. Only the officer that had been driving their car remained with them. The boat headed out towards the open sea. "Where are you taking us?" demanded Harry, now visibly shaken and upset. "What are you going to do with us? I demand to know".

The officer to whom he was shouting, just gave him a cold stare back, turned and went into the wheelhouse, and closed the door.

The three of them huddled together on the open deck. It was a chilly evening. Adrenalin and fear were now surging through their veins. After about thirty-minutes, Harry could see, silhouetted against the night sky, a large ship ahead of them. He could see light on the shore to the left and worked out that they must be somewhere near the island of Tomoga. As they approached the ship from behind, Harry could read what was written on the stern. It was the Kamakura Maru, a ship of the NYK line. The ship must be travelling at dead slow ahead, as it was hardly moving. A rope ladder was hanging over the port side, and the tender drew up alongside. Fortunately, the water was calm and there was little pitching. The crew of the tender put out the fenders and secured it to the larger vessel. Harry, May and Cecily were told to climb the ladder. Cecily went up first, followed by May with Harry behind. It was only a short climb to the rear deck, where they were helped by the ship's crew. As Harry climbed, he looked down behind him, the tender had already cast off and was heading back towards Kobe.

The three of them sat on a bench in a state of physical and nervous exhaustion. Was this the end of their ordeal or just the beginning?

An officer of the merchant marine was standing near to them. The deck-hands had gone. Harry, who had been comforting May and Cecily, broke away from them and approached the officer. The man gave a respectful bow, and before Harry could say anything, the man said, in excellent English; "Good evening, sir, if you and your family would care to follow me, the captain is waiting for you".

In no fit state to argue, they followed the officer up to the bridge. On the way, Harry noticed that the hum of the engines had changed, and that they were now picking up speed.

He also noted that there were no passengers on board and that most of the deck lights were out.

When they arrived at the bridge, they were welcomed by the captain; "Good evening, Mr. Cox, my name is Tatuya Kurita, and I am the master of this ship. I have been instructed by the company president, Mr. Otani, to give you this". He took an envelope from out of his pocket and handed it to Harry.

"Thank you", replied Harry. "Where are you taking us?"

Captain Kurita looked at him, and then at May and Cecily, who stood there staring at him, "My orders are to take you to San Francisco".

May fell to her knees and started sobbing. Harry and Cecily bent down and helped her back to her feet.

"I'm sorry Captain, we have all just had a rather unpleasant experience. We are all a little exhausted".

"Of course, I fully understand. One of my officers will show you to your quarters. You have the freedom of the ship and don't hesitate to ask if you have any requirements".

"Thank you, Captain".

They followed the second-mate. He led them to the first-class cabins, putting on the lights as he went along. "Are there any passengers on board?" asked Harry.

"No, sir. We have no passengers, nor cargo and only a skeleton crew. Our orders are to take you to San Francisco, refuel, and pick up some passengers to take back to Japan. I have never known of such a voyage".

"How long will it take to get there?" enquired Cecily.

"About ten-days miss".

They stopped outside one of the cabins and waited for the second-mate to open the door. He stepped in and put the light on. As they followed him in, their jaws dropped as they glanced around the room. All their belongings were packed into their trunks and just sitting there as if they were going on a holiday. Almost the entire contents of their house in Kobe, less the furniture, was there. Ornaments and delicate objects had been carefully packed into straw filled tea-chests. They really didn't think they would ever see any of it again. Harry rummaged around in one of his trunks and found the packet of cash he had been worried about. Not a note of it was missing.

"Excuse me, miss, your room is next door". Cecily followed him to the cabin and found all her luggage neatly packed. The first thing she found when she opened one of her trunks was two packets of letters tied up with a lace ribbon. One contained letters from Akira, the other, from Peter.

"Er, excuse me miss, if you'd like to come with me to the galley, we have something else of yours".

She looked questioningly at him.

"Follow me miss, it won't take a minute".

She was too tired to ask questions, so just followed him down the stairs to the deck below. They walked through the deserted dining room and into the kitchen area. There were a few of the crew in there, mainly clearing up. The second-mate called out and a large sweaty man appeared. A brief conversation was had and then the man, presumably one of the cooks, walked off.

Cecily stood there waiting for just a few moments, when she heard a familiar sound. She thought she was going to burst with the relief and excitement that rushed through her body. The sweaty man had just walked around the corner with D'Artagnan on his lead.

"My boy, my lovely boy", she cried, and bent down to him. D'Artagnan barked a few times, jumped up and licked her face, then rolled over on his back. This was against all the training advice she had given other dog owners for the last few years, but she didn't care, she was just so pleased to see him.

"The chef said that the dog has been well behaved. He gave it some scraps when it arrived", said the second-mate.

Cecily thanked the chef, and went back upstairs with D'Artagnan, to see her parents, and a very happy reunion ensued.

Before Harry went to bed, he opened the letter the captain had given him. It read;

My dear friend,

Firstly, I must apologise for not saying farewell to you in person. Our mutual friend told me it was imperative that, due to your position and knowledge, you should leave immediately. He says that the reason for this will become clear in due course.

He also apologises for not giving you any notice about your departure. Knowing how loyal you are to your staff, he has also asked me to arrange passage for them in due course, perhaps one at a time so as not to alert the authorities, who have started to make life difficult for Japanese people seen to be assisting or sympathising with those who they now consider to be undesirables.

Please give my regards to your lovely wife and daughter, and I hope that one

day we might meet again in more favourable circumstances.

Your friend,

Noboru

Reading between the lines, Harry believed that it was only a matter of time before they would have been interned. Yuzuru had put his neck on the line by helping them to escape. Tomorrow morning, it would appear that the three of them had disappeared without trace. He hoped that the rest of his friends and colleagues would be able to get out before it was too late.

The next ten-days were incredibly boring. They tried to keep themselves to themselves. The food was fairly basic, crew rations, but none of them complained. They were just glad to be heading in the right direction. Their son Charles was going to be very surprised to see them. He was now married and living in Hollywood of all places, working for a local law firm. They hoped that they would be able to stay with May's sister; Lucie, also in Los Angeles. Harry would have to contact head office in London, and wait to hear where they wanted him to go. Hopefully, he could stay in America and do the same job he'd done the last time he was there.

The hardest thing, was not getting any news from Europe, or not knowing the fate of his friends and colleagues back in Japan. Harry occasionally ventured up to the bridge, but got the impression he was not wanted there. The captain was always amiable, and the crew courteous, but there was definitely an atmosphere. Harry decided to destroy the letter from Noboru. If it ever fell into the wrong hands, it would prove most awkward for the pair of them and possibly Yuzuru as well. He tore it up and threw it overboard one night. I'm getting paranoid, he had said to himself. I've been reading too many Alexander Wilson novels. Cecily had D'Artagnan to keep her occupied. They would go on long circuitous walks around the ship, occasionally bumping into officers and crew she could have a conversation with. At one point, she even set up a dog agility course in the empty dining room, using a selection of tables and chairs. The kitchen staff would come out during their breaks, and cheer D'Artagnan on.

43 - Home in Sight

In the early hours of their tenth day at sea, the lights of the Californian coast could be seen on the horizon. By the time they had their breakfast, The hills of the San Francisco Bay area were clearly visible. It was a journey they had made before. Cecily had done it many times over the course of her schooling days in Canada and later at San Refael. Their excitement was palpable. With eyes full of emotion, they gazed at America, their saviour, their home.

Slowly, the now completed Golden Gate Bridge came into view. None of them had seen it before, and they marvelled at is beauty. It had been an ambitious building project the last time any of them had been here. They had seen pictures of it in magazines and newspapers, and the newsreels had been full of it when it opened just four-years previous. To see it for real, in its vermillion red splendour, was a spectacle to behold. A triumph of American ingenuity and engineering.

The ship sailed under the bridge and turned to starboard following the harbour pilot's boat. They docked by Japantown, in the shadow of the Bay Bridge, another recently completed infrastructure-project they had never seen before.

Harry thanked the captain for everything he had done. When the gangplank was in position, Harry, May, Cecily, D'Artagnan and an army of crew members carrying their possessions, got off the ship. As they watched the trunks being stacked against a nearby wall, a smartly dressed gentleman approached them. In a cheery voice, with a slight Scottish accent said, "Good afternoon, Mr. Cox and family I presume?"

Harry, slightly surprised, said "Yes, yes we are".

"Jolly good. My name is Millar, David Millar, I'm the Lloyd's principal surveyor here in San Francisco".

Harry's face lit up with a smile. "My dear chap, you have no idea how good it is to see you. How did you know we would be here?"

"We received a telegram in the office a couple of days ago, saying you would all be arriving here on the Kamakura Maru. It came as quite a surprise. We've been hearing all sorts of rumours coming out of Japan recently".

"Yes, it's all been a rather unsavoury experience. There was a moment I thought we were all going to be interned. It's been quite frightening. I'm certainly glad to be here. We haven't heard any news for ten-days. We have no idea how things are going in Europe".

"It's not looking too good at the moment. Churchill is trying his hardest to get the Americans involved, but they're not having any of it. I've taken the liberty of booking you into the Fairmont, it's probably the best we have to offer around here. I'll have someone take care of your trunks, and then I'll take you up to the hotel".

"Thank you, David. I shall come into the office tomorrow; there's a hundred and one calls I need to make. Bye the way, what day is it today? I've totally lost track of the time"

It's Saturday the sixth of December".

"Thanks. The sixth of December, 1941. That's not going to be a date I'll forget". Harry thought for a moment. "It's Sunday tomorrow, will anyone be at the office?"

"Oh, yes. It's been quite busy since the war started, I'll be there in the morning, around ten-o'clock, but the office staff will be in about an hour earlier".

The next morning, Harry, May and Cecily went down to breakfast together, just before nine-o'clock. As they approached the dining room, they could hear a loud hubbub of people talking loudly. May looked at Harry and said, "It's a bit noisy, isn't it? I hope it isn't always like this".

They were shown to a table. Everybody around them were deep in conversation, some had worried looks on their faces. Even the waiters that were not serving, stood around in groups conversing.

"Something's going on", said Harry.

"I wonder what it is?" said Cecily.

No sooner had the words left her mouth, the sound of the radio came over the hotel's public address system. Everybody fell silent.

People gasped and cried as a news bulletin was read out. Japanese aircraft had attacked Pearl Harbor in Hawaii. Many ships of the United States Navy had been damaged or destroyed, and the latest casualty figure stood at well over a thousand military personnel and civilians. The battle was still ongoing.

Everybody in the room was in shock. The whole country would be in shock. Harry put his hand on May's and gave it a gentle squeeze. "Yuzuru must have known, or at least suspected this was going to happen, that's why he got us out of the country so quickly. This is going to change everything", continued Harry. "The Americans won't stand for this. There will be retaliation and reprisals".

The broadcast finished. It left everyone in the room speechless. You could have heard a pin drop. Slowly, people started to take in the enormity of what they had just heard. People got up from their tables, breakfast unfinished and hurriedly left the dining room, in search of a telephone to call loved ones.

"Thank heavens you managed to contact Charles and Lucie last night. They would have been terribly worried about us", said May.

"I think I'd better get to the office now, and see if I can get in touch with London".

The three of them returned to their suite and Harry got his things together and went off. May and Cecily stayed in their room and started to write letters to friends and family, to tell them they were safe and well in San Francisco. How safe that was going to be in light of this morning's events, was impossible to know.

Harry spent the day in the office trying to get through to London. The telephone network across the whole country was at near breaking point. Radio broadcasts gave regular updates of the situation in Hawaii. Hour by hour the news came in of the destruction and the rising casualty figure. People were urged not to use the telephones in a bid to assist the military in getting information to its personnel.

It was mid-afternoon before Harry could speak to someone in authority at the London office. The message from James Montgomerie, Chief Ship Surveyor for the company, instructed him to set up a temporary office anywhere he could and wait for further instructions. Once the dust had settled, it may be that he would go back to the American headquarters in New York. In the meantime, Harry suggested that he make use of the office in Los Angeles, where he had family.

Harry walked back to the hotel. People were congregating in shop doorways, trying to listen to the news bulletins being broadcast at regular intervals on the radio. The look of worry that had been on everyone's face that morning, was still there. Rumours were going around that Japanese submarines had been seen in the harbour and that an attack on the west-coast mainland was imminent.

He got back to the hotel, and found May sitting in the hotel lounge with a number of other guests, listening to the radio. "Where's Cecily?" he asked.

"She's taken D'Artagnan for a walk around Huntington Park. Why, is everything all right?"

"Yes, for now. I expect you've heard the rumours that are flying about. If anything does happen, I want to make sure we are all together". He went on to tell her about his conversation with London. "At least if we're in Los Angeles, we'll be close to Charles and Lucie".

"I tried to call them today, but it was impossible to get through".

"We'll just have to sit it out here for a day of two, and then get the train south".

"I'm sure Charles or Lucie would offer to come and get us if we asked".

"Mm, I thought of that, but we have a lot of luggage with us. I don't want to leave any of it behind. We'll be all right here for a day or so".

Harry walked to the office the next morning. There was no longer a sense of panic in the air. but one of apprehension. Were they going to be in the firing line? What would be the government's response?

The telephone lines were not so chaotic this morning. Harry managed to make a few important calls. The first, was to the Los Angeles office in Wilmington, where he spoke to Fred Archbold, the ship surveyor for the area. He confirmed that there was plenty of free office space for Harry to use as he saw fit. He then spoke to his son Charles. They would see him as soon as they made their way down south. The last call was to Lucie. She had a big house in Whittier, and would be more than happy for the three of them to stay there.

While he talked to David Millar over a cup of tea, one of the office clerks came in and told them that the president was about to make a radio broadcast. They all went into the general office area and joined everyone, now huddled around a radio.

It was war. The Japanese were on the rampage in the Pacific, and Roosevelt vowed to put an end to it. All it needed was approval from congress. Only a fool would bet against it happening now. Harry had a sense of deja vu. He had the same feeling in his stomach as he did in 1939 after listening to Chamberlain.

He decided to leave the office and walk back to the hotel. The atmosphere going home was in stark contrast to the journey in. There was almost a sense of celebration in the air. Instead of scaring people, the president's speech united them. They had a belief, that collectively, they could overcome any adversary. They had God on their side and they were going to win.

A few hours later, it was confirmed on the radio, that the president had signed the declaration of war with Japan.

Harry, May and Cecily arrived at Lucie's house in Whittier later the next day. Charles, his wife Betty and son Jasper were waiting for them there. Also present were; Lucie's three daughters. A very emotional reunion took place. Despite world events, the Cox family had something to celebrate, and the champagne flowed. May now realised how much she had missed her family, and how important it was to have them near in times of adversity. Harry and May had kept themselves busy over the last twenty-years in Japan and had never considered leaving once. Now that it had been forced upon them, it was highly unlikely they would ever go back. Their future here, or anywhere else, would all depend on Harry's next posting. With a war starting in the Pacific, Europe and North Africa already at war, would there be anywhere safe to go?

Two days later, the United States of America declared war with Germany and Italy.

44 - To Canada

Harry returned home from his office in Wilmington. "I have an announcement to make", he said enthusiastically. "I have got my marching orders from London".

May took an audible intake of breath and put her hand to her cheek, her face the picture of worry.

"Don't worry, old thing", said Harry with a reassuring smile, "We're going to Canada".

"Canada?" cried Cecily, "Where abouts?"

"The capital, Ottawa. I have been seconded to the British Admiralty Technical Mission. I'm basically going to be doing the job I did in New York, during the last war. The Americans are going to be too busy building ships for themselves, now they are going to be fighting a war on two fronts. I was given the choice of Australia or Canada. I chose Canada because I thought it would keep us all together". He looked at May as he said the last part. She got up and hugged him, and said "Thank you, darling".

"When do we go?" enquired Cecily.

"As soon as possible really. It's going to take three or four days to get there on the train. We need to start making arrangements now".

"I was really looking forward to having a family Christmas with you all here", said Lucie, looking a little sad

"So was I", replied May. "People all around the world will be having to make far greater sacrifices this Christmas. It's a shame, but Harry has to go, and I have to be with him".

Arriving in the Canadian capital, Harry, May and Cecily arrived at the newly opened Lord Elgin Hotel. Their rooms were at the front, overlooking the Confederation Park and the Rideau Canal beyond. It was a cold, crisp morning and not at all what they had recently been used to in California.

Cecily and May started the arduous task of looking for a house to rent, while Harry went off in search of his new office. It was less than a mile away, in Lyon Street.

The officer in charge had the splendid name of; Captain Arthur George Wilkinson Stantan. It was an honorary title as he was in fact a civilian but trained by the Royal Navy and was now one of its senior naval architects. They talked in Arthur's office over tea and soon discovered they had mutual friends in London and had both trained at the college in Greenwich. Arthur was there two-years after Harry had left.

The Canadian shipyards were currently building ninety-two corvettes and minesweepers for the Royal Navy; most of which would be heading for the North Atlantic to protect the convoys.

"Oh, there's just one thing before you go, Harry", said Arthur, moving a bit closer and speaking in a lowered voice. "Churchill is coming to Ottawa tomorrow".

"Really?" replied Harry, also in hushed tones. "I thought he was visiting Roosevelt in Washington".

"He is, but he's popping up here to make a speech in the Parliament building. Rally the troops sort of thing".

When Harry, May and Cecily were having breakfast the next morning, there was a hum of excitement in the air. Red, white and blue bunting was being hung everywhere along with union jacks and the maple leaf flag. Churchill was due in at the station at about ten-o'clock in the morning and the procession to the governor-general's residence, Rideau Hall, would bring him quite close to the hotel. At just after ten-o'clock, the three of them made their way along Laurier Avenue and stood on the bridge over the canal. Thousands of people were waiting in anticipation. Being the Christmas holiday, most people were off work or school and it seemed as though the entire population of the city had come out to catch a glimpse of the great man.

The motorcade went past them and the crowd roared. Churchill had his trademark cigar in his mouth and waved as he went past. It only lasted a few seconds and then it was over. Those few seconds were all it took to lift one's spirits. The feeling of national pride and patriotism welled up inside and the three of them walked away feeling they had just witnessed a moment in history they would never forget. "It's quite remarkable" said Harry, as they walked back towards the hotel. "How one man can evoke such patriotic fervour in one. It really is astonishing".

"I'm glad he is on our side", said May, smiling.

The next afternoon, Churchill made a stirring speech in the parliament building, before going back to Washington. Such was the power of his words, that Cecily decided she wanted to do something for the war effort. She talked to her parents over dinner.

"I really think I ought to do something, do my bit"

"What do you have in mind?" asked Harry.

"I'm sure any of the services will have me, now national service for women has come in. I'm young enough, fit, and educated".

"What about Land Army or nursing or munitions work?" asked May

"Yes, I'm sure I could do any of it. What I need to do is go to a few recruitment centres and see if they are interested in me. Once I get over there, I'm sure I will find something".

"Over where?"

"England, of course".

"But I thought you meant over here. Why do you want to go to England?"

"Because I'm English. I'll be needed over there far more than I'll be needed here".

"But it's dangerous, darling. There are air raids almost every night".

"I know, mother, but I want to do my bit, for my country".

"Well, I think it's very brave of you", joined in Harry. "I think it sets a good example for all of your generation".

"Thank you, father, If I don't do it, I will probably regret it for the rest of my life".

"I suppose you have family over there you could stay with until you find something", conceded May.

"Aunts Lucia, Phyllis and Pauline, all said I could stay with them at any time. All I need to do, is get a passage across to England. I shall have to rely on you for that bit, father".

Harry used his contacts, and managed to get Cecily on a supply ship travelling between Halifax, Nova Scotia and Liverpool. May had got used to the idea of her going, but nonetheless, it didn't stop her worrying. The German U-Boats were having a lot of success in the Atlantic, and any such journey would be a risk.

She said goodbye to her parents at the quayside and gave D'Artagnan one last hug. A country that was experiencing regular air-raids and food rationing, was no place to take a dog.

If she thought that the ten-day journey from Japan had been boring, this two-week crossing was the most tedious experience of her life. The cabin was cramped, the food rations were inadequate, the crew were too busy to talk to her and no D'Artagnan to keep her amused. After a couple of days, she wondered if she was doing the right thing.

The crossing passed without incident. There had been a few false sightings of submarines and on one occasion a German plane had been spotted, too far away to worry about.

The first thing Cecily did when she arrived in Liverpool, was to find a half decent hotel and have a bath. The next thing she did, was to find the local post office and sent a telegram to her parents; 'ARRIVED SAFE AND WELL LIVERPOOL LOTS OF LOVE CECILY'.
The next thing to do was to get a train to London and hope that aunt Pauline had got her letter. Otherwise, she was in for a bit of a surprise.

Before getting the train south, she had a walk around the city. For the first time, she could see the actual devastation caused by the air-raids. All the rubble neatly swept away and piled up. Children playing in the bombed-out buildings, their skeletal remains lifeless and silent. It was hard to imagine that life would ever be the same for those that had lived there. It was hard to imagine any life at all. Yet, the people she saw going about their daily work stood tall, defiant. She now began to feel she had done the right thing coming over from the relative safety of Canada. If there had been any doubt before, there was none now. She was going to do her bit to help. Whatever that was going to be, she didn't know just yet, but she would stand next to these courageous people, and be counted.

By the time she got to London it was dark. Not just because the sun had gone down, but because of the blackout restrictions. There were plenty of people on the streets going about their business, but in darkness. She walked down Tottenham Court Road to Oxford Street and caught the number seventeen bus to Shepherds Bush. Traffic was very slow due to the added danger of driving in the dark. She changed at Shepherds Bush, and got the next bus to Perivale, near Ealing.

The house was in complete darkness. She wondered if there was going to be anyone at home. She rapped firmly on the door knocker. A few moments later, she could hear the door being unlocked and the sound of a curtain being drawn.

The door opened, and from within the darkness a face popped out. It was aunt Pauline.

"Cecily", she shrieked in excitement, "You're here, you made it. Quick, come in out the cold". Once in, the door was shut and the blackout curtain pulled across. "Cecily' is here", Pauline shouted. The hall light went on. It took a moment to get used to the light after spending the last hour in darkness. Uncle Henry and her six-cousins came into the hall to greet her. "We only got your letter the other day" said uncle Henry.

"I do hope it's all right, me coming here like this. I'm sure it won't be for long".

"Not at all my dear, you're welcome to stay as long as you like. Let's take that coat off and get you by the fire".

All nine of them went into the lounge and sat around Cecily and asked her questions about her trip from Canada and her earlier one from Japan. By the time she finished, they were in awe of her intercontinental lifestyle and bravery.

"I'm so glad you've sent a telegram to your mother. If she had to wait weeks for a letter, I'm sure she would be worried sick. I know I would be", said Pauline".

"What are you going to do now?" enquired Robert, the youngest cousin.

"I'm going to try for the Auxiliary Territorial Service, ATS. If they don't want me, I'll see about the WAAF's or the WRNS. I'm sure someone will have me.

"I'm sure they will my dear, you've shown a great deal of pluck and determination thus far", said Henry, encouragingly.

They talked long into the evening until it was time for bed.

"I've put you in the guest-room", said Pauline. "You'll be quite comfortable there. All this lot will be off to work in the morning, but I'll be around. Just get up when you're ready. It's so lovely to have you home".

45 - Cecily Signs Up for Adventure

Cecily sat in the kitchen the next morning with aunt Pauline. Over a cup of tea and a slice of toast, they planned their day. "The first thing we ought to do, is go down to the town hall and get you registered for a ration book and an identity card. It's quite handy that you were born in the district, they'll have your birth record to hand, that should save a bit of time".

"I have plenty of money with me, in case we need to pay for things. I shall give you house-keeping money while I'm here. I don't expect a free-ride".

"When we're in town, we can find out where the nearest ATS recruitment office is".

"Yes, I'd like to get that sorted out quickly. I don't want to be a burden on all of you".

"Don't be silly, Cecily, you're family. It's going to be great fun having you around. We're all very proud of you, coming over here to help with the war effort. You'll be an inspiration to all young women".

Cecily and Pauline spent the morning at Ealing town hall. A temporary identity card was issued, a ration book and a gas mask. Cecily then went off into London on the train by herself, to King's College, where she had been advised there was a recruitment officer for the ATS. Walking along The Strand on a sunny winter's afternoon, one could almost forget there was a war on. It was only when you looked beyond the cheery faces of passers-by, that you began to notice the bomb-damaged buildings, the sandbags, the scrim tape on shop windows and the multitude of different uniforms being worn.

She found the recruitment officer at the college, and sat in the queue. There were only two other girls in front of her, so the wait wasn't a long one.

Cecily introduced herself when it was her turn. The female recruitment officer was in the uniform of an ATS officer, the single pip on her epaulettes signified she was a Second-Lieutenant. She was very easy to talk to and showed such enthusiasm when Cecily told her the story of her recent arrival. As they talked, Army Form E511P was filled in. An eyebrow of interest was raised and a separate note made, when Cecily told her that she could speak Japanese.

"You've seemed to have lived a very interesting life, Miss Cox.

"I suppose I have, really. It is all thanks to my father's job, we've been able to travel around the world quite a bit".

"Well, I think I have everything I need from you at the moment. I expect you'll hear from our personnel department in a week to ten-days' time. What have you got planned for the rest of the day?"

"I thought I'd stop off in Notting Hill. I have an old friend there I'd like to see again".

They parted company, and Cecily walked off in the direction of Piccadilly Circus.

The place had very happy memories for her, it was here that she last saw Peter. She remembered that night in the Hungaria restaurant when he gave her his I.O.U. for a bottle of Champagne and a biscuit. The card was her pocket now. If he was at home, she would hold him to his promise.

She got off the train at Notting Hill Gate, and walked along the Bayswater Road to Clanricarde Gardens. It was a quiet little side street off the main road. All the houses were of the same, elegant Georgian-style architecture, very Peter, she thought. Number twenty-four was half-way down, on the right-hand side. The house was sub-divided into flats and an array of labelled doorbells indicated that Peter's was on the top floor. She pressed it and waited. She estimated how long it would take to walk down four-flights of stairs and added a bit. No answer. She tried again. No answer.

She started to rummage around in her handbag, looking for a pen and a piece of paper to write a message on when, a young woman walked up behind her.

"Hello, there", she said, "Do you need to get in?"

Cecily turned around. "Oh, no thank you. My friend doesn't appear to be at home. I was just going to write a note and slip it under the door".

"I know most of the people here, which flat does your friend live in?"

"The top one I think, I've never actually been here before".

"You don't mean Peter, do you?"

"Yes, that's right, Peter Ibbotson".

The young woman looked surprised. "How do you know Peter?"

"He's an old friend. We met when we both lived in Japan".

"Gosh", the woman looked even more surprised. She held out her hand, "Well, it's lovely to meet you, I've never met any of his non-army friends. My name is Joan, I'm Peter's fiancée".

Cecily gave an audible intake of breath. She stared at Joan, for what felt like a long time, but was actually a fleeting moment. She felt like she had just been punched in the stomach. She wanted to scream. She could feel the blood pumping in her ears. Was she going to feint, or vomit? In the blink of an eye, she regained her inner composure and simply said, "How nice to meet you".

Completely unaware of Cecily's true feelings, Joan asked if she would like to come in for a cup of tea. How could she refuse?

Once settled in the lounge, cup of tea in hand, Cecily asked, "How did you two meet?"

"We met at the start of the war. I was working at the Natural History Museum and Peter was a trainee officer, in charge of getting the place sand-bagged and ready for any future air-raids. He asked me out to dinner, and the rest, as they say, is history". She looked down at her cup, her face suddenly looked grave; "I'm very worried about him. He's out in the far-east, preparing for anything the Japanese might do. I normally get at least two-letters a week, but I haven't had any for weeks now".

"Where abouts in the far-east is he?"

"Somewhere around the Malaya, Singapore area, I think".

"I'm sure he will be all right".

"He wants me to go to South Africa. He keeps asking me to go there and stay with his parents. I don't want to leave England until I know he's safe. The rent on this flat is paid up until the end of March. I've got until then to make a decision about it".

Joan looked utterly heartbroken. Cecily, trying to come to terms that Peter was no longer going to be a part of her life, felt sorry for her.

"Would you mind writing to me at my aunts address, if you hear anything about Peter?"

"Yes, of course".

She sat on the bus, on her way back to Perivale and thought about Peter. The news of his engagement to Joan had come as quite a shock, but the more she thought about it, the more she realised he wasn't to blame for the way she was feeling. She told him she didn't want to go to South Africa with him and live his dream. When she met Akira, she barely even thought about him. Until of course, she learnt that Akira's parents had other plans for him. Plans that didn't include her. It was only then, she started thinking about Peter again. In the meantime, he had met a lovely girl, one who was prepared to be part of his dream, and prior to going off to fight for king and country, had proposed to her. She couldn't blame him for any of that. She just wished she could see him for one last time and tell him how much he had meant to her. I do hope he's all right, she thought.

46 - Peter's War

Peter was six and a half thousand-miles away, on the other side of the world, fighting for his life. When he had successfully completed his officer training with the Royal Engineers in August 1940, he was posted to the far-east. It was a four-month journey that took him to Sierra Leone, South Africa and India before reaching his final destination; Singapore. En route, he was transferred to the Training Battalion, Headquarters Division of the Royal Bombay Sappers and Miners. It was because of rising tensions in the region, that the British decided to strengthen its defensive positions in Malaya and the Singapore peninsula, from potential Japanese aggression.

For most of 1941, he had designed and built defensive positions in Singapore, Kuala Lumpa, Tanjong Malim and Sungai Patani. His hard work and effort had earned him a promotion to Captain, and adjutant to the Commander Royal Engineers (CRE). On the same day that the Japanese had attacked Pearl Harbor, they attacked Hong Kong and Malaya. The defences in the north of the country were no match for the Japanese onslaught, which formed a two-pronged attack, working Its way south, down the east and west coasts towards their objective; Singapore.

Peter's unit was part of the fighting withdrawal. The commander of British forces decided to get everyone back to the southern province of Johor, just north of Singapore. As British, Australin and Indian units fell back, it was the job of the engineers to blow-up the bridges and roads, and destroy anything that could be of use to the advancing Japanese army.

47 - A Trip to Bakers Street

Five days after her application to join the ATS, Cecily received a letter from the War Office, asking her to attended an interview the following day.

Wearing the smartest outfit she possessed; she made her way to Baker Street. Number sixty-four was a modern office-block with two uniformed commissionaires sitting at a desk just inside the door. One of them stood as Cecily walked in. "Good morning miss, how can I be of assistance?"

"Good morning, I have an appointment to see Brigadier Gubbins at half-past-nine". She handed him the letter she had received.

"Ah, yes, righty-oh, if you'd like to walk this way miss, I'll take you up". He turned to his colleague and said, "Just taking this young lady up to the fifth-floor, Albert".

He walked over to the lift and pushed the button. The door opened immediately. They got in. On the way up, Cecily asked, "What's the Brigadier like?"

"He's a gentleman, miss. Never heard a bad word said against him".

They got to the fifth-floor and entered one of the offices. "Good morning, Margaret. I have here a Miss Cox, for the Brigadier".

"Thank you, Fred. Hello Miss Cox, won't you take a seat, I'll see if the Brigadier is ready to see you".

Fred left and Cecily sat in one of the offered chairs.

A few moments later, Margaret returned and ushered Cecily into the Brigadier's office.

"Good morning, Miss Cox, please take a seat". The Brigadier was a tall, handsome man in his forties. He had an athletic build and reminded Cecily of a slightly older version of Errol Flynn. He was wearing a tweed suit and spoke with a soft Scottish accent. "Would you care to join me for a cup of tea?"

"Thank you, that would be lovely".

Margaret said she would get them, and left the room.

"Now then, do you mind if I call you Cecily? Miss Cox sounds so very formal. That's something we try to avoid around here".

"I don't mind at all".

On his desk, he had what looked like her application form she had filled out at King's College. "I understand from this, that you wish to join the ATS. Is your heart set on it?"

"I'm happy to do anything, I just want to do my bit, I would consider any of the services if the ATS won't have me".

"I see. That sounds like a good attitude to have. Now it says here, that you lived in Japan for twenty-years. I am particularly interested in that because I was born in Tokyo. I left when I was a wee bairn".

"Tokyo was my favourite place to visit. I went there many times with my mother and father. I have a vague memory of what it was like before the earthquake, but it's all been re-built and looks wonderful".

Margaret came in with two-cups of tea and put them on the desk and left.

The Brigadier consulted the paperwork on his desk. "So, you were born in London, went to New York, then to Japan. Your schooling was in Canada and California. Numerous trips to England over the years and you ran your own kennel business, all by the time you were twenty-five-years of age. That's some achievement. You're a very well-travelled young woman".

"Thank you. I've never really thought about it before".

"It says here that you have an older brother, what does he do?"

"He's a lawyer, in Hollywood. He became an American citizen a few years ago after he graduated from Harvard Law School".

The Brigadier sat there for a moment, stroking his chin, deep in thought. "I am particularly interested that you can speak Japanese", he said eventually. The statement hung in the air for a moment or two, and then he continued; "Now that Japan has entered the war, we need Japanese translators. You'd be surprised how few people in this country can speak it well."

"I must admit", said Cecily, "I didn't think the ATS would be particularly interested in foreign languages".

"They're not, but we are".

Cecily looked at the Brigadier in a slightly puzzled manner. "Is this not an interview for the ATS?"

"I'm afraid not. We're a fairly new outfit, recently put together by combining elements of a few specialist departments. We're called the Special Operations Executive, and I'd like you to join us".

Cecily sat there for a moment. "What is it you would want me to do?"

"Well, first of all, we would want to send you on some training courses to see how resourceful you are, see if your capable of working under pressure. You'd need to learn morse code of course, and how to defend yourself. Have you ever fired a gun?"

Cecily's eyes widened, "Er, yes. I've done a bit of shooting with my brother in Canada and America. Shotguns, rifles and pistols". Am I right in thinking, this is not going to be an office job?"

The Brigadier smiled. "Most definitely not an office job. We can't make you do it of course, it will be completely voluntary. If you'd rather be a chauffeur to a senior officer, or work the searchlight on an anti-aircraft battery, I will fully understand. The training in itself will be tough going, you may not even make it through, in which case we'll send you to the ATS, but I would very much like you to give it a go".

"Will I be in uniform?"

"Yes. On the outside, you will look like any other ATS officer, but in reality, you'll be working for us. You'd have to keep that bit secret of course. What we do is classified, but it is sanctioned from the man at the top, Mr. Churchill".

"Crikey. I saw him a few weeks ago in Ottawa. He gave such a wonderful speech; I think it was that which made me decide to come over here and do my bit".

"I wouldn't be asking if I didn't think you had it in you. We really need women like you in this service, women with experience of the world and with skills like yours. What do you say?"

"You are a very persuasive man, sir. Yes, I'll do it. I shall probably regret it if I don't".

"That's the ticket". He pressed a button on his desk which summoned Margaret to his office. "Miss Cox had agreed to join our merry band of Baker Street irregulars". He looked at Cecily, "If you would like to go with Margaret, she'll get you enrolled on the next ATS intake. Don't tell anyone you're working for us. As far as anyone else is concerned, you're just one of the regular girls. When you've passed your basic training with them, we'll put you on our more specialised courses, and see how you fare. He stood up and shook her hand. "Thank you, and good luck".

48 - Peter Saves the Day

Captain Ibbotson needed all the luck he could get. The British forces were doing the best they could with their fighting withdrawal. The Japanese had air superiority and could bomb anywhere they wanted to. The tactical retreat could become a rout at any moment.

On the outskirts of Ipoh, one-hundred-miles north of Kuala Lumpur, his unit had laid the demolition charges to bring down the bridge over the Kinta River. A General, his ADC, Peter and his Colonel were waiting on the safe, south-side of the bridge for the rear-guard to come across.

As they stood there waiting, the sound of motorcycles could be heard in the distance. The Colonel, looking through his binoculars said, "Here they come now sir, our two motorcyclists, the main column won't be far behind".

"Good", said the General, "As soon as they're all over, pull the plug on that bridge and head for KL. That should slow them down for a few hours at least".

"Yessir".

The officers stood around chatting as the motorcyclists approached. Peter, who had his back to the road, turned as they drew level.

"Christ", he shouted, "They're Japs".

Two Japanese soldiers on British motorcycles, armed with British Tommy guns, trundled past. Peter was the first to get out his revolver. He opened fire, and hit the nearest one, knocking him off the bike. The second one managed to get off his bike and jump down the bank at the side of the road. The Colonel opened fire with his machine gun and brought down the soldier.

While this was going on, the general and his ADC, ran down to the bridge and told the sappers to blow it.

There was an almighty bang, and within a few seconds, large chunks of concrete came raining down on their heads. Once the dust had settled, Perter, the Colonel and a handful of the infantry, started picking off Japanese soldiers on the other side of the bridge from their more elevated position.

49 - Cecily Starts Basic Training

Cecily made her way to Stoughton Barracks on the north side of Guildford in Surrey. It was the home of the Queen's Royal Regiment, but now that they were stationed abroad, the facilities were being used to train the ATS. By lunchtime, everyone who was expected, had arrived. After lunch, which consisted of potato soup and a wedge of bread, they were taken to the uniform stores and issued with their kit. It comprised of; Jacket and skirt, khaki shirts, underwear, cap, brown shoes and a raincoat. Depending on what role they would do after training, other items such as; overalls, wet weather gear and Wellington boots, would be issued at a later date.

For the first time since leaving school, Cecily was surrounded by women of a similar age. They were all there for the same reason, and from the start, there was a great sense of camaraderie. All the women were single, and for some, this was their first time away from home. A few were like Cecily and had been to boarding school, but none seemed to have had the truly international life she had lived. They were all here to learn how to salute, march, identify ranks of all military personnel, and how to walk, talk and sleep like a soldier. Some of it was going to fun, some of it boring, some of it hard, but they would all be doing it together. After a dinner of beef stew and potatoes, they went to their bunks. It really was like being back at an all-girls boarding school.

50 - Fortress Singapore

The sound of distant artillery was replaced by the sound of bagpipes. The Pipe-Major led the remnants of the Argyll & Sutherland Highlanders crossed the Johor Causeway. The Australian and Indian troops had already crossed, these were the last.

Peter found the whole spectacle quite moving. It never ceased to amaze him how the sound of the pipes could make one feel melancholy, yet uplifted at the same time. Once they were across, his job was to sever the link between the island of Singapore and the mainland of Malaya. It would become an island fortress that would have to be held at all costs, until reinforcements could arrive. These were truly dark days indeed.

Colonel Stewart and his ADC were the last across. Once clear, Peter received the signal to detonate the charges. The first took out the swinging bridge, the second blew a seventy-yard hole in the causeway, taking out the railway lines, road and all the water pipes. The Singapore peninsula was once again how nature intended; an island. With their backs to the sea, and thirty-five-thousand Japanese troops in front of them, they had to defend an area half the size of London. It was time to dig in, for one last stand.

51 - Cecily Moves On

One-week into her basic training course, Cecily was sent for by the Senior Commander. She couldn't think what she had done wrong. On all the other occasions recruits had been brought before the commander, it was because of some infraction of the rules, such as; wearing make-up, turning up late on parade or insolence towards a member of the staff.

She was marched into the office, saluted and stood to attention.

"At ease", said the commander, still looking down at the paperwork on her desk. "This is very irregular", she finally looked up at Cecily. "You've completed one-week of basic training, and already I have received your joining instructions for Special Operator Training. It's most irregular".

Outside, Cecily kept a straight face, but inside, she had a big grin on her face. She didn't want to leave her new found friends, they were all good fun, but she was excited and surprised about the idea of starting her 'other 'training" so soon.

"All the paperwork is in order, and has been signed off by a Brigadier. There is nothing I can do about it". The commander handed her a sheaf of papers. "These are your joining instructions and a travel warrant to Trowbridge in Wiltshire, you leave immediately. Go and pack your things and report to the guard house. A car will take you to the station. This is most irregular. Dismissed".

"Thank you, ma'am".

Cecily practically skipped back to her hut. Within thirty-minutes, she had packed and said a fond farewell to all the others she shared the accommodation with. The commander's car was waiting for her, driven by one of the instructors. Two train rides later, she was in Trowbridge.

There was no wasting time. The next morning, she would be sitting in a classroom with twenty-nine other ATS girls, learning morse code.

52 - Peter Gets a Promotion

"Peter".

"Yes sir?"

"I've had my marching orders. They want me to return to India and take over as the new commandant".

"Congratulations, sir".

"Lord knows how or if, I'm going to get out of this place alive".

"I'll be sorry to see you go, Colonel. Which way will you go?"

"I think the only way open to us now is; a boat to Sumatra, then overland to the west-coast and hopefully find a ship going towards India".

"As far as I know, the Dutch still have hold of Sumatra".

"Something tells me it's not going to be an easy ride".

"Good luck, sir".

"I'm appointing you the new CRE, you're Lieutenant-Colonel Ibbotson now. Just think what you'll be able to do with all that extra money".

"Thank you, sir", said Peter with a wry smile. "I hope I can live long enough to spend it".

The endless artillery barrages, and the aerial bombing by the Japanese air force, chipped away at the rock that was Singapore. Three of the five, south-facing fifteen-inch guns protecting the naval base from attack by sea, had been turned inwards towards the advancing Japanese army coming from the north. The armour-piercing shells that were supposed to be fired at ships, had little effect on advancing infantry.

The causeway had been crossed and the Japanese were now working their way to the city itself. The Royal Engineers had destroyed everything that may be of use to the enemy; fuel storage tanks, the docks, transport and communications infrastructure. Peter's men were now just filling the gaps in the line. Civilian and military casualties were mounting, and the fresh water supply was nearly exhausted. On Valentine's Day, the Alexandra Military Hospital, to the west of the city, had fallen to the Japanese. A massacre took place, in which three-hundred doctors, nurses, orderlies and patients were murdered. The unthinkable was about to happen.

53 - Cecily Gets the News

All of the other girls in Cecily's class, had done their full four-week basic course at various barracks up and down the country. She was the only one from Stoughton. Once again, she found herself among a group of women that had never left the country before, not even for a holiday. She hadn't realised that her life had been so different. Everyone she knew at school in Canada, America and her friends and acquaintances in Japan, had all lived the same life as she had. They were a jolly lot, and Cecily could see she was going to have fun with them.

Walking to the canteen that first morning was a bit of an ordeal. The cold and wet February weather had turned the place into a mud-bath. One girl had slipped and landed on her back-side, rather like Charlie Chaplin, much to the amusement of the others, and had to return to the accommodation hut to change her skirt and get cleaned up. After a helping of uninspiring porridge, they were just about to leave for the training hut, when the Senior Commander entered. Everyone got up and stood to attention.

"Sit down please, ladies".

Cecily was positioned quite close to her. She could see that the woman looked pale and her eyes bloodshot, the unmistakeable look of someone who had been crying, and was now putting on a brave face. Her voice shook as she spoke; "I have some bad news for you. I wanted to tell you all now, while you are all together, rather than have you finding it out from the rumours or gossip that is certainly going to go around the camp as the news spreads". She lifted up the newspaper she had was holding. It was a copy of that mornings Daily Mirror. "Singapore has fallen", she said in a loud voice.

There were gasps and cries all around. Cecily instantly thought of Peter.

When the hubbub subsided, she continued; "This has come as a great shock to us all. I know that some of you may well have friends or relations in the far-east who will be affected by this disaster. We must not let it weaken our resolve. It isn't our first defeat, I expect it won't be our last, but we must use this moment to remind ourselves, why we are here. Only by pulling together and working hard, will we beat our enemies and create a lasting peace". She got a cheer and an energetic round of applause. She put the newspaper down on the table in front of her and walked out.

They crowded around the newspaper. The headline read; *'Singapore Lost: Churchill Warning – I speak to you all under the shadow of a heavy and far-reaching military defeat. It is a British and Imperial defeat. Singapore has fallen. All the Malay Peninsular has been overrun'*.

54 - Peter's Escape

Peter stood in his office at the barracks. He had mustered all the Royal Engineers officers left under his command.

"Gentlemen, the GOC has signed the surrender. In half an hour, the fighting will stop, and we lay down our arms and become prisoners of war". There was a general murmur of disapproval from the assembled officers.

"However, I have far better things to do. It is the duty of all officers, not to become prisoners, or if they do so, attempt to escape where possible". This statement was met with approval from some of the officers.

I intend to have a shot for Sumatra. If anyone would like to join me, they will be most welcomed".

Conversations broke out between the men. The few Indian officers that were present said that they would stay and take their chances with the Japanese. One of the British officers asked; "What about the two wounded officers we have. sir?"

"We can't possibly take them with us", said Peter. "Ronnie Owen had a bullet through his shoulder and Scudamore's leg is pretty bad. They will have to stay in the sick bay".

"Right you are. Sir. None of us feel temperamentally suited to becoming a POW, especially a Japanese one. So, we're with you".

Shortly before nine-o'clock in the evening, Peter, and eight other officers got into the CRE's car and a truck. As they drove out of the back gates of the barracks, the Japanese were coming in through the front.

They headed south in the dark until they came to one of the canals that led to the coast. Abandoning and scuttling the two vehicles, they went in search of a boat that had a serviceable engine. Unfortunately, a few days before, their own engineers had made a very good job in decommissioning the engines on all the boats it could find, so as not to be of use to the Japanese. After a search lasting nearly two-hours, they re-grouped around Peter. "That's just our bloody luck, isn't it? We can't afford to waste any more time. We're going to have to take one of the sailing junks. Anyone got any experience of sailing?"

Nobody had.

Well, let's just get on and cast-off and see what happens. It can't be that difficult".

They got onboard and cast off. One of the junior officers found an empty bottle on the main deck, and proceeded to smash it on the side of the junk. "I name this ship, the Singapore Bitch, God help all those that sail in her". A ripple of laughter went around the boat.

"All right you clowns", said Peter, "It's time to get serious. We're drifting in the right direction, so keep an eye out for any obstructions in the water".

The junk proved almost impossible to control. For much of the journey to the coast, the ship went sideways along the canal, bouncing off other junks, boats and Sampans.

By one-o'clock in the morning, they had reached the Singapore strait and was a mile south of the city. Fumbling around in the almost pitch-black, they managed to raise the main sail half-way, before it became stuck and unmoveable in any direction. Their only means of navigation was with an army-issue pocket compass and a map, torn from a magazine in the barracks. They were going to have to navigate their way around the plethora of tiny Indonesian islands that lay south of the Singapore coast and east of Sumatra.

Just before dawn, a smaller boat was seen ahead of them, travelling in the same direction. It had onboard, an assortment of eleven British squaddies and sailors, who'd had the same idea of escape. As the Singapore Bitch was the larger vessel, Peter invited them to abandon their crowded fishing boat and join them.

One of the sailors approached Peter. He saluted and said, "Begging your pardon, sir, but you do realise that there are a lot sea-mines in these straits?"

"What?" gasped Peter.

"Yes, sir. The navy put out a load of mines to stop the Japs attacking from the south".

"Oh, great. Is there anything we can do about it?"

"Well, sir, these junks don't have a keel, so as long as we don't take on any cargo, and the ship sits high in the water, we'll just skip across above them. I hope".

"So do I", said Peter, "So do I".

As the sun came up, Peter estimated that they were about eight-miles from Singapore. Not bad, he thought, but still too close for comfort. Rather than finding a place to drop-anchor and wait for nightfall, he decided to press on. Stripping down to his khaki underpants, and making some sort of turban out of his shirt, he ordered everyone else on the ship below deck. It wasn't long before the occasional Japanese aircraft flew overhead. On one occasion, an Aichi dive-bomber swooped down low to have a good look at the ship. Peter waved. He will blow us out of the water if he doesn't like the look of us, he thought. The plane circled and came back the other way. This time, the pilot and the navigator waved back and disappeared back towards Singapore.

Sailing quite close to one of the islands, they came across a Malayan fisherman in a small boat. He was surprised to see a junk being sailed by an Englishman in his underpants. The fisherman spoke good English, and told them that he too was heading for Sumatra, to get away from the Japanese. On the promise that he could have the junk once they got there, Peter asked him to join them. He wasted no time in tying his fishing boat to the junk and climbing onboard. He took over the steering of the ship, and Peter was able to get out of the sun and join the others below deck. His arms, legs and back were quite burnt.

At midday, they were heading south-west between two small islands, when the boat started lunging from side to side in a most dramatic fashion. Everything that was not fastened down was being tossed about. They were caught in a rip-tide. Everyone was holding onto the rudder for dear life. There were rocks all around them, onto which they could be dashed with devastating effect. It was only the skill of the Malayan fisherman that saved the day. While the others were wrestling with the giant rudder, he managed to adjust the sail plan and balance the ship and avert catastrophe.

As the sun began to descend, they found a beautiful lagoon in which to drop anchor. By Peter's reckoning, they were thirty-five miles from Singapore and a third of the way to Sumatra.

Before it was dark, they had time to have a swim, catch some fish and pick coconuts. It was hard to imagine that they could be anywhere near a war-zone. The crystal-clear water lapped onto the silvery sand of the palm-fringed beach. It was heaven. Peter thought that if his Joan were with him, they'd happily stay there for the rest of their lives.

They sat on the beach and ate their grilled fish, washed down with fresh coconut milk. Just twenty-four hours ago, they were fighting for their very existence.

They had all slept on the beach, and had the best nights sleep for months. As the sun came up, Peter nearly started a mutiny, when he told everyone to wash their clothes and have a shave. After a fair amount of moaning and groaning, they got on with it, and afterwards, everybody looked and felt a lot better for it.

They set off at eight-thirty, but within two-hours, the wind had completely disappeared, and they spent the next four-hours barely moving at all. It was a worrying time for them as they felt completely exposed, like sitting ducks. There was nothing to do until the wind picked up. When it did, the Singapore Bitch sprang into action and rocketed along at about eight-knots.

As the light began to fade, they dropped anchor in a cove by a rocky island. It was considered too dangerous to negotiate these islands in the dark. They would spend the night on the ship as the sea was calm and would be far more comfortable than sleeping on rocky shore.

At about midnight, the wind picked up quite dramatically, and the ship started to drag its anchor. They were heading straight towards the rocks. Battered by waves that seem to come from nowhere, they were only yards away from disaster. If the ship went down there, they would be marooned on a tiny lump of rock with no chance whatsoever of going anywhere, except possibly a Japanese prisoner of war camp. There was nothing they could do.

The squall lasted for hours. Some said prayers as the waves crashed over the ship, others just sat in silence, holding on for dear life. The anchor held, the wind dropped, and by daybreak they were able to raise the main sail and set a course for Sumatra.

By midday, things were looking good and spirits were high; they had reached the east-coast of Sumatra. Heading north along the coast, they were looking for the Indragiri River. Soon, a large estuary was spotted, and they turned to port and sailed along the calmer waters of the river. A few miles upstream, they came to a small village, and after making enquiries, discovered that they were not on the Indragiri River but the Kampar River. They were thirty-miles further north than they thought they were. The locals were very hospitable and offered to take them further upstream in their more manageable sampans, where they could trek across country for about forty-miles to the town of Tembilahan, where the Dutch army were stationed.

The locals invited them to stay for dinner, which was graciously accepted. A banquet of fish curry, fresh fruit and coffee was had, along with a good night's sleep.

In the morning, Peter said goodbye to the Malayan fisherman and thanked him for his help over the last few days. It was fair to say that they probably wouldn't have made it without him. His plan, was to take his new ship further up the coast and sail across to Thailand, where he had family.

They all said goodbye to the Singapore Bitch and hoped they would never see it again.

From nowhere, a flotilla of sampans appeared, to take them upstream where they could pick up the track to the Indragiri River.

With two or three passengers per sampan, they set off on the fifteen-mile journey. In expert hands, the boats were quick and manoeuvrable, and they were soon there.

The 'good path' that they had been told about, turned out to be a bit of a misnomer. It turned out to be a hard slog through a mixture of dense jungle, mosquito infested swamp and ten-inches of mud. Barely any of it could be described as good. Peter was concerned at picking up another bout of malaria. He'd had the pleasure of that when he was stationed in Sungai Petani, this time last year. They reached a small village just as it was getting dark. Much to their amazement, the local store sold bottles of English beer. They bought every bottle of Bass beer in the place. It had never tasted so good.

The village was by a creek that led to the Indragiri River, so before they found somewhere to sleep for the night, they put the word out among the locals, that they wanted to go to Tembilahan by sampan in the morning. At first light, they awoke to find another flotilla of sampans ready to take them on the next leg of their journey. They left at sunrise, for a twenty-four-hour journey south through the almost un-navigable waterways of Indragiri Hilir.

The morning mist cleared, and the sun came out. It would soon become humid and sticky, but thanks to the movement of the boat creating a soft breeze, it would be bearable. The temperature in Sumatra was constant throughout the year, with only the amount of rainfall making any real difference. February was usually the dryest month of the year, with November and December being the wettest. Thank God he wasn't doing this in the monsoon season, thought Peter, as he sat in the shade of the sampan's canopy
Gentle, tree covered hills, no more than eighty-feet high, undulated down to the water's edge. The impenetrable, thick, lush, green vegetation would occasionally open up into flat areas of cultivated coconut groves. There was a surprising number of people about. Working the land, fishing, transporting goods, it was a scene that was being carried out on similar waterways, all over the world. It must have looked very strange to the locals, seeing eight sampans travelling in convoy, filled with pale skinned Europeans. Some just stood and stared, others shouted out to the rowers. Peter had learnt some Malay on the

ship from India, but he had no idea what dialect these people were speaking. Sitting in front of him was James Ralph, a fellow RE officer. "I bet they don't even know there's a war on".

"They soon will", replied Peter, "When Japanese gunboats start patrolling these rivers".

"I can't imagine the Dutch being able to put up much of a fight".

"Judging by the way the Japs went through Malaya, I don't think there is any chance of holding this island. They've already started air-raids in the south".

Every three or four hours, the sampan rowers would stop by a jetty for a drink, something to eat and a rest. The food and water were in plentiful supply, which they shared out to all their passengers. The strength and stamina of these rowers was something to be marvelled at. Some of them looked quite old. They were all skinny and appeared to have no muscles. Yet, they could row for hours without breaking into a sweat. On a couple of occasions, Peter and a few of the others tried the rowing. After a couple of hours, they were spent and had to lie down in the shade and drink copious amounts of water.

In the early hours of the following morning, they reached their destination; Tembilahan.

The rowers of the sampans, were very reluctant to accept any money from their passengers. They had rowed for over twenty-hours, and supplied them with all the food and water they needed. They did not expect anything in return. Eventually, they accepted what was being offered and said their farewells. Peter and his men were taken care of by the Dutch military and civilian authorities. They were pleased to hear that a number of stragglers had made it out of Singapore thus far. Regular truck convoys would be able to take them the two-hundred and fifty-miles to Padang on the west-coast, from where ships were still able to make the crossing to Ceylon.

They headed off the next day. The trucks moved slowly across the hilly terrain. Peter sat up front with two Dutch soldiers. He said it was 'privilege of rank' as all the others in the group complained when they were tossed around in the back. They stopped off at regular intervals, to let everyone stretch their legs and take on some water. Trying to drink water from a canteen while the truck was moving, usually ended with more water down their shirt than in their mouth. The journey went smoothly without incident, and they arrived at a small town called Air Molek, just as the sun went down. A camp fire was lit, rations issued, and another night's sleep under the stars.

This was the pattern for the next three nights until they arrived at a large coal-mining town called Sawah Lunto. The place was very quiet. People were moving out and dispersing into the surrounding villages. Japanese reconnaissance planes had been seen in the area, and it was highly likely that the coal mines would be a target when the Japanese got a foothold on the island. They spent the night in the vacated miner's cottages.

Padang was reached on the first of March. The city was in chaos. Thousands of people had congregated in the port area, trying to find passage on any ship that was leaving. Peter managed to find the officer in charge of the evacuation, and was told that an Australian warship would be taking military personnel to Colombo in Ceylon, later in the day. By midnight, after a short delay, His Majesty's Australian Ship – Hobart. left Padang with over five-hundred evacuees on board.

Four-days later it arrived in Colombo. They were safe. Three-days after that, Peter arrived in Bombay and headed to the regimental HQ in Kirkee. On the twenty-eighth of March, Sumatra fell to the Japanese.

55 - Cecily's First Mission

After three-months of intensive training, Cecily was dreaming in Morse code. What was so alien to begin with, was now part of her soul. She'd learnt the basics quite quickly but then they'd added the Wabun, Kana, Nigory and Nan Nigory elements into the course, and the sleepless nights began. And then one day, just as the instructors said it would, it all fell into place. It was, without doubt, the most gruelling time of her life. When the course had finished, she was summoned back to Baker Street to see the Brigadier.

Margaret Jackson, welcomed Cecily like an old friend when she entered the office. "Come straight through," she said "He's ready to see you".
Cecily picked up on the slight sense of urgency in the atmosphere.
"Good morning, Cecily. How the devil are you?" The Brigadier had stood up when she entered, and now he ushered her into a chair. "Two teas and some of those biscuits, if there are any left, please Margaret".
Margaret left the room and shut the door.
"How are things?" he asked in a fatherly way.
"Fine, now I've got Morse code drilled into me".
"I hear you were the star pupil when it came to learning the Japanese code".

"I wouldn't say that", she said modestly. "Although, it was a definite advantage knowing the language beforehand. I just hope I will be able to put it all to good use. I'd hate to think it was all done in vain".

"That's the spirit".

Margaret came in with two cups of tea and two small biscuits, and left again.

"I was going to send you on a couple of practical courses. Weapons handling, self-defence, that sort of thing. But they'll have to wait until later. We're going to need you in the field as soon as possible. You've heard about the situation in the far-east, I take it?"

"Yes". Cecily stared down at the tea cup she was holding. There was a momentary flash of sorrow across her face. "I had a friend who was stationed in Singapore. I have no idea what happened to him".

"The Japs are going through Burma like a dose of salts. If it falls, India and Ceylon will be next. That's why we need you over there".

"To do what, exactly?"

The navy has a listening station in Kandy. It's fine for tuning in to all the transmissions in the Indian Ocean, but we need something a bit more focused, a bit near the front line".

"Oh, I see".

"We have covert units operating behind enemy lines. A bit of sabotage and disruption to keep the Japs busy, that sort of thing. Your role will to be to monitor the enemy frequencies, and notify our units if they attract any unwanted attention".

"I assume that I won't be behind enemy lines myself?"

"No. To be honest, this type of role is normally carried out by one of the men in the covert units, but we're very short on Japanese speakers. If we had time on our side, we would have trained you up to go into Malaya to recruit and train local resistant groups".

"When do I go?"

"Tomorrow. You need to get up to Liverpool. There's a ship sailing as part of a convoy. There will be a flock of Wrens on board, going to Ceylon. You can attach yourself to them. If anyone asks, you're going to Army HQ to be a telegraphist. Margaret will give you a travel warrant and the usual documents. Keep up the good work, and good luck".

"Thank you, sir. From what I've heard about the Japanese, I am going to need it".

The ship left Liverpool late afternoon, The convoy formed up at Orsay, off the Argyll coast, and headed south to its first port of call; Freetown.

Cecily was one of a dozen young women, all heading for Ceylon. They were all Wrens, of a similar age, and had all recently finished their Morse code training. This was their first posting. For many, it was their first time abroad. Cecily had travelled around the globe on ships many times, but this was going to be a completely different experience. The captain had instructed them not to walk around the ship, or to fraternise with any of the ratings. They were to keep themselves to themselves, and out of sight. One of the ships junior officers was appointed liaison should they require anything. Meals would be served to them in their quarters, after the rest of the crew had finished and returned to their duties.

"This is going to be a bundle of laughs", said one of the girls after he'd left. "This journey is going to take weeks. We'll be pulling each other's hair out by the end of it".

The twelve girls occupied a space that four officers would normally be assigned to. It was certainly not like anything Cecily had ever travelled on. They spent their time reading, playing cards, practising their Morse code, and endless lifeboat drills, should they be attacked. After six-days at sea, they made it to Freetown, on the West African coast. They were going to be there for twenty-four-hours, and were advised not to leave the ship. They could however, go up on deck and sit in the sun, while it lasted.

Cecily thought the Wrens uniform was much more attractive than the ATS one she had to wear, especially in the sun. Her khaki shirts looked positively drab next to the other girl's white shirts. Their tunics and skirts looked better tailored as well. I suppose, where I'm going, khaki will be the better option in the long run, she thought.

After further stops in Durban and Mombasa, where they changed ship, they arrived in Colombo, after four-weeks at sea. It took a concerted effort to walk on dry land again. The girls laughed hysterically as they veered off course and bumped into things. By the time they got through customs and the various checkpoints and out of the dockyard, they had regained their land legs. Cecily said farewell to her travelling companions, feeling sad that she was unlikely to see any of them again. While they all went off to their new quarters in a Royal Navy truck, Cecily had to wait for a car to come and pick her up from army HQ. Fortunately, they seemed to know roughly what time she was due to arrive, so the wait for the car wasn't a long one. The sixty-mile drive to Kandy wasn't a particularly pleasurable one, but the driver was good company, and told her all she needed to know about Ceylon.

On arrival at HQ, she was shown to a small office. The sign of the door read; India Mission. A fresh-faced man in his early forties, sat behind a desk in the middle of the room. He wore a beige linen suit and a white shirt with open collar and a silk cravat. He looked every inch a businessman rather than a military man. In a soft Scottish accent he said,

"Hello my dear, won't you take a seat? You must be exhausted after that tedious journey".

Cecily sat down.

"My name is Colin Mackenzie. Excuse me for not getting up". From somewhere under the table came the sound dull metal thud as he tapped his left leg. "Gammy leg, lost it during the last war. Slows me down a bit, but my darling wife is never far behind. She keeps me on track".

He reminded Cecily of the gentlemen that would tell her war stories when she was at her father's yacht club in Kobe. Colin wasn't the sort to brag about anything, he was underplaying it. There was a glint in his eye that gave her the impression, that he was no fool.

"As you can see, I'm not military, but a civilian. I was asked to set up an Indian mission for our friends in Baker Street. I started off in India, but for my sins, I am now here".

An orderly brough in some tea and sandwiches. Cecily's eyes lit up. She had hardly eaten anything all day. When they had finished their tea, Colin suggested that she went off to the women's quarters and get some rest for a couple of days. She would need to get acclimatised and swap her hot, khaki drill uniform for some of the cooler jungle green dress.

"Come back and see me in a couple of days, and we'll discuss what happens next".

"Thank you. Sir". She was about to salute, when he said;

"Don't worry about any of that nonsense. Call me Colin, or Mr. Mackenzie, whichever you prefer, and definitely no saluting, especially outside of the office".

Once at the accommodation block, the first thing she wanted to do was have a shower and wash her clothes. It was almost impossible to stay dry in this heat. Afterwards, she went to the common room and found a couple of ATS girls lounging around, listening to the gramophone. Cecily introduced herself, and asked, "What does one do for entertainment around here?"

"Well," said the youngest, "It all depends on how much time off you have. Anything less than twenty-four-hours, then you may as well just stay here".

"If I have longer?"

There's a proper R and R camp over at Diyatalawa. It's sixty-miles away, so you'll need to stay the night. There are sports you can play, and even a theatre. And of course, lots of men".

"That's all she thinks about", said the other girl, playfully throwing a cushion at her".

"I'm young free and single, and we all might be killed tomorrow, so why not have fun now?"

"Do you have a fella, Cecily?"

"No. The war messed up two relationships I was having. I've sort of given up for the time being".

"Poor thing, we'll look after you".

Cecily found the uniform stores and was issued with her tropical uniform. It wasn't as well tailored as her khaki one, but it was a lighter material and a looser fit which would be ideal in this climate. The next day, she went and explored Kandy. She'd never seen so many different uniforms. Apart from all the British ones, there was; French, Dutch, Indian, Australian, it was all very cosmopolitan.

The following day, she reported to Colin Mackenzie. "Good morning, Cecily. I trust you are suitably refreshed?"

"Yes. Thank you, I feel almost human again".

"Good show". He opened a file on his desk "I have an assignment for you". He looked her straight in the eye. She could see the intensity of that glint now. It was almost mesmerising. "The person I had in mind originally for this job has broken his leg on a parachute jump. We can't afford to wait two-months until he's fit again, time is of the essence. Apart from the combat side of things, you have all the skills we're looking for. Fluent in Japanese, and a good signaller".

"I'm not sure I could I could parachute". Cecily started to wonder, what on earth she was getting involved in.

"That's all right, we plan to drop you off by submarine".

"Submarine?" Cecily raised an eyebrow, fear and excitement showing in her eyes.

"We want you to go to the Anderman Islands, and set up a forward observation post. You'll be our eyes and ears over there. Just report back whatever is going on. There's a strong possibility that the Japanese will use the islands to launch an attack on Ceylon or India. Of course, I can't make you go. It will have to be a voluntary decision". There was a long pause. "Will you do it?"

Cecily thought for a moment and then smiled at him; "I have been on every sea vessel imaginable, but never a submarine. I suppose there is a first time for everything".

"That's the spirit. Now, you will need to talk to Major McCarthy. He got off the island just as the Japs took it. He was a policeman on the island for many years and has the best up-to-date knowledge about the place, and contacts. Go and see him, and I'll arrange a first-class ticket on the next available sub".

Major McCarthy was found in the map-room. He sat down with Cecily and explained the lie of the land and gave her more details about the mission. "It's a sort of a feasibility study really". He offered her a cigarette, which she declined, and lit one for himself. "I'm currently planning a sizeable mission to the Anderman's, but before we can commit man-power and resources to it, we have to know exactly what's going on over there. You'll be with three of my best men from the Sikh Regiment. Once they've set up base camp, they will go off in search of some old friends on the island that are sympathetic to our cause. Your job will be to monitor the enemies signal traffic, and report back to us anything you deem useful. My men will also gather intelligence for you to send back. Three-weeks should do it, and then you'll be extracted. In an ideal world, you would have had months of training, but it just can't be done. Your knowledge of Japanese is your greatest asset. Just do what my men tell you to do, and it will be a walk in the park. Oh, bye-the-way, have you ever rowed a kayak?"

Because the answer to that question was; no, Cecilly spent the rest of the day on Kandy Lake with a soldier from the Indian Army, practising getting in and out of a two-man Foldboat, and rowing up and down the lake.

The following morning, Cecily met her new travelling companions; Jemadar Kohli, who was the OIC, and two Naiks; Dhaliwal and Mahal. They spent an hour checking their equipment, and loaded it into a truck. By late afternoon, they had reached the docks in Colombo, where the Royal Netherlands Navy had a submarine moored.

Lieutenant-Commander De Vries of the Dutch Navy introduced himself, and ran through the safety procedure and the things they could and couldn't do on his boat. Basically, sit there, be quiet and don't touch anything. He advised them that they would be leaving as it got dark, and the journey to the Anderman Islands would take four-days. Their equipment was loaded, and they got onboard.

There were no first-class suites here. The space available to her was no bigger than a coffin. A poor choice of words, thought Cecily as the thought ran through her mind. It was hard to imagine that anyone could last the day in a space like this, let alone for weeks, even months at a time. Trying to imagine what it would be like at battle-stations, was too much for her to contemplate.

56 - Andaman Islands

Much of the journey across the Bay of Bengal was on the surface. Only when un-identified ships or aircraft showed up on the radar, and when they reached the drop-off point, did they submerge. Cecily was amazed at how close to the coast the submarine could get. It would have been a short swim for anyone, so long as they weren't carrying a wireless set with extra batteries. After a considerable amount of time, studying the shore-line through the periscope, De Vries gave the command to surface. Within a few minutes, the two Foldboats had been assembled and loaded with their equipment and supplies. The only light to work with was the light of the moon. The water rippled with a silvery glow as they paddled silently, skirting the rocks, towards the shore. Cecily turned back to look behind her. The submarine was gone. It had left as silently as it had arrived.

When they reached the shore, they dragged the boats into the jungle, completely out of sight of any foot patrols or passing boats. Once unloaded, they were dismantled and hid. They would be needing them again in three-week's time for the exfiltration. Now, they would have to wait for first-light before they could head off to look for a suitable place to build a base-camp.

They had landed on the west-coast of the island, about twenty-miles north of the capital; Port Blair. Not long after day-break, they found a suitable spot on a piece of high ground with a fresh-water stream running near-by. A couple of bashas were set up on string-lines tied to trees, and Cecily's home for the next three-weeks was ready. She set up the communication equipment and sent a test message, which was received and understood.

Jemadar Kohli, and his subordinates would now move on to a village about ten-miles away called Ferrarganj, where they hoped to find Major McCarthy's contact. From there, Kohli and Dhaliwal would press on to the Port Blair area to gather intelligence, and recruit more sympathisers to the allied cause. Mahal would act as a go-between, to ferry the gathered intelligence back to base-camp for onward transmission.

Cecily's first night at the camp was eerie. She was completely on her own, with nothing but the sounds of insects and the occasional grunts of foraging wild pigs. Her days were spent monitoring the Japanese frequencies. There were naval vessels in the harbour at Port Blair, and a squadron of eighteen flying-boats. The garrison on the island amounted to six-hundred men. The Japanese were very formal in their transmissions, and correct procedure was followed at all times. It was very easy to follow and understand, if a little boring. Cecily sat there one morning during a quiet moment and thought about her current situation. Look at me, I'm sitting here, in a jungle, looking like the Wild Man of Borneo. Surrounded by the Japanese, nearly a thousand miles from anywhere I'd consider safe, and I'm actually enjoying it. I'm doing something worthwhile. Not a single member of my family knows where I am. They probably think I'm in a typing-pool somewhere in London.

She heard the snap of a twig behind her. It made her jump. She swung round, and standing behind her, was Mahal. He stood there with a large grin on his face. He'd snapped the twig deliberately. "Jesus", cried Cecily. Her heart felt as if it was in the back of her throat. "You frightened the life out of me, Mahal".

"I am sorry to scare you, ma'am, it is my training, everything has to be silent".

"Well, you're very good at it, I had no idea you were there".

"Thank you, I do my best. I have some intelligence for you from Jemadar Kohli. He says he would like it sent immediately. It is already coded".

While Cecily transmitted the message, Mahal filled his canteen at the stream and disappeared back into the jungle, saying he would return in another few days.

After a week, Cecily was well into the routine of it all. The naval vessels would practice drills at regular intervals, and the flying boats would go on reconnaissance missions over the Bay of Bengal, the Andaman Sea and the Malacca Straits. The garrison seemed to do little except raid villages and round up suspected spies and put them into the Cellular Jail – the large prison in Port Blair built by the British to house political prisoners.

The next time Mahal came back to the camp, a few days later, she heard him a mile off. She didn't think for one moment that her ears were getting more accustomed to the sounds of the jungle, but more likely, it was Mahal treading heavily so she could hear him coming. Once again, with more messages to send, he stayed for a few minutes, before setting off again. Quite remarkable, she thought, how he just keeps going. He was just skin and bone, and carried a sizable backpack and a machine gun all day, without so much as a bead of sweat on his brow.

57 - In the Bag

Every few days, she went down towards the coast to check the Foldboats were still in their hiding place. She would wash and carry out her ablutions in the sea, careful to leave no trace of her activities behind.

The best part of a week had gone by before she heard the heavy footsteps of Mahal approaching. When he appeared, she could see something was wrong, terribly wrong.

He stood in the clearing of the camp. His head hung down but it was clear that he'd had a beating of some kind. His clothes were in ruin, bloodstained and torn. His hands were tied behind his back. She was standing about twenty-yards from him when a shot rang out. His body arched backwards violently and he fell heavily to the ground. Standing ten-yards behind him was a Japanese officer with a pistol, and a number of infantry soldiers. Cecily fell to her knees and put her hands over her head. Half in terror and half to make herself a smaller target should the bullets begin to fly. Over the sound of a thousand birds taking flight, came the sound of footsteps towards her. She looked up. The officer stood over her and pointed his pistol at her head. She stared into his cold, soul-less brown eyes. There was no hint of humanity in them. He ran the fingers of his left hand through her hair and clenched tightly, dragging her up into a standing position.

Turning his pistol over in his right-hand, he began to pistol whip her until she was a bloody, unconscious mess on the floor.

For the next few hours, she fell in and out of consciousness. She was aware that her hands were tied and that she was being dragged. At one point, she was aware of being dragged along a sandy beach and bundled onto a small motorboat. After that, she remembered lying face-down in the back of some sort of truck with men kicking and stamping on her as they went along. The last thing she remembered, was the sound of metal doors slamming shut.

When she fully regained consciousness, she found herself in a dimly lit room. The first thing she noticed was the horrendous smell. It almost made her wretch. Her head throbbed, and every inch of her body felt bruised. She slowly moved her limbs one-by-one, to see if anything was broken. Her hair was matted with dried blood and her lips and eyes felt swollen. She sat on the floor and leant against one of the walls and waited for her eyes to get accustomed to the dark. Eventually, she could see that she was in what looked like a prison cell. The walls were of stone and the heavy iron door, with a peep-hole, looked like something from the middle-ages.

She sat there for what felt like an eternity but was probably no more than twenty-four-hours. Occasionally, she heard the sound of Japanese voices and the distant, blood-curdling screams of people obviously in pain. Two or three times, she heard the peep-hole being used, but nobody entered, and nothing was said

After another twenty-four-hours, she was feeling feint with hunger and thirst. She couldn't remember the last time she'd had food or water. The thought that she was not going to get out of this place alive, started to take hold. She was going to be another casualty of war. Her family would never know what happened to her. She would just be one of the missing, like so many who were never found in the last war. She would just be another name on another memorial in another cemetery, far from home. She wept uncontrollably.

On the third day, two guards came crashing into her cell and started shouting at her. She cowered into one of the corners of the cell and made herself small and prepared herself as best she could for a beating. In Japanese, they were calling her an English dog. The shouting stopped, and she was picked up by the guards and dragged out, down a dark corridor and into another cell-like room.

This time, there was a table in the centre of the room, over which a bright light-bulb hung, making her squint. She hadn't seen a light this bright since she arrived. Sitting at the table was a Japanese officer. It could have been the one that captured her, she couldn't be sure. She was manhandled into the chair opposite the officer and her hands tied behind her back. She sat there with her head down, hair hanging down in front of her face.

"What is your name?" The officer spoke English with a slight hint of an American accent.

She raised her head and said, "Please, I need water, I must have water".

"You will get water when you answer my questions. What is your name?"

"Cecily".

"So, Cecily, the British have resorted to send women to fight their battles for them, have they?" He said the same thing again in Japanese to the two guards standing behind her. They both laughed.

"The honourable and noble British army send their women to live like dogs in the jungle to do their spying. No wonder they do not have the spirit to fight. They surrender at the first opportunity. This war will soon be over, and you will live like the dogs you are".

All Cecily could think about was water. "Please, I beg you, I must have water".

"Silence". As he shouted, he stood up and gave her a hard back-hand slap across the face, sending her crashing to the ground.

The two guards stepped forward and put her back on the chair. She could feel her face stinging with pain and the taste of blood in her mouth. Her head lolled about and she groaned incoherently. The officer instructed one of the guards to get some water. He returned with a bucket of what looked like ditch water. He filled a tin cup and put it on the table, in front of

Cecily. Her hands were still tied behind her back. The officer and guards laughed as she tried to pick up the cup with her teeth and tilt it backwards to drink the foul-looking water. She managed to get a few sips into her mouth before the cup fell onto the table and splashed over her and the officer. Once again, a heavy, back-handed slap across the face sent her onto the floor again. She lay there, unmoving. With a command from the officer, one of the guards picked up the bucket of water and poured it over her head. She tried to lap-up the water before it soaked into the stone floor. The guards laughed as the officer started barking like a dog and said, "Look, the English dog drinks like an animal, woof, woof".

Cecily was dragged back to the chair. "What is your name?" shouted the officer.

"Cecily", came the almost inaudible reply.

"How many others are with you?"

"Just me, and the man you killed".

He instructed one of the guards to untie her hands and hold one down on the table. As this was being done, he removed a knife from a scabbard on his belt. He stood up and put the point of the knife on the back of her hand, and applied just enough pressure to break the skin. Her entire body went tense, waiting to absorb the imminent pain.

"I know you are lying", he said in a slow, menacing, sadistic voice. "We shot another two of your men the day before we found you and the other. How many were in your group?"

The realisation that she was now completely on her own hit her hard. She slumped in the chair. I am going to die. This is where it ends, she thought. In this God-forsaken hole. She quickly stiffened as the pressure on the knife was increased.

"How many of you are there?"

"Just the four of us".

The officer looked at her, his eyes narrowed. He didn't know whether she was telling the truth or not. The point of the knife digging into the back of her hand made her whole arm throb. Under the table, she used her other hand to pinch her leg as hard as she could, to try and somehow divert the pain.

"How did you get onto the island?"

"Parachute".

"Where did you land?"

"Ten-miles north of where you found me, in the jungle".

He started to increase the pressure on the knife. The pain was excruciating. Cecily cried out in pain, her body going into a spasm.

"You are lying little dog. Nobody parachutes into a jungle. There are no clearings in that area. You would get caught up in the trees".

"We were supposed to land on the beach. We got blown off-course".

"What was the object of your mission?"

"Just to report back your strength. Ships, planes and troops".

"How long have you been on the island?"

"Two-weeks, before you found me".

"How were you going to get off the island?"

"Boat".

"Where?"

"North of the island".

"When?"

"I don't know, it hasn't been arranged yet".

"Liar", screamed the officer. As he did so, he put all his weight onto the knife. The sound of breaking bone could be heard as the blade went through Cecily's right-hand and into the table beneath it. She screamed in agony. It only lasted a split-second before the room went dark and she collapsed, unconscious on the table.

Cecily came round, and found herself in her dark, damp, humid, stinking cell, her hand screaming with pain. On the floor was a cup of the putrid-looking water and what passed for a bowl of rice. She scoffed it down.

In the darkness, using her teeth and left hand, she managed to tear a strip off the bottom of her blouse. She wrapped it around her injured hand as best she could. It was only a matter of time before infection set in, but at that moment it seemed to be the least of her problems.

A few hours later, the cell door crashed open, and the officer stood there grinning at her. She was curled up into a ball in one of the corners, shaking and sobbing.

"I have some good news for you, my little English dog", he sneered. "One of our best interrogators will be coming to see you tomorrow. He has a reputation for getting answers quickly. His methods will be a pleasure to watch. Sleep well, you filthy dog, it may be your last".

It was impossible to sleep. The pain, the thirst, the hunger, the sheer terror of her situation, and the hopelessness, how could anyone sleep. Since she had been in this place, she'd had no idea if it was day or night, what day of the week it was, or how long she had been there. It was a living hell. She wasn't particularly religious, but she had begged God for mercy and sought forgiveness for her sins. She was ready for death. It didn't matter what they did to her, she knew next to nothing. No names, no secrets, nothing that could possibly benefit the enemy. The only thing she wanted to keep quiet about, was the submarine. It would mess up future operations if she let on about that.

58 - The Interrogation Officer

She heard voices in Japanese outside her door. One said, "The commander has arrived". The other replied; "He has a fearsome reputation".

Soon, there was the unmistakeable sounds of junior soldiers snaping to attention when a senior officer appears in their vicinity. After a few minutes, the cell door opened and two guards came in and half carried, half dragged Cecily down the corridor to the brightly lit room. Her head hung down. Her filthy hair, matted with dried blood, hung down in front of her face. She clutched her blood-stained, shattered hand with the other, trying to protect it, wincing in pain at every footstep she was forced to make. Blinded by the bright light, she kept her head down as she was pushed into the chair by the table.

She sat there for a few moments, shaking with fear. The trembling of her beaten and bruised body creating wave after wave of pain. She sat there, waiting. She wasn't going to start talking first, for fear of getting a slap in the face for insubordination.

"What is your name?" It was a different voice. This time, it was educated, with a noticeable English accent to it.

"Cecily", her voice not much more than a broken whisper.

"Cecily what?"

"Cecily Pauline Cox".

She was aware that the man sitting opposite her stood up. She felt a hand being placed under her chin. Slowly, her head was raised until she was looking at a blurred outline of a man. With his other hand, he wiped the hair out of her face and away from her eyes.

In Japanese, he said; "My God, it is you".

Slowly, her eyes began to focus. First, the navy uniform, and then the face. It was the face of Akira Hiraga.

Suddenly, Akira was shouting at the three other men in the room to get out. Cecily collapsed, face first onto the table. She was delirious, and wailed uncontrollably. Once they were alone, Akira got down on his knees and held her, taking care not to touch her damaged hand. He managed to calm her down and then went in search of the junior officer. He gave him instructions to fetch a doctor and to sort out cleaner and more comfortable accommodation.

While his orders were being carried out, Akira sat with Cecily and tried to find out how she ended up in the Andaman Islands working as a British spy.

It was a very one-sided conversation. Cecily could barely speak. She desperately needed food and drink, but that would be done on the advice of the doctor.

Two hours later, Cecily was lying sedated, in a clean bed, having been washed by a nurse. A local doctor had set the broken bones in her hand and bandaged it. For the benefit of the guards and their officers at the prison, Akira told them that he was going to turn her, and get her to become one of his double agents. This would give him time to work out a way in which she could escape back to her own people. He left instructions that he was to be called immediately she regained consciousness and could talk.

Twelve-hours later, Akira was notified that Cecily was awake and was eating small amounts of food under supervision of the doctor. On arrival, he told everyone to leave the room. When they had gone, he sat on the side of the bed and held her left hand. "I am very sorry they did this to you. I give you my word, I will help you all I can, to get away from here".

"My family already owes your family a debt of gratitude. It is becoming a habit".

Akira smiled. "My father told me what he said to you, about my mother wanting me to marry into an honourable Japanese family. It was not my decision. I had no say in the matter. Can you ever forgive me?"

"Of course".

"A lot has changed in the world since I last saw you and your family. Are your parents well?"

"Yes, they are living in Canada. How is your father?"

"He serves his country well, but his heart is not in this war. He is first and foremost, a man of peace".

"Am I your prisoner, now?"

"No. I want you to return to your family in Canada. War is no place for a lady".

"Thank you for calling me a lady. I don't much look nor feel like one at the moment. I, like you, had a patriotic urge to do something for my country. I didn't think for one moment I would be behind enemy lines. It doesn't feel right calling you, my enemy. I want to think of you as my friend, and remember the happy times we shared. I am sorry, Akira. I am so tired. Please let me sleep".

"I will stay and watch over you".

A few hours later, Akira was awakened by Cecily pulling at his arm. After she had something to eat and drink, she asked; "So what is to become of me?"

"I need to find some way of getting you off the island".

"What is the date today?"

"It is Wednesday, twelfth of August".

Cecily thought for a moment. Simple mental arithmetic proved very difficult in her present state. She had been given morphine when the doctor had worked on straightening out her right hand.

"If you can get me to the place your people found me by the evening of the fifteenth, I can make the rendezvous with a submarine that is due off the coast, as planned".

Akira looked at her with a mixture of amazement and respect in his eyes. He said; "If I am found to have helped you escape, it will be a firing squad for me, you do realise that, don't you?"

Over the next forty-eight-hours, Cecily worked on building her strength up, by eating, drinking and going for short walks with the nurse. She found out that she had been in the Cellular Jail, but since Akira's arrival, was now in a small private hospital that was reserved for the Japanese military. Fortunately, Akira was now a commander in the Tokkeitai, and no-one would dare question his authority, or what he was doing with an English female prisoner. He came to see her on Friday evening, to discuss the next day's plan.

"I will come to you in the morning, after breakfast. I have some ladies' clothes for you. We will get a rickshaw out of the town. Anyone that sees us will think we are going on a picnic. I will have a hamper with our lunch in it and some torches. A few miles south, I have found a fisherman with a junk for hire, and he has agreed to take us up the west coast, near to where you were captured. Once you are on your submarine, I will return to Fort Blair. Nobody will ask questions. Promise me one thing?"

"Of course, what?"

"Don't come back here".

"Don't worry, I have no intention of ever doing that".

"One other thing", he looked deadly serious, "Your people will want to know how you escaped. Please do not give them anything that will identify me. If my name appears on enemy intelligence reports, and those reports fall into our hands, well, you know what will happen to me?"

"I will tell them I was rescued by a knight in shining armour, my guardian angel".

Surprisingly, Cecily slept like a log. She was given a small breakfast by the nurse, and had the bandage on her hand changed. When Akira arrived, he ordered the nurse to leave them. Once she had left the room, he opened the bamboo hamper he was carrying, and got out the clothes he had bought for her; a simple yellow dress, some sandals and a wide-brimmed sun-hat. It was a goof fit, but difficult for her to get on with only the use of one hand.

"Are you ready", said Akira

"Yes, but please don't walk too fast. If I feel unsteady, I will need to hold your arm".

It was only a short walk to where the rickshaw was waiting. Akira helped Cecily climb on to it as gracefully as circumstances would allow.

Cecily kept her head down as they went through the busy part of town. She still had bruising all around her face. On seeing a rickshaw approaching them, carrying an officer, soldiers in the street would stand to attention and salute as Akira went past. Once out of the town, they continued south to where there was a series of jetties with boats moored.

They stopped next to a junk, where the owner greeted them in good English. Akira helped Cecily off the rickshaw and onto the boat. Without wasting any time, it cast off.

The journey was going to take seven or eight hours. That would give them a three-hour window in which to retrieve one of the foldboats and signal to the submarine. She just hoped that HQ in Kandy hadn't cancelled it, after not hearing from her for a week. Only time would tell.

Cecily sat in the shade of the canopy for the most part. The water was calm, and in any other scenario, it would have been an enjoyable trip. It was certainly not one she was ever likely to forget, no matter how hard she tried. After lunch, Akira fell asleep and gently snored. Cecily couldn't get comfortable enough to sleep, so she talked to the boat owner.

"This boat has a very interesting name", she said, looking up at the nameplate above the canopy. "What made you choose it?"

"It was chosen for me, ma'am".

"Oh, how so?"

"This boat was taken by British officers escaping from Singapore. It is the name they gave it. They said, if I help them to get to Sumatra, they would give it to me".

"How wonderful. It must have been terrible when Singapore fell. I had a friend there. He was in the Royal Engineers".

"Most of the men on this boat were from the Royal Engineers. They were all officers. The man in charge was a Lieutenant-Colonel. A very honourable man".

"Cecily smiled, "Can you remember his name?"

"Yes, of course, Lieutenant-Colonel Ibbotson, Royal Engineers".

Cecily's body went tense, her heart started to pound inside her chest. "Do you know his first name?"

"No, ma'am, everybody called him Sir".

"My friend was called Peter. Can you remember anything else about him?"

"I heard him talking to another officer one night, about a lady called Jean".

Cecily thought for a moment. "Could it have been Joan?"

"Yes, it could have been".

"Anything else?"

"I remember he said that after the war, he was going to live in South Africa with this lady".

Cecily, filled with a mixture of conflicting emotions, asked; "What happened when you got to Sumatra?"

"We stayed in a fishing village for the night, and in the morning, they were taken upstream and I was given this boat. I never saw them again".

Cecily sat there with tears in her eyes. Oh, Peter, she thought, I do hope you made it back home.

Akira had brought a map with him, showing the area where Cecily's base-camp had been. She studied it for a while and pointed out where the foldboats had been hidden. Akira instructed the boatman to tie up at a jetty about one-mile south and to wait for his return.

Cecily and Akira walked along the shoreline until they came to a spot Cecily recognised.

They soon found the hidden boats. Akira dragged one down to the shore, where, under Cecily's supervision, it was quickly assembled.

"I am going to have to row you out when the time comes. You will never be able to do it with one hand".

"Yes, I think you are right. You're going to have to take that uniform off. If it's spotted by anyone on the sub, they might open fire on us".

Akira took his shirt off, which revealed a khaki vest underneath. "What happens now?" he asked.

"Just before it gets dark, I start sending an intermittent signal with a torch. When they're happy, they will surface, and we row out".

The sun dropped quickly in the west sky. Cecily started to flash her signal, and repeated it every few of minutes. A quarter of an hour went past, when suddenly, from the darkness of the sea, a light flashed. Cecily's heart leapt for joy. They had come for her. They had come for everyone, but it would only be her they were going to get. She started to send the pre-arranged coded signal, as Akira dragged the boat into the water. Within a few minutes, the submarines conning tower rose up from beneath the sea, and sat there, silhouetted against the darkening sky. Akira pulled Cecily into the boat and started to row. It was hard going; the boat was designed to be rowed by two-persons. Cecily could do nothing to help.

Akira was young and strong, and made good progress. As they approached the sub, Cecily could see the captain on the tower and three sailors standing on the deck awaiting their arrival.

As they got close, Captain De Vries shouted down to them; "What about the other boat?"

"It's just me", Cecily shouted back.

They finally reached the submarine, and with the help of the sailors, Cecily got out and stood on the deck. She turned to Akira, who was still sitting in the boat, and said; "How can I ever thank you?"

"Go home, and don't come back. I don't want to see you hurt again". He smiled and started to head off back to shore.

As Cecily was climbing through one of the hatches, the sound of machinegun fire filled the air. She heard the sound of bullets hitting the steel hull of the submarine. It was coming from the shore, just north of where they had set out from. She heard the captain shout "Dive", and all the sailors on deck scrambled down into the nearest hatch. As Cecily looked on, bullets riddled Akira's boat. She heard him scream and fall into the water.

59 - What Next?

Five-days later, Cecily was sitting in a quiet room, at the Royal Navy Auxiliary Hospital in Colombo. She was being de-briefed by Major McCarthy. His police training was very much in evidence. His questions were relentless and left no stone unturned. He finished off by saying; "I don't suppose we'll ever know what happened to Kohli and Dhaliwal. Shame, they were good men".

"Who do you think opened fire on the submarine?"

"I have absolutely no idea. Possibly a foot patrol that got lucky. From what you've said about Commander Hiraga, I doubt very much if he had anything to do with it".

"He asked me not to mention his to anyone, in case it found its way back to the Japanese".

"Would you have told me if he hadn't of been shot?"

"Yes, definitely. I loved him once. My family owes his father a debt of gratitude, but after what I experienced over there, I am going to find it hard to ever forgive them or their kind". She wiped a tear from her eye, "I know that isn't very Christian of me".

The Major put his notes into an army issue briefcase. "One thing is clear from this mission, the Japs aren't planning an invasion of Ceylon or India from the

Andaman Islands at this moment in time, which is good".

"Does that mean it will be classed as a success?"

"We got something out of it, that is all we can ever hope for in this game. We have to chip away, bit-by-bit, until we get the breakthrough that finally puts an end to the war. It will be a long game".

Half an hour after Major McCarthy left, she had another visitor; Colin Mackenzie.

He came in carrying a large bunch of fresh flowers. How are you my dear girl? These are from my wife, Evelyn".

"Thank you, they're beautiful".

"The doctor tells me that you are making good progress. Your hand will be out of action for a while, but he's sure it will make a full recovery".

"Yes, I won't be playing tennis for a while", she said jokingly.

"I've just been talking to Major McCarthy, we both agree that when you're up to it, a little rest somewhere quiet would be in order".

"Thank you. I don't think I'm going to be much use to anybody until this hand gets a bit better".

"Is there anything I can get for you, or anything I could do?"

"A typewriter would be useful. I could send some letters to my family. I've tried writing with my left hand but it's almost unreadable".

"I'm sure I can arrange that. Anything else?"

"There is one thing. A friend of mine may have escaped from Singapore via Sumatra. I would dearly love to know if he made it. His name is Lieutenant-Colonel Peter Ibbotson, Royal Engineers".

Colin wrote the name down in a little notebook. "Leave it with me, I'll get someone to check for you".

"I would really appreciate it, thank you".

"I'll come and visit you again an a few days, see how you are. Take care".

Cecily liked Colin. He reminded her of her father; the well-travelled, genial, colonial type.

A typewriter appeared on a table near her bed a couple of hours later. She spent the rest of the day typing letters to various members of her family with the fingers of one hand. Fortunately, they only needed to be short letters. Just a few words to tell them that she was safe and well. Details of where she was or what she had been doing wouldn't have been allowed.

The following afternoon, an orderly delivered a note from Colin. It said; Lieutenant-Colonel Peter Ibbotson of the Royal Bombay Sappers & Miners, had arrived in Colombo from Sumatra, and was now at his divisional HQ in Kirkee, India. The post-script read; I will come and see you on Monday. Have you decided where you want to go next?

She was so happy that Peter has escaped and got home safely, she cried.

She spent the next twenty-four-hours contemplating whether she should go to India and see him. She wanted to, but what was the point? It would only upset her further. He was engaged to Joan. Lucky Joan. No, she had to forget about him. It wasn't going to be easy to forget the first love of her life but she would have to put it all behind her and move on.

When Colin came to see her the following week, he was very surprised at her decision. "Are you sure you want to go back to London?"

"Yes. I've given it a lot of thought. I have family there, and it's only a hop, skip and a jump to where my parents and brother are. I am only going to be of use in a clerical role for some time. I don't think that even you could talk me into going on another mission ever again. I'm sorry, but I think my confidence has taken quite a knock, I just want to go home and be with people like me".

"I will be very sorry to see you go. You are an asset to us out here, but I fully understand your decision. You are a remarkable young woman".

A week later, Cecily was on a troop ship heading for home. She had been promoted to Second Subaltern, the lowest of the officer ranks, but it did mean she had slightly better accommodation than she did on the way out. The hardest part of the journey was being in Bombay. She was seventy-five-miles from Peter. That was the closest she had been to him since before the war.

On arrival back in Liverpool, she sought out the hotel she had stayed in previously. After sending a telegram to her aunt and uncle in London, she enjoyed a good night's sleep in a comfortable bed.

After breakfast, she received a reply from London, saying all was well and they looked forward to seeing her that night.

It was the end of summer and Cecilly loved the cool fresh air in her face as she stood by an open window on the Euston-bound train. The English countryside looked green and lush. Almost every field was sown with crops and pockets of Land Army girls could be seen doing the jobs men had done only three-years ago. She noticed more bomb-damaged buildings when she arrived in London, but not a lot else had changed.

Her aunt Pauline and uncle Henry made such a fuss of her when she arrived at the house in Perivale, Cecily broke down and cried uncontrollably. She had spent the last six-weeks trying to hold in all her emotions, putting on a brave face, keeping a stiff upper lip. It all came flooding out, wave after wave of emotion, until she was totally exhausted by it. She was able to tell them some of what happened, but not all. Some of it, she didn't want to re-visit in her own mind. Some of it would probably be locked away for ever.

When she had regained some control, she asked where everyone was. The three boys had joined up and were serving in the army, and the two eldest girls were married. Only Betty remained, but she was getting married next year. "It will be just the two of us rattling around in this big house", said her aunt. Henry had poured everyone a brandy when Cecily had got really emotional. He now raised his glass and proposed a toast; "To family, and all those men and women doing their bit".

In the morning, Pauline brought Cecily a cup of tea in bed. She also handed her a bundle of letters. "These are all the letters that have come for you since you went away. I think most of them are from your mum and dad in Canada".

Cecily read the ones from her parents first, in the order in which they were date-stamped. Father was working hard and doing long hours. Mother was keeping herself busy doing clerical work for the Red Cross a few days a week. A letter from her brother in California intimated that he was thinking of joining the United States Navy, in their legal department. A few letters from various cousins, aunts and uncles dotted across the country, and finally, a letter posted in London and addressed in a hand she didn't recognise at all.

It was from Joan Nevill, Peter's fiancé. It said that Peter was alive and well and had got out of Singapore in the nick of time, and that she was going to live in South Africa with his parents until such time a wedding could be arranged. Cecily smiled. Lucky Joan, she thought. Now it really is time to move on.

A few days later, Cecily received an appointment to attend the Quenn Alexandra Military Hospital in Millbank. The doctor gave her hand a thorough examination. "You're very lucky", he said, making his notes.

"Am I?" replied Cecily, thinking how having a hole in your hand could be regarded as lucky.

"Yes, If the blade of the knife had been turned ninety-degrees left or right, it would have cut a tendon or two. You would probably have lost full use of it forever. As it is, once the bone has knitted together properly, there is no reason why it won't make a full recovery".

"Yes, I see. Thank you, I suppose I was lucky".

"Keep it strapped up, wiggle your fingers if you can do so without it hurting, and I'll see you again in a couple of weeks".

"Will you write to my CO and tell him?"

"Yes, of course. Leave all that stuff to me. See you in two-weeks".

Cecily was not good at sitting around and doing nothing. She helped out as best she could at the local church, where her uncle was the organist and choirmaster. She potted about in the garden and read books. What she really wanted was a dog. Not many people had them at the moment, what with the rationing and air-raids to contend with. One day, she thought, if this war ever ends, she would start up her kennels again. Forget about men, and that silly notion of getting married, her best friends were dogs, they always had been.

Two-weeks went slowly by. When she went to see the doctor again, she was ready to tell him she wanted to go back to work. She didn't yet know what that work would be, but she had to do something or else she'd go mad.

"The wound has closed up nicely" said the doctor, wiggle your fingers for me. Yes, good. I think you're ready for light duties now".

"Thank heavens for that. I'm bored to death sitting at home all day".

"Your CO sent me a message, to say that as soon as you're up to it, go and see him in Bakers Street".

"Are you happy for me to go?"

"Yes, of course. You can keep the strapping off. I would wear a leather glove on that hand, just to remind yourself to be careful with it. If you do something that makes it hurt – don't do it".

"Thank you doctor, I will go to Bakers Street now. Good bye".

"Good luck to you".

Cecily got the bus to Baker Street, arriving just before lunch. Margaret, the Brigadier's secretary, was delighted to see Cecily. "We heard what happened to you", she said in hushed tones. "I don't know that there would have been many women that could have done it".

"I wonder how I got through it myself" replied Cecily, "I don't think I would be able to do it again". She held up her right hand, "Physically or mentally".

"Come through to the Brigadier, he told me to show you in as soon as you got here. To be honest, I thought you'd be off a while longer".

"My dear Cecily". The Brigadier leapt up from his desk and pulled a chair out for her, plumping-up the cushion, "Come and sit down and tell me how you are".

Cecily smiled to herself; it was all rather paternalistic. "Thank you".

"Is there anything I can get you? Tea, a sandwich, a biscuit?

"I'm fine, thank you".

Pleasantries over, they spent some time talking about the details of her assignment and subsequent capture and escape.

"I'm absolutely furious that they thought it wise to send you behind enemy lines without the proper training. I shall make sure it doesn't happen again".

"I don't think any training would have prepared me for what happened in the prison".

"Yes, I see what you mean". The Brigadier picked up a file on his desk. "How would you like something a lot closer to home? The only risk will be getting caught in an air-raid, like the rest of us".

"I would consider anything that occupies my mind. I need to keep busy.

"Some friends of ours in military intelligence need a Japanese translator".

"Where would I be based?"

"Just down the road in Berkeley Street, about twenty-minutes' walk from here".

"It sounds ideal".

"I'll tell you what, why don't we take a walk down there now, and I can introduce you?"

"All right, then".

The Brigadier introduced Cecily to Commander Denniston. A nice, amiable man, she thought.

"I read the file you sent me", said Denniston, looking at the Brigadier. Then turning to Cecily, "You're just the kind of person we are looking for. Your Japanese language is obviously excellent, and the fact that you lived there for twenty-years, will help you to read between the lines, as it were".

"Thank you for your confidence in me. What exactly do you do here?"

"I like that. Straight to the point. Well, we intercept the diplomatic and commercial communications of all the axis powers. They use different cyphers to their military, and are just as variable. Information between two Japanese steel manufactures, for example, could give us insight into what the military are planning. We need to keep on top of it at all times.

"It makes perfect sense", smiled Cecily. When would you like me to start?"

The answer to that was; straight away.

60 - Epilogue

After the war, Harry, May, Charles and Cecily were reunited in Washington DC. Harry retired from Lloyd's Register of Shipping and was given a generous pension for his service to the company. Charles had joined the United States Navy in 1943, working as a lawyer in the legal department. In 1945, he became a civilian employee of the navy, before returning to California. In 1950, Harry and May retired to Santa Barbara in California.

Cecily worked at Berkeley House for military intelligence until the end of the war. In December 1945, she was seconded to the Pentagon in Washington DC, where she worked for the North Atlantic Military Committee. After her commission in the ATS was relinquished the following year, she remained in Washington as a civilian employee and worked for the British Joint Services Mission and the British Embassy.

Shortly after the death of her father and mother in 1955 and 1958 respectively, Cecily returned to England, where she fulfilled her dream of running a successful kennels. She set up the 'Dufault' Kennels, and became a champion breeder of Deerhounds, and an international judge. She died on the 14th December 2003 in the village of Quenington, Gloucestershire.

Peter Ibbotson went on to serve in Madagascar and Africa. He married Joan Nevill in 1944, and spent the rest of the war training soldiers in jungle warfare at Bukoba in Tanzania. He fulfilled his dream of settling in South Africa, and had a successful career as a civil engineer.

Thank you to those of a certain generation who found it within themselves to rise and shine. We will be forever in your debt.

Acknowledgements

Freda and Annice Collett – for rescuing Cecily's personal effects from the recycling bin.

Louise Bloomfield and the staff of the Lloyds Register Foundation – Heritage & Education Centre – for showing early interest in my project and providing a wonderful on-line archive that proved so useful in the writing of this book.

Doug Cox – for useful information regarding the Cox family.

Peter Eastman and family – for allowing me to recount the heroic wartime experiences of Peter Ibbotson.

Patty Holbert – for sharing with me family photographs and information about the Baynham and Cox families and helping me to put faces to the many names.

James Kirby – for reigniting my interest in this project that had sat on the back-burner for far too long. Also, for his tremendous research at the Japan Society and the Institution of Civil Engineers in London.

Lys Kirby – for proof reading and reminding me not to write a chronology but a story.

About the author

Steve Kirby was originally from north-west London and has spent the last thirty years living in the Cotswolds, in Gloucestershire.

It was when studying for his degree with the Open University that a tutor complimented him on the conversational style of prose in his essays. It planted a seed which gave him the confidence to write a book.

Now retired, he spends much of his time on his two main hobbies; genealogy and photography. He also runs a social media group which takes a nostalgic look at his old hometown of Harrow. He is married with two children.

Rise and Shine is his first novel.

Printed in Great Britain
by Amazon